BURNING HEART

DOCTOR WHO – THE MISSING ADVENTURES

Also available:

BURNING
HEART

Dave Stone

THE MISSING ADVENTURES

First published in Great Britain in 1997 by
Doctor Who Books
an imprint of Virgin Publishing Ltd
332 Ladbroke Grove
London W10 5AH

Copyright © Dave Stone 1997

The right of Dave Stone to be identified as the Author of
this Work has been asserted by him in accordance with the
Copyright, Designs and Patents Act 1988.

'Doctor Who' series copyright © British Broadcasting
Corporation 1997

ISBN 0 426 20498 0

Cover illustration by Alister Pearson

Typeset by Galleon Typesetting, Ipswich
Printed and bound in Great Britain by
Mackays of Chatham PLC

*All characters in this publication are fictitious and any resemblance
to real persons, living or dead, is purely coincidental.*

This book is sold subject to the condition that it shall
not, by way of trade or otherwise, be lent, resold, hired
out or otherwise circulated without the publisher's prior
written consent in any form of binding or cover other
than that in which it is published and without a similar
condition including this condition being imposed on the
subsequent purchaser.

Author's Note

In an immediately previous book, *Death and Diplomacy*, I mentioned that it was the second part of a trilogy and that the third part would follow in the fullness of time. This isn't it.

I have to acknowledge several people, without whom this book would have taken an entirely different course. So in particular, in no particular order: Kate Orman for making me remember the Vermicious Knids, the Bottersnikes and Gumbols and the crack about Peri's brain. Andy Lane, who builded a Dreddful, as it were, Church into the Who continuity. Marcus Morgan, for letting me shelve my half of the TV pilot for a while – *Mutually Beneficial Arrangement* is gonna be huge.

Rebecca J. Anderson, for helping me to clarify certain thoughts, and stopping me from making at least one serious boo-boo in actual print. P.J. Merrifield. Ben Aaronovitch. Gareth Roberts. Frobisher. Jackie H, without whom my personal stories would be a hell of a lot less interesting. The guy who wrote the book I was given once at Sunday school, the title of which I can't recall, but which had chapters along the lines of 'Timmy Builds a Treehouse and Finds God'.

The entire bunch in rec.arts except the obvious one or two. Everybody at the Fitz, even if the beer *is* like love on a lilo. People of good will and kindness everywhere, of whatever stripe, and all my various sources – if you rip one person off it's plagiarism, you rip a whole bunch of people off and it's *research*. Natch.

And, forever, Laura, without whom a light would not be in the world and we would all be that much nearer to the dark.

Blame them.

D.S.

'I believe that no man or group of men is good enough to be trusted with uncontrolled power over others. And the higher the pretensions of such power, the more dangerous I think it both to the rulers and to the subjects. Hence Theocracy is the worst of all governments. If we must have a tyrant, a robber baron is far better than an inquisitor.'

– C.S. Lewis, 'A Reply to Professor Haldane', 1946

SANJAYA:

9   And when Krishna, the God of Yoga, had spoken, O king, he appeared then to Arjuna in his supreme divine form.

10 And Arjuna saw in that form countless visions of Wonder: eyes from innumerable faces, numerous celestial ornaments, heavenly weapons without number;

11 Celestial garments and vestures, forms anointed with heavenly perfumes. The Infinite Divinity was facing all sides, all marvels in him contained.

12 If the light of a thousand suns suddenly arose in the sky, that radiance might be compared to the radiance of the Supreme Spirit.

13 And Arjuna saw in that radiance the whole universe in its variety, standing in a vast unity in the body of the God of gods.

14 Trembling with awe and wonder, Arjuna bowed his head, and joining his hands in adoration he thus spoke to his God.

– The *Bhagavad Gita*, Chapter 11

Section One

Investigation and Arrest

One

The planetoid of Dramos was as sterile as when people had first come: flat grey rock as smooth as glass, polished clean of even micrometeoritic dust by the ionospheric traces of Titania, the unstable gas giant around which it spun.

In itself Dramos had no atmosphere, no fossil water reserves, no carbon reserves, no assimilable silicates, nothing to support life. It was untenable: nothing here for humans or the myriad sentient races that were broadly comparable to humans. Races with the more extreme forms of physiognomy might have found some purchase here, but such races were a galactic rarity and there was nothing on Dramos to interest them.

There was nothing particularly interesting about Dramos at all. Or at least nothing save in terms of its position.

Dramos orbited the gas giant of Titania, which in turn orbited the sun designated K7A–00741–417b–16. This sun was a scatterling, a statistical anomaly, one of those few small, stray specks of matter poised equidistant between the secondary and tertiary spiral arms of the Galaxy.

K7A–00741–417b–16 was the vital staging post and crossover point for intergalactic travel. Titania was the single coherent planet in its system. Dramos was its single solid, stable body. That was the sole reason it was colonized, and the reason why it thrived.

People in their billions, from races in their millions, from species in their hundreds of thousands, made use of its facilities. Billions upon billions of tonnes of cargo went

3

through, the legal and the illegal, from weapons caches intended for a hundred intergalactic wars to famine shipments of grain. Over the centuries since First Landing, humanity, and the myriad species roughly comparable to humanity, converted Dramos into the largest, most extensive port that the Galaxy had ever seen.

And ports the Universe over have hinterlands.

As Dramos Port had established itself, the Habitat had grown: a pressurized, geodesic canopy extending itself step by step across the flat terrain. Originally the site of the Port Authority and minimal layover facilities, it now covered fully a third of the planetoid's surface area and tunnelled through a third of its mass. Thousands of cubic kilometres of interconnected modules that had been built, and built over again, and again, and then again; intestinal towers rising up under the dome in an unchartable tangle. A three-dimensional maze crammed with transients, and those who serviced them, and those who preyed upon them.

As with ports through history, in any time, in any place, below these surface processes there existed an underclass. The criminals who took advantage of the slave routes. The stranded and the dispossessed. The exiled and those running from the justice of their various worlds and of the galaxy at large. The flotsam and jetsam of two whole spiral arms of the galaxy.

The slugs smacked into the copper wall behind him, stitched and spattered across it wetly. Craator hit the floor hard, forearm and flat hand slapping it to take the impact, free hand hauling a monomolecularly polymerized cowl over the exposed areas of his face.

The 'slugs' were literally what the term implies – tiny, gastropoidal, artificial lifeforms, generated by and ejected from the alien weapons system. Their digestive processes were microcustomized and force-accelerated, so that they ate through the living tissues of their target like a blowtorch through a block of lard. It was just one of the many

4

blanket-kill solutions to a species-mixed environment. It also removed the living targets whilst leaving any inert valuable personal property more or less intact. If you worked it right it could end up paying for itself.

Such biotechnology was cumbersome, far too cumbersome to be carried, and was commonly used in static security installations. The eject module in the ceiling tracked Craator as he rolled, and opened fire again. Now fully sealed inside his suit, Craator was relatively safe – but even through the kevlar, polymer and teflon of the uniform it was like being hit by an unending series of slightly squashy Varloon deathmatch balls. It jarred and momentarily disorientated him – and the living security now had time to react. The guards around Ragho ak Areghi, after their crucial moment of shock when he had come through the doors, were reaching for the flenser guns that were perfectly capable of liquefying the soft tissues of Adjudicator Joseph Craator and blowing it off his bones.

'Bike!' he roared to the floating Micro-Antipersonnel Vehicle, which had been hovering dormant on its impellers since he had dived from it. 'Take out the gun!'

The MAV was in no way sentient, but its control vocabularies were sophisticated enough to pull the meanings out of voice commands. Its integral impact cannon – the same cannon that Craator had used to blast through the titanium-teflon club sandwich of the doors – now swung around and up and took the eject unit out. It left a gaping hole. Control cabling and burst delivery tubes prolapsed from it.

The security guards were still going for their flensers. Craator was still on the floor and slathered in a squashy, wriggling spatter of quasi-living projectiles, but the thought of getting off it never so much as occurred to him. In Adjudicator combat training the instructors clubbed you back down if you tried to get up off the floor once on it, and kept on clubbing you until you bled.

The big MFG – the Multi-Function Gun that was the

trademark of an Adjudicator on the streets – was out of practicable reach, slung as it was across his back, but there were other weapons he could use. Instant, unconscious pattern recognition had told him that the security guards were human. He raised a hand and depressed a certain point on his gauntleted palm, twice with a finger, sweeping his hand in the approximate direction of the guards and stitching them with fléchette needles.

The guards went down juddering and choking and clawing at their eyes as the nerve toxin took effect – riot-control IG pacifiers boosted to produce almost instant collapse, with only a minor and acceptable increase in the deaths from allergic suffocation. When the chamber was silent save for the odd aspirating gurgle, Craator climbed to his feet, brushing the slimy, dead remains of the bio-cannon projectiles from him. They weren't and had never been meant to be viable, and had given up what little actual life they'd had after hitting him and finding themselves with nothing to eat.

The entire explosion of violence, from coming through the doors to taking out the guards, had taken no more than seconds. It was like throwing a switch and then throwing it back. Only now, now that his Adjudicator-honed reflexes and senses detected no immediate threat, did Craator consciously allow himself to take in his surroundings, noting the elements that had impinged but had been instantly dismissed as irrelevant.

A tracery of verdigris and fungoid growths crawled around the copper walls, sluiced by rivulets of water that pooled on a steel floor sludgy with rust, eventually trickling down through sluice gratings. The air was dank and clammy, condensation droplets flecking and blooming the surface of Craator's cowl and sliding off.

Plinths, scattered seemingly at random, supported human figures in contorted, leering poses reminiscent of the most irredeemable and brutal pornography, some dating back to the barbarities of century twenty; the sort now seen only through the static haze of an

6

nth-generation holovid transfer copy to distortion-fouled, centuries-superannuated synthetic music. The figures were obviously handcrafted, sculpted, cast in solid bronze. The loving and expensive recreation of them seemed to make it all the worse. The other furnishings were slightly more extreme – seemingly here for no other purpose than to cause revulsion, as though whoever had furnished this place had known precisely the effect that it would have, and had gloatingly enjoyed it.

Ragho ak Areghi might at first glance have been taken for just one more, if particularly repulsive, example of the sculptures. A corpulent and sluglike quasi-humanoid amphibian, about the size of a small human child, with glistening grey-green skin and a swept-forward bony head crest. A Mentor from Thoros-Beta.

He squatted immobile, his lower torso ending in a larval tail. The plinth on which he squatted bubbled with a greenish fluid behind its clear glass ports: the nutrient fluid that was no doubt plugged directly into somewhere horrible inside him. He was unarmed and presented no immediate threat – Mentors disliking direct physical violence and being largely incapable of it in any case. His symbiotic chattel – the huge and musclebound, humanoid combination of servant and slave that served him as a pair of hands – was currently curled up in a corner and whimpering, having fled there the moment Craator had come through the doors. He seemed to have wet himself, though that might have just been the normal condition of the floor.

Craator pulled the monomolecular cowl off his face, and strode over to the plinth. Ragho ak Areghi looked up at the half-visored face of the Adjudicator with resignation, sardonically calm rather than anything else.

'It would appear that you have the better of me,' he gurgled. He gave a little unconcerned flick of a hand like a slimy baby's fist. 'It's a fair cop, as I believe the human saying goes.'

7

Craator pulled the comms pack from his belt and punched up Areghi's data page. 'Ragho ak Areghi, you have been Rightfully Adjudged to have contravened the Laws and Statutes of the Dramos Habitat Under God. Four hundred and seventy counts, illegal trafficking of Earth Reptile pituitary-analogue extract. Three hundred and twenty-one counts, trafficking in illegal biological limb grafts. Seventeen counts, conspiracy to commit murder of –'

'Ah well.' Areghi shrugged his diminutive shoulders. 'I suppose it was all too good to last. I have to wonder, though, how it was you finally caught up with me. I was aware that the Church of Adjudication had suspicions, but every scrap of evidence relating to my more, shall we say, *nefarious* activities was locked away most carefully in my transputer systems. Safe from spiders. Protected by some extremely scrupulous Data Protection laws.' He looked up at Craator steadily, beady eyes narrowing. 'Your laws.'

'These laws have now been rescinded,' said Craator.

'I rather imagine they have.' Areghi smiled sardonically. 'I seem to recall how the argument goes – hideous villains like myself are let free on technicalities because the good, honest policemen's hands are tied. Ah, well. So much for the hideous villains like me.

'I rather wonder, though,' he continued, looking up at Craator with that strangely quiet and knowing smile, 'if the Church is quite going to leave it at that. What about the millions of others? We're none of us entirely clean, after all. We're none of us pure. We all have something, some-where, to hide. What of those who cheat a little on their tithes, or take the occasional recreational drug, or own a dubiously incorrect data-wafer? I wonder how the Church is going to use these sweeping new powers on them.'

'Each case will be Adjudged by the Adjudicator con-cerned,' said Craator.

'Ah, yes.' Ragho ak Areghi sighed wetly. 'I was rather afraid that it might.'

* * *

Of Titania itself little was known. It was a 'hot' giant, very nearly a small sun in its own right. Indeed, the geostationary, automated energy-mining rigs that hung above it comprised the entire power source for the Dramos Port, together with replenishment for the ships that it serviced.

Seen from Dramos, the surface of Titania was a churning mass. Vast, unstable gravitational and electro-magnetic forces resulted in planet-wide gas storms, the forces unleashed by them of a magnitude that was almost nuclear, blurring the distinctions between energy and matter. The entire planet seemed to exist in a state of energy–matter flux. This had proved an invaluable resource, and ships had mined its energies for the second leg of the galactic voyage.

The only distinctive feature in the chaos was what people called the Node, a darker, reddish vortex that seemed to crawl across the surface, in much the same way as the Red Spot had crawled across the surface of Sol System's Jupiter, for all that half-forgotten planet had an entirely different albedo and energy slope.

Sometimes, this swirl of darker, reddish matter would seem to pulse. Sometimes it would change its course for no apparent reason.

Almost, some would say, as though it were alive.

Out in the chaos of the Habitat again, in Sector 3, nosing his MAV through the interways running through the hab-stacks, Craator kept a wary eye on the traffic and the crowds. Up above, through the tangle of the stacks and through the polymer of the Habitat dome, something pulsed redly in the Titanian chaos that filled the available sky.

Crazy season. The presence of the Node directly over-head always seemed to destabilize the Habitat. Mass-psychosis vectors elevated markedly, domestic murderers finally snapped, crimes of violence went through the geodesic roof. It was as though the whole Habitat burnt with a low-grade fever. The only bright spot, if it could be called that, was a slight dip in the traffic of certain narcotic substances – but that was simply the knock-on effect of the increase in people tripping out, killing others and themselves, and never purchasing any certain narcotic substances ever again.

The Curia, the control/dispatch arm of the Church of Adjudication, was working overtime, redirecting and optimizing forces to deal with the crazy-season fallout.

It was early on in the current cycle, the Habitat equivalent of morning, and the Habitat was waking up. But it was like waking up with a violent hangover, of the sort where one is still drunk and racked with abdominal cramps; the state in which one might scream in loved ones' faces and bludgeon them to the ground, and then just keep on hitting them, over and over again. Just to make them go away.

His attention fixed firmly on his immediate surroundings, Craator listened to the static-hazed wide-band casts of the Curia with half an ear, pulling together a sense of the Habitat's mood in the same way as his lungs pulled in the reek of millions going about their lives and deaths. Someone in Sector 4 was sniping from a hab-stack with a laser cutter – an even more serious threat since he was in danger of puncturing the geodesic. A pulldown squad was on its way. Riot Control forces were being mobilized and stockpiled in the Church's bunkers around the Sector 3 Concourse nearby, where the Human First activists would be holding a mass rally. They were holding it to protest at new Statutes saying that they couldn't hold it in the first place. Church of Adjudication vector psychometrists were predicting trouble, and had recommended that it be nipped in the bud, but in an uncharacteristic climb-down the High Churchmen had decided to let it go ahead anyway. A suspected pathogenic accelerated retrovirus, remarkably similar to parahydrophobia, was spreading through the Fnarok community of Sector 7 . . .

10

Thousands upon thousands of crimes and disturbances and their Adjudicator response became an unending, violent, Red-Queen-racing dance kept from spinning off into catastrophe only by the Church's OBERON systems – the semi-AI processing network that controlled and coordinated the forces of Adjudication absolutely. It was an absolute control made possible only by the fact that the communications and the life support of the entire Habitat itself were routed through the OBERON.

Even so, resources were currently stretched to the limit. Over the past Habitat year increasingly drastic measures had had to be crash-implemented by the Church – measures of which the rescinding of the Data Protection laws and the prohibition of mass gatherings were only the most recent. Stop-and-search procedures. Probable Cause. The war of attrition that every policing force wages against the rights of those it polices had been stepped up violently in this past year; it could only be a matter of time before these so-called 'rights' were obliterated entirely.

And this was all for the good, in the opinion of one Adjudicator Joseph Aaron Craator. People must be forced, if necessary, to recognize the difference between right and wrong. These new measures might seem to be harsh but they were also scrupulously fair, administered by Adjudicators steeped in long traditions of morality and honour. Only those who had committed crimes would have the slightest thing to fear.

This was one of the more homogenized areas of the Sector. Run down, shabby storefronts and stalls sold a farraginous mix of human and alien products and foodstuffs, clothing, ritual jewellery, religious fetishes, medical and ceremonial compounds. The crowd that thronged the walkways was no less mixed: human and hominid forms cheek by masticatory sac with the tentacular or segmented or polymorphic. Craator ran a trained eye over the confusion, without fear or favour, the mass of forms and bodies mere background noise to

11

the specific gestalt-trigger pattern of posture and motion that would mean something he could –

Something there.

'You!' Craator swung the MAV towards the walkway, flicking a stud on the control stick with his thumb to power up the pacification systems.

Two Dobrovian youths were fighting. The species was basically humanoid but with concentrated muscle mass, so that their bodies looked like oogli fruit haphazardly attached to skeletal stick figures. They were fighting over the worn and roughly repaired remains of a VR headset several centuries old, of the sort that had been used by Strikeout XIV assault pilots during the Earth/Draconian wars and had been subsequently war-surplus recycled as cheap subsistence-level entertainment. The larger of the Dobros had snatched it from the smaller, and the smaller was loudly and violently wanting it back.

As the MAV swung in, Craator reached out a hand and shoved the larger of the Dobros off his feet, sending him crashing back into a small pile of discarded packaging shells. He caught the headset as the youth let go of it with a double whoop that was the Dobrovian equivalent of a dismayed cry.

No point in thinking arrest and charges here. 'Pick on someone more your own size.' Craator hefted the VR and turned his attention to the smaller Dobro – and was shocked when the boy straight-armed him in the stomach.

'Leave my brother 'lone!' the alien child snarled, face flushed, segmented insectoid eyes flashing with pure hate. 'Dirty God-love Jood! You leave him '*lone*, yeah?'

Even without body armour there was no way the kid could have hurt him – that was largely the reason why Craator had been startled by the attack. Now, what seemed to be a simple case of siblings squabbling was threatening to get out of control to the point where Craator might actually be forced to do something official. If the boy tried to hit him again that would be Wilful

Assault on the Person of a Curate of the Law, which carried a mandatory two thousand lashes, and fifteen years in the Church's holding complex if he survived.

Using the MFG even on its stunner setting never crossed Craator's mind. An Adjudicator's shok baton, however, could be set to give a slight sting. Just the thing to scare some sense into the kids before either of them did something they would regret. Craator was pulling his shok rod with just this in mind, when a large exploding Jersey cow landed directly in front of him.

Two

_____

You couldn't see the stars here. The sky just burnt.

Mora Cica Valdez could remember being five years old and seeing the stars for the first time, looking up, huddled in undecomposed polymer sheeting, in the ruins of what had once been Nova Santa Cruz on Rensec IX. She had lived all her life in the underground caverns of the planet before catastrophic seismic activity had ruptured them, and it was like looking up at the stars through a hole in the sky as big as the world.

The vectors of Mora Valdez's life had mirrored those of almost any other refugee. She wasn't important. Nobody cared about her. That was the point.

The old Earth Empire was in the process of being dismantled from the outside in, abandoning countless systems colonized during its expansion to their fate. The powers that be — powers Mora Cica Valdez had never fully comprehended — had declared Rensec IX inviable for cleanup and reclamation, had dispossessed her and millions like her. Flung them up the gravity well as a shoddy alternative to simply leaving them to die.

The ragged survivors of the world had no place in the system outside. They had been simply shipped, en masse, to the decommissioned, dormant staging-post facilities of Puerto Lumina — the planetary satellite that had caused the Rensec disaster in the first place. There, a combination of faulty life support and a hamfisted attempt to chemically sterilize the survivors had introduced oestrogen into their artificial micro-ecology in terminal quantities. Mora remembered how she had

14

haemorrhaged, how a hundred thousand others had died.

The only way out had been the Mitor Line, packed into cryogenic cold-sleep canisters, originally designed for genetically mutated pigs, shot to hit the Outreach rigs on Mitor and the hope of hopping a ship out into the Galaxy at large, before the calcium depletion cracked your bones beyond all repair.

She had worked her way off Mitor, doing things she didn't want to remember, bartering off the expense of periodic lymphatic-system swap and cellular repair. It was a simple, win-all, lose-all gamble – she was counting on making enough to get her well away from the Rensec system in one jump rather than drifting into the slow death of a disrupted local economy. She was seventeen years old by the time she had saved enough. Then Mora Cica Valdez went out, and never came back.

She wandered and, after a while, she stopped. She never found a home, she never put down roots: she simply, in a way that she could not quite get her head around, ended up.

She was twenty-one years old. She was on Dramos. There were no stars here.

The geodesic over the entire Habitat was polarized and depolarized over a thirty-hour cycle, giving an approximation of day and night. It was morning now, and the Node was pulsing overhead. It was like two jagged slivers of glass hammered straight into the living brain behind the eyes.

This was an area of Sector 3 given over to transit stacks: thousands of credit-operated self-contained living-modules lashed to scaffolding, originally intended as cheap accommodation for the mass-transit liners running between the two galactic arms. The shuttles hadn't run for more than a Habitat year now.

It was that magic time of day when the stacks seemed dormant, almost deserted. The day people forced to live

15

here had gone about their business, while the night-people majority who had colonized the capsules were already curled up asleep or staring, muscle-locked and speeding, at the wall. Mora stumbled through the ground level, giggling a little, heading for the ladder to the capsule that she currently called home.

The gaiety was entirely physical and automatic. Her body was just doing it; she wasn't feeling anything either way. She had ended her shift the night before and a customer had wanted to party. Middle-grade Exec-type, working for one of the control-incorp subsidiaries. Seemed he was a good customer, very special client. Volan had gone along with it like a shot, and one Mora Cica Valdez better go along with it too if she wanted to keep her credit fix.

Hadn't been a total loss. The very special client had access to some serious Janies, and Janies went with every-thing. It was funny how the Joods kept on saying how they were *narcotics*, like they were endorphin-triggers or something. Endorphin-triggers screwed you up and Janies weren't like that at all. They made you bigger, in your head, like you knew everything. Like you could see every-thing that ever was, and everything that ever will be, and it was like it was all made of these little jewels and filled with love.

They made you feel like a goddess.

Until the point when you came down off them, of course. Mora had pulled out of the crash somewhere out there on the pneumatique, sandwiched between the partition and some human dosser pressing the crusty growth on his bald grey head into the side of her neck. She had started laughing and couldn't stop. It was just the vestigial effect of the drug. Her daily credit tags were gone from her pouch, but in the mindless chaos of finding her way home, back here through the morning rush hour, she had begun to wonder whether she had ever got them or not. One thing was for sure, though, if nothing else was. Volan would have already taken his cut. Volan would have taken it right off the top.

It was as if the pulsing of the burning sky was slamming at her head like fists. The giggling turned into racking heave of the lungs on the suddenly oven-hot air. Her heart accelerated and hammered.

Mora leant against a scaffold piling, staring absently at the big blue box that sat discreetly to one side of it, until her breathing eased. After a while, the purple and black explosions behind her eyes faded, and her eyes registered what she was seeing:

POLICE PUBLIC CALL BOX

– in blocky white letters on a notice on the box.

Some sort of new call-station for the Joods? Lots of stuff like that had been appearing recently: camera installations, holding posts, things that looked a bit like holding posts but were bigger and sort of in the shape of a T with two crossbars.

Mora knew that the Joods were putting the heat on the lap-bars and the clubs, even making oblique passes at Volan. Nobody had ever done that before. It was as if the Joods had simply decided they could do what they liked. Anything they liked.

That didn't change anything at all for Mora, naturally, because she was one of the people to whom the forces of authority had *always* been able to do anything they liked. She had the vague idea, though, that larger and more complex forces than she could comprehend, subtle pressures and arrangements that had previously maintained the status quo, were being violently overturned.

Maybe it was just the comedown from the Janies, but Mora had the distinct and crawling feeling that the blue box was watching her. Not something inside the box – the box itself. Watching her specifically and speculatively. Like it was deciding whether it wanted to eat her up.

Very carefully, though she was still unsteady and weak, she walked on past it. Walked away without looking back once, though she could feel – she could really *feel* –

its intangible attention on her like a cold-burn prickle between her shoulderblades.

As she walked, she stuck her hands in the pockets of her jacket and felt a sudden elation as her left thumb hit the small shape of a pill lodged in the lining, felt the distinctive double Godhead embossed on it, the design that gave Janies their name. That would at least soften the comedown for a little while.

Her mind on other things, Mora Cica Valdez entirely ceased to wonder about the blue box. If she had recollected that plunging, disorientating instant when she could have sworn that there was nothing there, and then it *was* there, she would have no doubt put it down to the lingering aftereffects of the drug.

A minute later, the door of the TARDIS opened and a young woman walked out, glancing around warily, instinctively hugging herself.

Unaccountably, she felt vulnerable on some basic level – one of those *self* moments, when you suddenly, chillingly realize how naked and unprotected you really are under your clothes, and find yourself wishing for a heavy jacket, if not body armour and three extra vests. This looming pile of modular capsules in the weirdly pulsing light didn't help. They made her think of clustered mutant growths lit by the firelight of hell. There were things sleeping in them, she could feel it, and any minute now they were going to wake up.

Movement behind her.

Perpugilliam Brown snapped her head round to see the Doctor, slouching in the door of the TARDIS, hands thrust deep into the voluminous frock coat of patchwork primary colours and tartan that seemed a sloppy parody of the clothing *he* had worn in the past, let alone of human clothing. Once again – yet again – Peri felt that edgy mix of disappointment and annoyance. Once again, on some deep emotional level, she had expected to turn and see the friendly and engaging, utterly decent and trustworthy

18

man she had once known – only to find that it was, well, *him*. The Doctor. It always slightly disorientated her, kept her on the wrong foot. The fact that she had now known this version of the Time Lord longer than the original just seemed to make it all the worse.

Now he looked at her with that little supercilious sneer she had come to know and loathe. 'You're quite all right I take it? You're displaced more than you've ever been before, temporally speaking, at any rate. Earth has changed a lot. Everything's different on the subliminal level and you don't have quite the right mental toolkit yet. I don't want you going to pieces on me because your mind can't cope.'

Peri thought of the Time Lord's erratic behaviour of late, thought of one or two pertinent comments about correct mental toolkits, and forbore to comment. The real Doctor must still be in there somewhere. That was the only reason why anyone would stay with him and put up with him. At least, any other reasons for staying with him were just too horrible to contemplate.

Peri hugged herself and looked up at a visible sky that seemed a mass of pulsing, swirling red. 'So when *are* we?'

The Doctor gave a little sniff. 'That's what I'm talking about. You're thinking in the wrong terms. "When" compared to what? There are thousands upon thousands of sentient, semisentient and quasi-sentient species and entities in the Universe, each with their own terms of reference.'

'When are we in human terms,' said Peri.

'How very anthrocentric of you.' The Doctor totted rapidly on his fingers. 'Well, the Aztec calendar tells us that today is a nine-*Ehecatl* day, but that's hardly either here or there after all that unfortunate business with Cortez – who always got something of a bad press, I felt, by the way, since before he came along they were already ripping hearts out on a ziggurat-industrial basis . . .'

He visibly caught himself and came back to the point. 'The Islamic calendar gives us the year 2594, but then

19

again the *Hebrew* calendar gives us a rather impressive 6934. If we take the French Revolutionary calendar, on the other hand, of course, we come out as . . .'

Oh dear God, Peri thought. He's doing it with the lofty child-superiority routine again. Any second now he's going to ask me if I'm stupid or what.

'Give me something I understand,' she snapped. 'Something I can feel. Anno Domini. Christian calendar. Guy with a beard who got nailed to a tree, remember that?'

'Gregorian or Julian?' said the Doctor.

Then he finally seemed to notice the expression on Peri's face. He shrugged and sighed. 'By that particular system it's the year 3174. That's what it would be on Earth, of course, if we were on it, which we're not. I never actually said we were on Earth.'

'OK,' said Peri. 'Fine.'

For almost half a minute, arms still folded, she glared at the Doctor with a slow burn as he simply lounged there, fishing the TARDIS key from his pocket, insouciantly fiddling with it and whistling soundlessly through his teeth. She was damned if she was going to say it, even if she did want to know where they were. After a while, the Doctor spun round and pulled the door of the TARDIS shut with a decisive clunk. He turned back and gave the wicked little grin that somehow had you liking him again despite yourself. For about a split second.

'The planet we're on is called Dramos,' he said. 'The place we're in is called the Habitat. I'll tell you all about it as we go along.'

The smells you couldn't smell were the worst part.

During her degree course at Boston U, Peri had learnt the important part that scent played in the differentiation of biological matter – and she had also learnt about the effects of secondary ketones, esters and pheromones, the complex molecules that triggered receptors in the olfactory nerve, plugged directly into the brain, microscopically re-engineering it without conscious awareness. The receptors

20

triggered recollection, chemical keys unlocking whole cascades of memory and association so that, for example, the recollected wet crunch of your leg under motorwheels could leave you pretty much unaffected, while the smell of dust and dried oregano could have you remembering some summer's day, long ago, with such an intensity that it could have you bursting into tears.

The process was subconscious. It took something on the cruder level to make you consciously aware of it, in the same way that one might drift towards a man one likes, and not really be aware one likes him until he turns to you, and looks at you, and smiles. Peri recalled a field trip to Madagascar, a year before she had met the Doctor. There had been a frightening, formless, seemingly sourceless sense of dislocation – until her eyes and mind had registered the specifics of the jungle around her, and she had realized that she was in an evolutional environment unlike any she had ever known.

This was like that. When she had walked out of the TARDIS, the receptors in her brain had been hit with smells she couldn't smell and didn't know, had *never* known, and it was only now that she could consciously recognize why.

The streets – if you could call these precarious, twisting catwalks and walkways and ramps streets – were packed. Such human figures she could see moved wrong, and dressed wrong, and spoke with utterly the wrong cadences and sounds. There was nothing so very much different about it than if she had suddenly been plonked down in, say, Delhi or Siam – but this was merely the least extreme end of the scale. There were other humanoids of increasing strangeness, to the point where they ceased to be recognizable as humanoid at all, and then animal, or reptile, or even *vegetable* at all – things that perhaps should not be alive.

The combined reek of them – the smells she *could* consciously assimilate – made her want to throw up, but she couldn't, because her body simply didn't know how to cope with them and failed to trigger even this simple reflex. It was as though the floor was continually being pulled out from under her; perceptions became slippery. She thought she saw something made of wooden sticks and greasy rope disembowelling a human, and was about to scream when she realized that the 'human' was in fact a simulacrum of some kind. The alien creature, a trader, she guessed, had simply opened a hatch in its chest to show what might or might not have been the alien equivalent of jewellery to a passer by.

There were spindly, glassy, motionless things that seemed to appear and disappear at random through the crowd – until she realized it was one thing, moving incredibly fast then standing stock still, simply going about its business. In a blur of motion she saw what she thought was a flock of reptilian, winged creatures falling vulture-like upon some victim. Then she perceived that they were connected by fleshy tubes to the thing itself, the meat they chomped out with their jaws pulsing down the tube and back into its main mass. The entire arrangement wandered around on a ring of little legs that rippled like those of a centipede, and if it was in distress then it made no sound about it, save for the slavering chomps as it continuously ate itself.

The things she could actually recognize didn't help.

'Don't worry about it,' the Doctor said, seemingly catching her mood with one of those sudden insights she had missed lately. Far from being out of his element in this chaos, the Time Lord seemed utterly relaxed and at home, surveying the scene with a cheerful, even gleeful, interest, as though it were giving him something he was hungry for. He had briefly sketched the situation of the Habitat to her, pointing out small details that seemed of interest to him and him alone, and given her some indication of the state of the Galaxy at large.

'Earth went through something of a bad patch with the destruction of the Overcities,' he said. 'Some form of mass psychosis that pulled them down, and damned good riddance, frankly. They're rebuilding, and I think they're practising some rather basic eugenics in the process. Not a nice place to visit. I was never that interested in going to find out.'

He gestured to take in the swarming Habitat. 'The core population of humanity is retrenching and consolidating itself. It'll lead to a more stable Federation in the end, but for the moment it's left a great yawning gap in the Galactic culture. The results are being felt, even out here. Interspecies, interstellar trade's entirely disrupted – and this place was built for interstellar trade. The ships have stopped running this far now. Everybody's stranded here. It'll just be some time before they know it.'

'So what's going to happen to them?' Peri said.

The Doctor shrugged. 'Mass starvation, catastrophic civil unrest. Food riots, mostly. Mass cannibalism. They'll either deal with it or die. These things happen.'

Peri turned to look at him. A horrible thought had struck her. 'You're not going to do anything, are you?' she said. 'You're not going to do anything to help.'

The Time Lord frowned. 'Perhaps I haven't explained it properly. These things *happen*. Will have happened. Start messing around with the key points and you pull the whole shooting match, as it were, down around our ears.'

'There must be something,' Peri muttered.

'Oh yes?' The Doctor sneered at her. 'Tell you what, why don't we start with something easy and work our way up? Go back and assassinate Adolf Hitler as a child, maybe?' He snorted. 'The literary executors of Anne Frank would have the shirt off my back.'

Peri stared at him aghast. She simply couldn't believe that he had said something so hurtful. Suddenly, irrationally, all she wanted to do was slap that snide, superior face and wipe the smirk off it.

The Doctor, meanwhile, seemingly oblivious, continued, 'We're here for something else. The databases in the TARDIS are remarkably specific on the history of this place – except for the three-month period we're in now. Something crucial happened here, but it's completely locked out from her extrapolatory banks – which rather leads me to suspect that *I* was directly involved. I've been meaning to investigate it for a while now, and this seems as good a point on my timeline as any. The only thing I really know is that it's linked some way to these chaps . . .'

The Time Lord nodded briefly towards a pair of helmeted, body-armoured figures marching along a walkway. Those in front of them, of whatever species, were moving smartly aside and in some cases leaping violently out of the way – avoiding what were presumably their eyes behind the one-way half-visors.

It was obvious from their body language that these two were human, as opposed to merely humanoid, for all that could be discerned of their actual, living forms were their chins and scowling mouths. Their body armour was reinforced at the shoulders and joints by heavy padding. Jointed nunchuk-like nightsticks hung from their belts. Bulky firearms were strapped to their knee-length boots.

Their insignia, in silver chrome on their helmets and chests, at first sight seemed to be crucifixes somewhat reminiscent of those of the Knights Templars – but on closer examination they could be seen to be based on a T with two crossbars.

'Adjudicators,' the Doctor said. 'Priests of the High Church of Adjudication. The Masonic elements in the police forces of your own time cohered and evolved into a holy, monastic Order – but that devolved over the centuries into an almost purely policing organization again. They lost their blanket jurisdiction on Earth after the collapse of the Overcities. They briefly had a stronghold on the Uranian satellite of Oberon, but then the Neo-Reformation pushed them out of the Sol system entirely. There are vestigial sub-sects of the Order scattered through the Galaxy now, but I gather that somehow the sect here have somehow become incredibly –'

24

He seemed to become aware that Peri was simply walking in a stony silence, pointedly looking at absolutely everything and everyone but him. He shrugged and lapsed into silence himself.

After a while, though, he said, 'Things seem to be opening out a little. Some kind of open space, I think. It seems to be a gathering of some kind. If you feel up to being on your own for a while, Peri, I don't suppose you'd like to mingle a little and let me know what you see?'

'Sure,' said Peri. 'Fine. Anything you say.'

She'd had enough. Possibly for ever. This was the perfect opportunity to get away from him before she had to scream.

The Doctor leant against a steel piling with two crossbars bolted to the ledge of the walkway and watched Peri as she stalked off, noting with approval that the anger he had instilled in her had countered and overridden the severe culture shock that might well have threatened to tear her mind apart.

Hopefully, it would protect her for a while yet.

'Like a little clockwork terrier,' he mused. 'Prime her, wind her up and watch her go.' Then he frowned. 'I hope I didn't wind her up too tight.'

Then he shrugged and wandered off. He had better things to do.

Three

In the Habitat, in Sector 3, people ran screaming as bits of burning debris rained down on them. The Dobrovian boy was on the walkway, hit by shrapnel and on fire. Craator slapped at the smouldering skin and pulled a field dressing from his belt, all the while staring upwards at the forms ejecting themselves from the hab-block above. The smart systems in his visor tracked and targeted them, zoomed in on them. Readouts should have been able to identify any known projectile weapon, but they persistently flashed CONFIG UNKNOWN.

But Craator could see exactly what they were.

'Sheol!' Craator switched in the mike that allowed him to hook into the Curia, patching in the view from his visor. 'Are you getting this? *Sahajyia* Block. Somebody's throwing animals off there!'

Through the visor, magnified, in succession, three hogtied sheep, a Vietnamese pot-bellied pig, a squirrel and an extremely surprised-looking hippo flew through the air and exploded.

'What the Sheol's going on here?' Craator growled.

'We're checking,' the voice of the Curia operator said in his ear.

There was a two-second pause as various factors were run through the OBERON systems. It seemed longer. Then: 'The animals are identified as being stolen from the private menagerie of one Marvin Gabon Wopat,' the voice of the Curia said. 'Genetically recreated, genuine Earth livestock. OBERON further advises that you check the date today.'

Craator glanced at his visor readouts. 'So?'

'OBERON says that on Earth that translates into the fifth of November.'

'Oh,' said Craator heavily. 'That.'

In the centuries since humanity had made it to the stars, a large number of humans had converted to various alien religions: Ice Warrior *Sklacki* rituals, Oolonian toe-worship, even joining in the Rite of Exterminating Everything That Isn't a Dalek. Said alien races, naturally, found these sad attempts extremely pathetic and highly amusing. This must have been so, because the sword of belief cuts both ways, and a large number of aliens had attempted to convert to human beliefs. And without exception they had got them completely and utterly wrong.

There was a Fnarok sect, the Twenty-fourth Day Adventists, who believed that every year their young should be tied up in sacks and left up the chimney. They built chimneys wherever they lived for this especial purpose. An entire race of quasi-arachnids from Praxis XIV, on the other appendage, had obliterated themselves over a centuries-long argument about whether Roline had really scratched Joey's surfboard in episode 2487 of the twentieth-century Australian soap opera, *Bondi Blues*. A fundamentalist sect of Darian septilateral gestalt entities now firmly believed that the Universe had been created in seven minutes, and everything in it was descended from Adam, Adam, Adam, Adam, Adam, Adam and Jeremy. But all of this, comparative paratheologians agreed, was as nothing to the Piglet People of Glomi IV.

These otherwise remarkably amiable and stable creatures had latched on to the idea of the Hebrew scapegoat – that is, an animal taking on the sins of the tribe, which then die with it upon its slaughter. They had then confused it with that Ur-scapegoat, Jesus Emmanuel, who had been born in a stable with a lot of animals around him.

They had *then*, for some obscure reason, confused it all with the Terran English tradition of Guy Fawkes night. The practical upshot of this was that every Earth year, wherever they were at a date and time calculated to be eight thirty in the evening on 5 November, Greenwich Mean Time, they stuffed high explosives up assorted livestock, catapulted them a hundred feet in the air and exploded them.

Ordinarily, of course, such a happy spectacle might provide hours of fun and glee for all concerned – but in the crowded, pressurized environment of the Habitat it was a lethal liability. The practice had been banned some years before, due to an unfortunate incident involving an overzealous Piglet People sect, a herd of elephants and a number of decommissioned dirty cobalt bombs. The sect, however, still flourished underground, surreptitiously gathering its materials and waiting to burst forth again in all its pyrotechnic glory.

And in the domed sky the Node flickered and pulsed with unknowable energies. There was something hypnotic about it; you could lose yourself in it. And what came back was slightly different from what went in.

(*In the washrooms of the Sector 7 transit racks, a Silurian named Kogh du Hak, in the middle of scouring his hands with a soapstone, found himself unable to stop. He simply could not make himself stop. The cuticles of his claws were now flayed and raw. The scaly skin of his palms was flaking. The more delicate scales on the back of his hands were already gone.*)

Craator hauled himself on to his MAV. 'I want backup,' he told the Curia control. 'Divert me a pulldown squad and some Riot Control.'

Again, there was a brief pause from the Curia. Then: 'No can do, Craator. Sector 3 riot control is completely tied up with the Human First thing.'

'Everything?' Craator was surprised. Taken together

28

the Adjudication riot control forces were capable of fighting a small war. 'This is a mostly peaceful demonstration we're talking about. Strict assurances and sanction, I thought.'

'They've been revoked as of the last hour,' said the voice of the Curia. 'Emergency conditions have been declared. High Churchman Garon directs that all mass meetings of any kind are now *verboten* for the duration of the Emergency.'

'Emergency?' Craator said. 'What emergency?'

'Crazy season. High Churchman Garon also directs that all unoccupied personnel make themselves available as reinforcements.'

Up above, a genetically resurrected ostrich went to glory by way of some tens of pounds of home-made Semtex.

'I'm not exactly unoccupied,' said Craator.

'As and when available, Craator.'

'I'll let you know.'

Adjudication MAVs were designed so that they could convert their power charge on to one short overload burst, boosting them for short periods of flight. Craator cycled the power up and braced himself against the crash-bars, flipping the cover off the switches that would fling the bike several hundred feet into the air.

The effects of the Node were being felt throughout the Habitat, burning into minds and brains: pseudo-epileptic and aphasic fits abounded as synaptic and neurological systems were damaged in a thousand subtle little ways.

(*In the bedroom of her con-apt in Sector 5, a human woman named Liora Jadron gave a choking sob as a growth on her forehead split open like a ripe boil to reveal the clotted socket of a vestigial eye.*)

And in some the effect was far more drastic. Race or species did not seem to matter. Those with the precisely correct biomorphic signature were disrupted on the cellular level. Taken apart. Put back together.

(*In the middle of a Sector 2 hypermart, in the* DEATHLESS MEAT *section, by the stacks of freeze-dried placenta, a man named Michael Case found himself screaming the word 'mouth', over and over again.*)

Transfixed and transubstantiated by the power of the Node.

(*In her credit-operated capsule, on stained, worn polyfoam picked to shreds with fingernails, Mora Cica Valdez moaned and scratched at the skin under her collarbones and armpits, the sudden itching of which had broken into her dreams.*)

Four

The open space was a platform some half a mile square, suspended between the towering modular blocks and fed into by several walkways: a pedestrian concourse with no vehicles allowed. It was packed with people.

Peri wandered through them, feeling at ease for the first time since she had arrived here in the Habitat. Possibly it was because these people seemed to be entirely human – or as relatively near to it, given a thousand-odd extra years of evolution, as made no odds.

In her travels with the Doctor, Peri had come to notice that, in a particular place and time, while people might not wear uniforms as such, their clothing had a kind of uniformity, a certain cut that stamped them. Here there was no such unity: a woman or a man might be wearing anything from a single string of jewels to multiple layers of polymer robes, or a suit of twinkling lights and a snood. This was probably a result of the Habitat's recent status as a transit nexus. The styles of half a galaxy were clustered here.

There was, however, a general air of seediness, of grubbiness, of things running down. This tended to corroborate the Doctor's summing up of the Habitat as a place for the stranded. Wherever they had come from, whichever colony world or culture had made them, nobody was going anywhere, now.

Several of these people were clutching placards and banners made from scavenged materials. The written language seemed to be predominantly of Cyrillic script, with the occasional recognizable letter standing out like an English trademark in a page of Cantonese. The images on the banners seemed to be those of what the Doctor had pointed out as Adjudicator insignia, defaced by slogan scrawls.

The atmosphere was one of surly anger – but even this was like a breath of fresh air to Peri, after spending far too long with someone who had become intangibly but increasingly alien. Someone who, she sometimes felt, could not honestly care less if she lived or died. He would go into paroxysms of grief, seemingly for the hell of it, about a sparrow falling out of a tree while leaving entire civilizations to their deaths. It was as if he simply didn't care any more. She remembered a time, a subjective month ago, when some now characteristically erratic bit of Time Lord tinkering had left the TARDIS stalled in the Vortex, seemingly with no way out. She remembered what the Doctor had said: 'You're just going to grow old and die; *I'm* going to have to live on through regeneration after regeneration.' Peri had been forced to come up with a way out of their predicament, more or less out of spite.

As she made her way through the crowd, Peri noticed a number of uniformed Adjudicators, watchfully patrolling the crowd. Those they passed seemed to be studiously ignoring them, but she heard random snatches of conversation from those around her:

'. . . dirty shame. I mean, It wasn't as if she'd *done* anything . . .'

'. . . let those skags run around. That's what I can't stand. Just like they was real . . .'

'. . . should be on our *side*; I mean they're . . .'

A number of people had white bands tied around their upper arms; they seemed to be the organizers of the gathering, talking with and liaising between the various individuals and sub-groups. Peri drifted over to a pair of them, a young man and woman in woollen smocks and dreadlocks, passing out and collecting back slightly crumpled, grubby fliers.

'I was supposed to be here with someone,' she said, 'but he, uh . . .'

That was always a good opener. Looking for someone who had invited you somewhere without explaining why, and now feeling a little lost and alone. It had people telling you what was going on, without quite triggering the suspicion that you were a true outsider. And the fact that it was, in a sense, the absolute truth tended to inspire trust.

As one, the couple turned bright, warm, friendly eyes to her. 'Do you know which group they're with?' said the girl sympathetically. 'Do you know if they're members of the Party?'

'I don't know,' Peri said. 'He just said I might learn something important.'

'Oh you'll learn something, all right,' said a voice behind her from the crowd.

Peri glanced around sharply to where a man stood, seemingly a little aloof from those around him, hands thrust into the pockets of a leather jacket. Though the words had seemed to be directed at her, he wasn't looking in her direction.

Peri turned back to the couple. 'Party?'

'Oh, *yes*.' The woman looked happily at her, delighted at the opportunity to espouse some deeply held enthusiasm. 'For too long we have laboured under the yoke of the oppressor! For too long we have allowed their treacherous words to enslave us! It is time for humanity to finally break the chains that bind us! To realize our true potential! To finally be free!' She sounded as if she was quoting, probably from the leaflets in her hand.

'It is time to put Humanity First!' chimed in her similarly attired companion.

'A little humanity wouldn't go amiss, certainly,' said the sardonic voice from the crowd again.

This time, when Peri turned, he was looking at her. Tallish, youngish, his face set in a kind of lopsided sneer. Then he winked at her and looked away.

33

The man from the couple laid a hand on her shoulder, and gestured with the other towards what seemed to be the focus of the gathering. Peri could see nothing but a couple of figures on a higher level moving back and forth. Probably a stage of some kind, in itself obscured by the press of people.

The figures on it were erecting large flat panels on masts, like sails.

'Avron *Jelks* will be speaking now,' he said. The emphasis, plus the sudden look of worshipful awe in the eyes of the girl, suggested that this Avron Jelks must be someone very important indeed.

'He'll tell 'em what's what,' the girl said firmly.

'Things are changing,' her companion said. 'Things are changing soon, and Avron Jelks is going to change them.'

Leaving the couple to continue handing out their fliers, Peri wandered off in the direction of the stage to get a better look. This was easier said than done. At last, wedged by people either side and in front, she could go no further. If she craned her neck she could make out the faces of the technicians putting up the display screens.

They were testing them now. Bright patterns swirled across their surfaces and pulsed.

She became aware of a presence behind her, almost but not quite touching her.

'You still seem a bit lost,' a voice said. 'If you don't mind me saying so. A little out of place.'

She turned her head to see the tall, sardonic figure she had seen in the crowd a little earlier.

'Do I know you?' Peri said. The man was utterly unfamiliar, but given the added element of time travel the question wasn't quite as stupid as it might have been.

'Never met you before in my life.' The man grinned at her. 'The name's Kane. Old Earth name, Australian. Aborigine hero-god. Lived on a floating island and carried the wind around in a bag.' He shrugged. 'Highly indicative if you ask me.'

'Right.' Peri turned her back on him and pointedly

34

studied the stage. The last thing she wanted to deal with at the moment was a clumsy attempt at a pick-up.

It was at this point that the mood of the crowd abruptly changed.

Before, it had simply been a large collection of people, a random sea of faces, with its waves and currents and squalls that might follow some complex Brownian process but with no humanly comprehensible unity. Now it was as if every single face, by sheer chance, had simultaneously turned towards the stage. The susurration of thousands of random conversations died. The sounds of several thousand people simply existing and breathing was like silence in comparison. There was an air of excitement, of expectancy.

Someone was climbing on to the stage.

Something about him, the pattern signature of his form and movements as opposed to the unobtrusive, barely noticed movements of the technicians, seemed to wrench the eye towards him with a physical shock. He stood there, alone, on a level slightly higher than the crowd. Then the screens behind him flared with the close-up image of his face.

'My name is Avron Jelks,' he said. 'I have a message for you.'

The Doctor, in the meantime, had turned his back upon the human gathering and was wandering the brawling streets. Humans were probably his favourite species, but you could have too much of a good thing.

It was their fundamental and unshakable belief that they were, both individually and as a race, the centre of the entire Universe. They tended to see the world as divided into themselves and the monsters. The fact that human history was littered with monstrous atrocities that would make a Cyberman's head spin round on its bearings seemed to go entirely over *their* heads. They were Good, the monsters were Evil, and there was an end on't.

It was good to come to somewhere like the Habitat and

remember in the bones that things should not necessarily be thought of in human terms. Far too many periods of history – and especially human history – had been reduced to the blunt *absurdum* of two forces going at it hammer-and-tongs, head-on. As if that ever, ever solved anything.

It was nice to find oneself somewhere slightly more cosmopolitan, with any number of factions. It kept things interesting, made the processes more entertaining. Of course, it didn't make the suffering and death any less prevalent – suffering and death were, after all, the ultimate natural state of anything and everything that lived. It simply made the processes of them more palatable. A million individuals, each suffering their individual thousand natural shocks that flesh is heir to, was preferable by far to some external sur-agency wiping out the lot of them in a second flat. It spread the individual process out by years, or centuries, or even millennia, and made it easier for the mind to –

It was at that point that, from the distant concourse, there came a roar of voices in their thousands, in unison. It was like the howl of some massive pack falling upon some prey in triumph – and, if the humans and aliens, here on the walkway, hadn't glanced in that direction in startlement, they might have noticed a tallish, unkempt, blond man in a garish overcoat and waistcoat suddenly jerk bolt upright, wild eyed, as though he had been slapped in the face.

'Oh, by Rassilon's grey and hairy beard!' the Time Lord snapped, his voice rough with sudden self-directed anger. 'I'm doing it *again!*'

It was that last damned regeneration again. He remembered the feel of the spectrox toxaemia back on Adrozani Minor, the feel of the things in his blood. He remembered again what it felt like to die, in some fundamental sense, before his proper time.

Oh, he had tried not to blame Peri for it – would do the exact same thing again if it came down to it – but the complications of the trauma had remained. He had recognized the symptoms all too well in others over the years. If you survived, you switched it off and dissociated yourself from the world. You became cold and distant. You pushed people away – manoeuvring them into hating you, detesting you so much that they never wanted anything to do with you again.

You pretended that you were not alive – just a collection of functions and processes and systems – and if you were not alive, how much less alive were others? They were just things that moved and made sounds and sometimes went away and came back. They were the walking dead. And if they were dead then you could do anything to them. You could do anything you liked.

The Doctor shuddered. He had started to come to terms with these feelings over the past subjective months, recognized them for what they were and tried to counter them – but denial is a slippery business. You lock and bar the cerebral door and chain it, pile the furniture behind, and they come up through the serving-hatch of the backbrain.

He looked up at the geodesic sky. The pulsing mass on the planet above seemed to have triggered a kind of intangible sunstroke in him – something no dwarf star like the G2 sun of Earth's solar system could have done.

Some kind of secondary radiation? Some purely visual pattern that triggered some analogue of epilepsy in the odd connections of a Time Lord brain? Or was it something else and utterly unconnected with the sky at all?

Without further extensive study it would be difficult to say, but either way something had disrupted him a little, like an incipient migraine, and allowed all those negative feelings to again burst forth.

His every thought had been overlaid by a kind of bleak desolation – a sense, an *intimation*, that something bad was coming. Not immediately, not on this particular excursion, but quite soon now. Something that was quite possibly worse than he had ever known.

It was literally formless: a sense of some approaching, absolute oblivion that he would not experience for the course of some time – possibly for months or even years to come – and this very formlessness seemed to have permeated him. He had forgotten on some level that life is of the moment, and must be lived for the moment in hand.

God, despite rumours to the contrary, was not the abstract of the whole vast churning machine of the Universe, the butterfly-effect progression of all its component parts. God was the specific, glorious scintillation of the butterfly's damned *wing*, and how it made you catch your breath. Or a sunset. Or a smile. Or for that matter a fire-iron or a small uninteresting rock. God was in the details.

He recalled, in complete mnemonic detail, the expression on Peri's face as he had manipulated her into going off and doing what he wanted, to set in motion certain processes. At the time he had thought he was working for some ultimate and greater abstract Good. Now he realized how much he had hurt and damaged a specific, living, breathing, frightened woman who had desperately needed to trust him, a woman of whom he was supposed to be a friend.

He had lost the specific in pursuit of the general, forgotten friendship, love and pain in the implacable process of Good. Start going down that road and you end up building camps for the extermination of the not quite 'good' enough.

It was as simple and as trite as that: the ends never justified the means. It was the truth of what he had said to Peri earlier, for quite other reasons than he had meant. You could go back in time and kill Adolf Hitler as a baby, but only if you were the sort of person who could kill a baby in the first place. Vague and hypocritical posturings about the workings and processes of History weren't even in the *Sklaki* arena.

If the Doctor had been capable of it, he would have blushed. As it was, he slapped himself so hard that he did something human hands weren't capable of and raised a slight bruise.

'That's for forgetting what's real, here and now, and what isn't,' he told himself sternly – oblivious to a passing polyp-brood of polymorphs who looked at him askance. 'The next time you start thinking like that, go and kick a stone or something to remind you.'

And with that he turned on his heels and set off back towards the concourse where the gathering of humans was taking place, to rescue Peri from the processes that he himself had set in motion. It complicated several plans he had, but he'd just have to sort something out.

As an afterthought, he pulled a dog-eared notebook from his pocket and jotted down the thought about kicking the stone. There was a chap in Hellenic Greece who collected such inveterately ephemeral stuff and he might be interested.

Five

The Temple of the Church of Adjudication was the largest freestanding structure in the Habitat: fifty levels of bloody-minded functionalism in the centre of the Dome, garlanded with a bolt-on fretwork of insignia and iconography so that, from a distance, it looked like some overgrown burial mound, from within which the corpse-lights burnt.

The bulk of the Temple contained armories and the communications centre of the Curia, dormitories and living quarters for the rank-and-file Adjudicators. There were equipment stores, vehicle depots and enough stockpiled food to make the Adjudicators, as a cohesive force, independent of any outside factor for more than a century. The very topmost floors were given over to the OBERON central processors so that, in addition to the fibreoptic landlines that linked the system to its subsystems, it could transmit and receive data via laser in the infrared. Directly below these floors was the domain of the High Churchmen, those who operated OBERON. The High Churchmen wielded, so far as any faction could wield, supreme power over the Habitat. They were the highest-ranking Adjudicators, who remained in monastic seclusion, attended by a retinue of hand-picked Adjudicators known as the Hands of God, never leaving the Temple, to protect themselves from undue influence and temptation. To keep themselves pure.

And if, in a sense, Heaven was above, then Hades was below. The installation extended downward into a vast

40

complex hollowed out from the crust of Dramos. These were the Holding Cells, built to contain those whom the Adjudicators did not summarily execute, and which had extended until they were almost a city in their own right.

In the Curia central control, an operator named Nadia Chong watched a bank of screens displaying readouts from five Adjudicators on the streets – five being the optimax per controller, being the maximum number of people one person could keep track of, and it being statistically likely that only one of them would need support at any one time.

At the moment, though, the operator was doing a precarious juggling act. A lot of auxiliary forces had been taken out of the loop to back up the Adjudicators seconded to Riot Control. The few personnel still on street duty – some thousands of them, admittedly – were out there on their own. They were out on their own in the middle of the Crazy season.

Around her, hundreds of other operators frantically worked their own consoles, but Chong was too busy to pay them any heed. She was currently directing one Adjudicator through the sewerage system and security systems of the Marvin Beeny block on the trail of some absconding Cutter runners, whilst simultaneously trying to keep another Adjudicator talking while he held his stomach together and waited for a medevac that, she knew, quite simply would never arrive.

In between, she was keeping an eye on her other three charges, flipping between them for a second at a time. One was on the riots and waiting for the go signal, the second didn't seem to be in any trouble at this point, and Craator was the sort of Adjudicator who could look after himself.

'You take the second on the left,' she said to the Adjudicator in hot, or, rather, horridly warm, pursuit. 'That should put you on one of the main shafts, and blueprint files say there should be rungs . . .'

'But there's a *hole!*' the voice of the gutshot man broke through into her ear. He sounded more like a frightened child than anything else. 'There's things *inside* it!' It was as though he were fussily complaining about the mess someone had made of something he owned – that state of utter agony wherein pain and fear and higher association simply shut down.

'It's all right,' she told him. 'It's going to be all right.'

The Adjudicator in the sewers had reached another junction, so she fed him another track to follow based on best-guess data taken from the plans.

Then she switched momentarily to Craator.

Biosigns relayed from heart mikes and the blood-test unit clipped to his ear were up; adrenochrome levels had spiked off the scale. The juddering image from his helmet microcam showed him dodging exploding animals in mid-air. He probably wouldn't take kindly to an inter-ruption at this point.

As Chong flipped back to the dying Adjudicator, the razor-cut hairs on the back of her neck bristled. No shadow had fallen over her, but she felt the crawling presence of someone standing rather too close behind her.

She glanced back to see High Churchman Garon.

If the High Churchmen were the body of men – and they were exclusively *men* – who had dominion of the Habitat, High Churchman Garon was the man who had dominion over them. Ostensibly, the upper stratum of the Church was run on a collective basis, but in actual fact it moved according to his will. Things he wanted to happen happened. Things he didn't want to happen *un*happened. It was as though he had a direct line to God, and from him to the Church, and from the Church to the world.

When he wasn't in seclusion, in the upper levels of the Temple, Garon stalked the levels beneath. His official duties included the running of the underground complex of the Holding Cells, and he could turn up anywhere, as if in passing, and make his wishes known. No one ever countermanded him. Part of his remit in the Holding Cells was the Inquisition and interrogation of prisoners; he had never, so much as anybody knew, actually put an Adjudicator to the Inquisition for disobeying an order – but there was an air about him, something in his eyes and smile, that had nobody ever deciding to risk it.

Chong concentrated on her work, trying to ignore the presence behind her, the minuscule sensation of warmth on the nape of her neck, all the while praying to God that she didn't screw anything up.

'. . . seem to be coming up to a grille of some kind,' said the Adjudicator in the sewer.

'. . . think my legs have gone to sleep,' said the Adjudicator with half his internal organs on the ground.

'You're running Craator?' said Garon, moving closer. Now she could actually feel his breath.

She nodded towards the status panel on her display. 'I'm running him.'

'I think I'd like to see what he's doing,' said Garon.

'What?' Chong waved a hand at the other panels. The people who actually needed her help. 'I have to –'

'I would like to see what he's doing. Now.'

Later, thinking back, Chong considered how she could have flatly refused. The order was nonsensical and downright dangerous. There was no way it would have held up under inquiry. At the time, she found herself obeying, switching the displays to Craator, her hands shaking a little as she realized that she was literally abandoning at least two people to their fate.

Later, thinking back, she would wonder why she had ever done it. That was because she couldn't quite recapture that black and icy chill of terror that Garon's voice had sent through her. You are nothing, it seemed to say. You are here to do my will and nothing else, and you will do it. It held no threat of what might happen if things

43

were otherwise, because there was no possible way that things could *be* otherwise.

You did what he told you to. And that was it.

The view from Craator's helmet-cam now showed the roof of a hab-block: a tangle of piping and cabling, clumps of water tanks and forests of comms dishes, the vane-like arrangements of the expulsion fans and heat sinks of cooling units. Another, newer structure had been built here: a large catapult arrangement seemingly cobbled together from cannibalized junk. Bright forms swarmed around it, and as the camera drew closer they became distinct: Piglet People dressed in the garish Hawaiian shirts that was their ceremonial garb, several of them holding tethered animals.

As the camera fell closer, travelling very fast now, it focused on a group of figures leading the lumbering form of what might or might not have been an elephant.

'Let me talk to him,' Garon said behind Chong.

'Sire?'

Even given the Authority of Garon, distracting an Adjudicator like this would be an Inquisition offence. Chong hesitated.

The High Churchman simply reached forward and pressed the switch that activated the external comms of the console. 'Craator.' There was no hint of questioning.

'What?' The image from the helmet-cam jolted as if in startlement. 'What the Sheol d'you think you're playing at?'

'This is High Churchman Garon. I have new and direct orders for you.'

'Yeah, well cruk off and give them to me later. I'm busy.'

Chong was shocked – not so much by the language itself, as by the angry contempt in Craator's voice towards a High Churchman, whatever the circumstances. Garon, however, continued as if the

Adjudicator hadn't spoken. 'You will dispose of your current duties with all possible dispatch and report for secondment to Sector 3 Riot Control. I repeat, Craator, with all possible dispatch.'

Chong repressed a little shudder. The Piglet People, for all the havoc their religious practices had caused, were not inherently violent criminals or murderers. Standard practice would be to subdue them, restrain and then Adjudge them for whatever damage, injury or death they had ultimately caused. Garon, now, was ordering that they be summarily executed, by any means, regardless of any civilians who might get in the way. An Adjudicator's MAV was equipped with heavy-duty missiles capable of taking out an entire block, and Garon was ordering Craator to use them.

The roof of the block filled the monitor now. Craator's arrival was bare seconds imminent.

Then the image jolted and strobed and blanked out completely. The comms pack relaying it had probably been damaged on impact.

'What was that?' Craator's voice was almost drowned out by static. 'You broke up on me. I didn't get that last bit.'

Chong glanced back to see Garon open his mouth to speak, and then shut it as Craator's transmission was drowned out by the static entirely.

For a while Garon regarded the blank monitor silently. Then he turned his steady gaze to Chong.

'I believe I shall have to take an especial interest in our Adjudicator Craator. I feared I would. I'll have to watch him close.'

He reached out a hand and touched her. She felt the dry, cold skin of it against the side of her neck.

'Things are changing, Technician Chong,' he told her solemnly. 'If we are all to be saved, then we in the Church must act together for the greater good. And those who are not with us are against us.'

* * *

45

In her credit-operated capsule, Mora Valdez coughed and rolled over on her mattress.

Her lungs seemed loose and viscous, detached on some subtle level that had her worrying about the effects of a serious coughing fit. Like that guy she had seen once, on Jadriis IV, up on adreno-acs cut with some kind of locally mutated willowfine.

The bloated sense, the sense of things sloshing about inside her, puzzled her. You came down off a Janie buzz dehydrated and rasping. Had she bloated herself with water before crashing and simply blanked it out?

No. The feeling was more like . . . hot and greasy and electric. Like when you used a spiky massage oil that made your skin tingle – only now it was inside her, permeating her. Filling her up.

The mushy feeling in her head made it difficult to think. She had never felt like this before. Was it some kind of skaggy alien disease she had caught at Volan's, or on the pneumatique? Was it serious? Was it fatal? Was she finally going to die?

Mora Valdez rolled over again, reaching for the pitifully small collection of objects that was the entire material sum of her life: costume jewellery, cosmetic disposables, Juanita, the now long-headless doll that had somehow followed her around for as long as she could remember, the shard of chromed polypropylene that she used as a mirror.

There was something nagging at the back of her mind, something she could not quite put her finger on until she saw the boil-like growths on her face.

Then she put her fingers on the growths on her arms. The ones that covered them, that she had seen but had not let herself notice, because if she *had* let herself notice them she would have started coughing (*screaming*) and not be able to stop.

The growths felt mushy, not quite solid, sliding around as if they were not quite flesh. As if they were not quite *real*. They felt like the things sliding around inside her.

46

Mora Valdez moaned quietly, because she desperately wanted to scream. In her eyes, in the mirror, a reddish energy glow pulsed.

Six

___

Avron Jelks now prowled the stage, tracking microcams relaying his face to the screens behind him. It was a blocky face, solid as a rock, but unremarkable. The face of any man on the street. The face of Everyman.

Ah, but his eyes . . .

They were pale blue and clear and rock-steady, beaming out of his unremarkable face as though gazing, unflinching, into the troubled future that only they could see. And then, without moving, they would somehow change and it was as though he was looking at *you*. Just you, out of thousands, and there was fire in them. Burning into you, burning off the layers of fear and indecision, burning into your very soul, transmuting and igniting it.

Making it burn.

He had been detailing, with calm precision, the most recent atrocities and repressions of the Adjudicators, culminating in the suppression of the right to congregate that this rally had been expressly called to flout. Peri, as she watched and listened, had been struck by the sheer degree of courage this involved. Not only for resisting these unjust laws, but in making himself the focus of this resistance. It reminded her a little of the Governor on Varos, a man who had occupied his position in a system that would kill him for the simple reason that it had to be done. Admittedly, the positions were reversed here – authority on one hand, dissident on the other – but the nobility of action was the same: knowing what was coming, and what must be done, and quite calmly, without

48

regret, accepting it because there was no other way.

'They have taken our right to say no,' Jelks was saying now, perfectly calm but with the rumble of barely constrained, cataclysmic passion. 'So we will not say no. We will say *yes*.' He struck his palm firmly and with a regular beat on every 'yes' to emphasize his words. '*Yes*, we will meet, as is our right. *Yes*, we will make our voices heard, as is our right. *Yes*, we will demand the freedom that is our right and given destiny!'

Peri felt the *surge* as the crowd began cheering – and would have responded herself, too, had not the sardonic man behind her, Kane, spoken in her ear again.

'Nice bit of construction,' he said. 'Rule of three.'

He snapped his fingers three times rapidly.

'Bang, bang, *bang*, and get 'em all cheering. Notice how they started shouting on the beat? He could have told 'em they'd have toast three times a week and twice on Sunday.'

With everyone else cheering around her, Peri suddenly felt cheated and sick. She rounded on him with something like hatred. His voice had been modulated so that it cut *under* rather than through the ovation around them, as though it were some little, quiet and mocking voice inside her, and Peri found she couldn't catch the trick.

She settled for aiming a slap at his face. It wasn't like her at all, but he had made her so furious. It was as though all the irritations and the worries of the last few months had come out in a single, vicious lump. He casually flicked his head to one side so that her fist barely grazed his cheek. Her momentum carried her forward and into him and she smelt old sweat and leather.

She shoved him roughly away from her, so far as he could go against the press of people behind. They and the rest of the crowd were winding down from their outburst now. She could just about make herself heard.

'Get away from me,' she snapped. 'Just get away.'

The man, Kane, held up his hands and smiled placatingly. 'Hey, I don't mean anything. You do what you like.'

Peri turned her back on the man and her eyes back to the stage, where Avron Jelks was about to continue speaking.

As she did so, she thought she caught a flash of something under the man Kane's smile. It didn't seem particularly threatening, but she hadn't seen it before, and she didn't know what it was. It was only later that she identified it as distaste.

In the same way that secure lines run through a telephonic system, the physical communications of the Habitat, its interways and walkways, were paralleled by heavily armoured tubeways and underground tunnels given over to the Adjudicators. You could travel from any point to another faster than was possible any other way. At strategic points throughout this subnetwork were large bunkers for the deployment of riot control forces, vehicles and equipment, and Craator piloted his MAV out of the tubeway to find that the Sector 3 bunker was packed to capacity.

In addition to street Adjudicators and the more heavily armed and armoured Riot Control, Craator saw several squads of Shok-TAC – exosuited soldiers who were ordinarily kept in reserve for some ultimate emergency like an invasion or a full-scale war. In addition to the common MAVs there were heavy-duty armoured hovs and fliers, up to and including a big, military-spec Strikeout XIV. The assembled forces were ranked before the heavy butterfly shutters that would open out on to the Sector 3 streets. Something about them, the tension they gave off, the smell in the air, reminded him of the genetically boosted mastiff-lemur hybrids in the Animal Handling Division straining at the leash.

Riot Control were running things, and Craator recognized Command-Adjudicator Gloathe, commander of operations, talking with the leader of one of the Shok-TAC squads. Or, rather – since Shok-TAC was made up almost exclusively of violent and irredeemably psychopathic criminals, mind-wiped and implanted with basic identity constructs – shouting at him and hitting him with his nightstick until the soldier got what he wanted.

Craator climbed off his MAV and headed for the commander, fixing his face rigid to disguise his distaste. Like Craator himself, Gloathe ranked as high in the Church as it was possible to go without being a High Churchman, but there the resemblance ended.

Gloathe was a vicious brute, working within the letter of the Statutes, but using those Statutes as the remit for his brutality. He currently held the Church record for deaths, both before and during custody, and the recent toughening up of the Church procedures had been something of a Godsend to him.

As Craator approached, Gloathe finished belabouring the Shok-TAC and shoved him away to wander mindlessly back to his squad. He turned to Craator and sneered. 'You took your time getting here.'

'Yeah, well I had better things to do.' Craator pointedly glared about the bunker – not to take it in, but to make his perusal obvious. 'Seems a little over the top for breaking up a demonstration. Looks like you're gearing up for a small war.'

'The time for leniency is past,' Gloathe said with a pompous and self-conscious attempt at the portentous tone of High Churchman Garon, from whom the phrase had probably originally come. Gloathe was fond of quoting High Churchman Garon. 'The Human Firsters decide to flout our Statutes, we give them a telling.' He grinned wolfishly. 'And, because we want to be clear about it, we tell them very loud.'

Craator kept his face immobile. 'So where do you want me?'

Gloathe gestured towards the street Adjudicators, who had congregated slightly apart from the other forces and were scowling at them with contempt. Even in their helmets and uniforms there seemed something more *human* about them. Possibly, Craator thought, it was

51

because their proper function was more to deal with people on the human level, on an individual basis, than as a faceless mass. It stopped them from becoming truly faceless in themselves.

'You take your people and look after the perimeter containment,' Gloathe said. 'You seal it and deal with the peripheral disturbance. Human or . . .' He made the little zipper gesture across his mouth that, among the Adjudicators, had become the code for the derogatory term 'skag'. 'Anyone comes out, anyone goes in, you take 'em down. Nobody gets through.'

For a split second, Craator was speechless. The result of a tactic like that would be so obvious that only a certified moron would even so much as consider it.

A certified moron or a cold-blooded butcher.

'High Churchman Garon?' he said at last.

Gloathe grinned again. 'Express orders. He's ordered Minimum Necessary Force.'

Even concentrating on the individual and particular, it was possible to discern the larger forces at work here as you reapproached the concourse. Out on the interways and walkways the humans and other lifeforms were mixing, if not in peace and harmony, then at least with as much as any general crowd. The concourse, on the other hand, was filled entirely with humans – and, crucially, humans of a certain type. Those who followed a cause and were focused on it. The unified and aligned.

As you approached it the basic, not particularly noble but occasionally halfway decent human faces vanished – the unaligned owners of them simply didn't care and they had better things to do. This was not some festival or entertainment which one might casually wander into and out of. You were either in or you were out.

The practical upshot was that what might, ordinarily, have been a buffer zone between some mass event and the world outside was now a sharp delineation. This was where the innately violent gathered, in the hope of confrontation. At the access points and ramps, surly, armed, paramilitary-looking human thugs glowered with dislike at anything nonhuman, self-appointedly determined to keep these elements away with whatever force they had at their disposal.

Oh, well. This was going to be one of those times when looking precisely like a human was a distinct advantage. The Doctor brushed down his patchwork coat and did up a couple of buttons the right way round and let surface several of the human mannerisms and quirks he had worked hard to acquire over several lifetimes. He marched towards the armed thugs with a disarming grin on his face.

'You!' one of the thugs bellowed. 'Where d'you think you're goin', skag?'

This was such a dramatically apposite punchline that the Doctor was about to answer – until he realized that the thug was addressing someone else: a segmented multipedal creature some five feet long and reminiscent of a centipede walking on its back nine rows of legs. It had wandered, seemingly entirely aimlessly, too close.

Its five frontmost sets of legs were adapted into different kinds of manipulatory appendage. Rows of chameleon-like, directional eyes ran along its entire length, vestigial to the rear, fully developed at the front. Its tail ended in a sharp and dangerous-looking barb, which glistened with some viscous alien ichor. A strap ran around its body, securing a boxlike arrangement of polished wood and brass, with brass keys reminiscent of those on a typewriter immediately after they had been invented. Three ivory speaking horns, of differing lengths and curves, protruded from this. The creature's lowermost manipulators were typing frantically on it, and complicated clockwork whirred within.

'Most profound enquiries as to the express purpose of your most welcome felicitation,' the box said, 'but might one's good self prognosticate to the effect that said esteemed felicitation was perchance intended for the

53

reciprocatory awareness of one's good self?'

The armed thug looked at the creature for a moment, trying to work this out. Several others joined him. During the interim, the mass rally beyond erupted into sustained applause.

'What?' he said at last, and some time after the applause had died down.

Again the manipulators typed frantically.

'One was merely attempting to ascertain the intentionality pursuant to the –'

The lead thug, however, had had enough. He swung his jointed baton – the same sort as were commonly carried by Adjudicators – at the creature and smashed open the box.

The others moved in.

'Oh damn,' the Doctor said, to himself, off to one side on the sidelines and totally ignored. 'Enough of the pontificating on the nature of specificity in a polyfractal universe. I suppose it's time I stepped in and actually *did* something.'

In his spartan, bare-walled quarters in the Temple of Adjudication, High Churchman Garon sat in a hard-backed chair, his elbows on the high rests, fingers steepled before him, eyes staring into nothing.

He wasn't praying. He had more direct ways of communicating with his God. His mind was a perfect blank. It was as though he had switched himself off.

He was broken from his reverie by a voice from the METATRON, the internal communications system that was slaved to OBERON.

'Personal communiqué received from Command-Adjudicator Gloathe,' it said.

There was no sense of transition. Garon simply turned his head and began to speak. 'Put him through. Are you quite prepared, Gloathe?'

'Locked and loaded. We're ready to go.' The Command-Adjudicator sounded excited.

Possibly too excited, Garon thought. Possibly, after careful consideration of the matter, after he had served his purpose, Gloathe might have to be purged. It was a stern duty, but it might just have to be done.

'Then by all means proceed,' Garon said. 'And remember, Gloathe, this is something of a test operation. The way you comport yourself and your men might well be vital to the continued supremacy of the Church as an administrative force. Please don't fail me, Gloathe.'

'We won't, sir. I only wish we were going up against the skags this time.' Gloathe's voice became more heated. 'We could really show 'em. Take them to the –'

'All in good time, Gloathe. All in good time.'

But not for you, Garon thought, coming to a decision. Better the open insubordination of a Craator than the mindless zealotry of a Gloathe. The one you could predict and contain, the other was like the pus from some infection: you could direct the flow, but sooner or later it had to burst out.

That reminded him. 'Have Craator's recent detainees been brought into the Church?' he asked the META-TRON unit.

'Yes,' the unit said with no humanly perceptible pause. 'Seventeen porcines indigenous to the Glomi system. Detained pending damage assessment and reparation.'

'Ah yes,' Garon mused. 'The famous law-abiding Piglet People of Glomi IV. Aside from their unfortunate religious practices, of course.' He pondered the matter for a moment. 'However, their actions did not exactly constitute a *secular* crime, and an example must be set. We have, after all, our duty to the one true God.'

He pondered the matter further, until he was struck by a happy inspiration. 'I believe that it's time we began implementing our more, ah, *public* appliances of punishment. The Lorraine crosses, I think. It might serve as some small example to others.'

Seven

On the access ramp on the edge of the concourse, emboldened by the lack of overt resistance, a thug extricated his club from the clockwork-prolapsing remains of the box strapped to the creature, and brought it back to apply it to the carapace of its owner. He brought it down with a meaty smack – as it landed solidly in the palm of the tallish, slightly odd-looking man, who was now somehow positioned between himself and his intended victim.

'An interesting weapon,' he said, grinning at him amiably. 'Do you mind if I take a closer look?'

The tall man simply seemed to tug on the interesting weapon lightly – and the thug gave a gasp of pain as it was wrenched from his grip with a seemingly inhuman strength. The tall man examined the baton critically, turning it absently over in his hands and regarding it from under raised eyebrows.

'Very nice,' he said. 'The joint transfers the power of the stroke transversely. It must take a certain amount of skill to use it to its best advantage.'

But by now the thug had entirely had enough. He swung his fist in a bludgeoning backhand arc at the tall man's face – which suddenly wasn't there any more. The momentum of the swing carried the thug around, and he was only dimly aware of a tall and brightly coloured presence to the other side of him, before a finger planted firmly in his exposed inner arm deadened it. The thug lurched back, colliding with one of his comrades, who, taking up on his original lead, had closed in for the attack. Instinctively, this other thug lashed out with his own baton, smacking the original thug squarely in the mouth. There was a crunch and a small spray of teeth.

In the meantime, simultaneously, a third thug was landing flat on his face – having somehow tangled his feet in a jointed baton that the tall man seemed to have absently dropped. This now left two of the original group still standing – the thug who had inadvertently disabled his leader and one other. These two now bracketed the tall man – who now simply stood there, hands in his pockets, looking around cheerfully as if he hadn't a care in the world.

They swung their sticks. They hit him and the blows rebounded, leaving him apparently undamaged, returning with impossible force to smack the two surviving thugs dead square in their respective foreheads, and knock them both out cold. They went down as though they had been poleaxed, which in a very real sense they had been.

The entire altercation had taken perhaps three seconds. Two thugs were unconscious, their leader on his knees, clutching at his bleeding face and shouting, somewhat indistinctly, 'Moush! Ooo groke my moush!' The thug who had tripped and fallen on his face was climbing furiously to his feet. He took a look around, worked out the available odds, and backed surlily off.

'I said you needed a certain degree of skill.' The Doctor shrugged and flicked an imaginary fleck of dust from the lapel of his coat. Then he strolled over to the alien creature, which was hastily attempting to repair the broken mechanism strapped around itself.

The creature typed something on the keyboard and the clockwork ratcheted and clicked: 'Skrek bloork ta *whirr* tickticktick . . .' the box said. 'Fugger buckit ticktick-tick-*skreak!* What an inconvenientualizational funt.'

The creature made another small adjustment to the mechanism and started typing yet again: 'Investigation, experimentation, analysis, *uno, dos, trés . . .* excellent! Immoderately laudable, *ou quoi?*'

It turned several of its extensible eyes towards the Doctor.

'Must impart profoundest and most meaty recognition and thankfulness towards your very person. One was upon something of the precipitational point of entertaining dubiety as to the viability of one's continuational and corporeal actuality.'

'Think nothing of it,' said the Doctor, one wary eye on the temporarily disabled thugs.

'One regrets that one cannot impart one's legitimate and veracious appellation with the correct and justly warranted degree of verisimilitude,' said the creature. 'Unhappy same tends towards irreparable unspeakability upon the hominid palate.'

The Doctor smiled a secret smile. 'You could try me.'

The creature hammered on its keyboard. For the next twenty seconds there was a sound like a freight train with a live whale strapped to it, ploughing through a series of cratefuls of chickens, with ground-shaking sonic booms in the background for good measure.

After the final explosion and squawk had died away the Doctor shrugged. 'Point taken,' he said. 'I don't suppose you have a kind of *nom de plume*? Something someone vaguely humanoid can get its tongue around?'

'Affirmativity towards an extreme exquisitationality!' the creature declared. 'One has stipulated for the appellation, pursuant to the comprehensibility of the hominid ear, of Queegvogel Duck Duck Duck Duck Duck Seven!'

The Doctor raised an eyebrow. 'Duck Duck Duck Duck Duck Seven?'

'Ah! Apologatory exposition. One's voder/vocoder portmanteau-apparati would appear to be slightly more debilitationally challenged than one provisionalization-arily presumed.'

The creature made another adjustment. 'Queegvogel Duck Duck Duck Duck Duck *Duck* Seven.'

'How about,' said the Doctor, carefully, 'if I just call you Queegvogel? Or even Queeg?'

'One might tend to allow such familiarizationality of address,' said Queegvogel, or even Queeg, magnanimously. 'One is, after all, perpetually and positionally in a state of debt.'

'Which reminds me . . .' The Doctor looked at the three disabled thugs, who were now showing signs of movement and recovery. The fourth could be back at any second with reinforcements. As a man of peace, he really didn't feel up to, as it were, precipitately effecting a further educationally edifying interlude. 'I think we'd better get you somewhere safe,' he told Queegvogel. 'I have the distinct feeling that this might not be a healthy place to –'

Quite what it might not have been a healthy place to do exactly, Queegvogel never learnt. Overhead, several dark shapes streaked by with a whine of impellers, and in the human-filled concourse and the more homogenized surrounding sector, all culturally and biologically applicable hells broke loose.

'Minimum necessary force', like so much of the terminology of the Church of Adjudication, had its roots back in the police forces of twentieth-century Earth. In the same way as a 'cleaning' or 'hygienics' squad had been a euphemism for the slaughtering of dissidents and street children, 'minimum necessary force' had been and was a euphemism for what the criminal circles, with a slightly greater degree of accuracy and honesty, had called 'extreme prejudice'.

On the concourse, Peri looked up as a shadow fell over her. Above her, silhouetted against the pulsing geodesic sky, hanging in the air and banking slowly round, were four large craft comprising globular modules bolted to a scaffolding framework.

For a moment Peri was caught wrong-footed, in a way

that almost nobody from her planetary time period would have been. Whereas another twentieth-century human might have to go through a mental gear change, Peri knew in her bones and from personal experience that *this* was what spaceships really looked like. Her first, panicked thought was that this was some alien attack force, smashing through the dome and killing everything and everyone under it by explosive decompression.

The fact that this was obviously not happening registered itself almost instantly, and then she saw the silver markings on the craft: the insignia of the Adjudicators. She wondered why she had instinctively thought in terms of alien attack. Having been on the wrong end of quite a few of such things, she knew that the actuality of it was nothing like the portrayal of old B-movies. The mother ship might hang menacingly over the defenceless kingdoms of the world, but the simple mechanics of scale meant you would never actually *see* it.

She didn't have time to wonder about anything else for the moment, though, because at that point eject hatches opened in the craft and armoured figures dropped from them. They had heavy-duty, wide-snouted guns, seemingly too big for a human to possibly handle, but supported by hydraulic rack-and-hinge mechanisms bolted to their body armour, and they used the guns before they landed in the crowd. Pepper-gas canisters detonated, incendiary slugs flared.

The people on the concourse began to burn and choke and scream.

In the miasmic chaos that followed, Peri's throat became closed and raw and clotted, and a searing pain gripped her eyes as though they had been dashed with acid. She found herself feeling strangely detached and focused at the same time. Focusing on the way a girl got hit with a baton round that stove in the side of her head, focusing on how it changed her in interesting ways and noting in passing that she was the woollen-clad girl she had talked to earlier. Gazing at the gas-hazed forms of people as they caught fire, or jerked under small-arms fire, or went down under the weight of the armoured figures simply landing on top of them, but not really feeling anything.

It was as though her body was functioning and making itself move, but there was nothing inside her actually doing it. It was only later that she realized she had been suffering profound psychological shock.

Somebody grabbed her by the arm and wrenched at her.

She looked at him and realized he was Kane – and felt absurdly grateful. Despite, or even because of, her dislike of him, he was someone she could think of as *real*. It cut through the trauma and confusion that threatened to engulf her. Off to one side, someone else went down, hit by the baton round that had zipped past her left ear. That almost hit me, she thought absently, without making any sort of real connection.

Kane was shouting at her, but her ears felt mushy inside and she couldn't make out what it was. She looked at him with eyebrows raised in polite enquiry. Kane mouthed something that sounded like, 'Offer ducks *snake*!' He took his hand off her and pulled it back and for a moment Peri thought he was going to hit her. She felt frightened.

Then Kane lowered his hands and took hold of her again. He roughly pulled her round and with his other hand pointed to some figures through the smoke who were working their way through the carnage in loose formation. Something about their movements triggered recognition in her. She was reminded of the freedom fighters she had met in the maze on Varos as they beat a tactical retreat from the Guards. These people moved with the same watchful, responsive, sure-footed caution of trained fighters living to fight another day.

These people, Peri realized, knew what they were doing – and the thought cut through her torpor that if she was going to survive, here and now, she could do a

61

lot worse than go along. She nodded to Kane, who was desperately trying to haul her towards them, and let him take her along.

As the concourse erupted into violence, the access ramps swiftly became little more than deathtraps, jammed by people trying to get out. They piled up and tore at each other in panic and smothered.

The Doctor and Queegvogel, having been caught ahead of the crush, found themselves joining in the haphazard efforts of those in the surrounding sector to help these people out. Due to recent events they might not have much love for the people on the concourse, but, as the Doctor pointed out, if you only tried to save the things you loved, you ended up with the same kind of situation as on twentieth-century Earth – where the great white shark had been allowed to become extinct while little fluffy bunnies laid waste to an entire continent.

Queegvogel had merely been of the opinion that it was the civilizationarily decent office for those purporting to a sentient and cultivated frame of mentation to do.

Now, as the Doctor hauled a body from the pile, he noted that it was one of the thugs he'd encountered earlier on. He checked the pulse and respiration and decided against giving him the kiss of life. A Time Lord's oxygenation system used almost every atom of available oxygen, so it wouldn't do any good for one thing. The Doctor thumped the inert body's chest until it spasmed and drew rasping breath, then passed it down the line.

Looking around, he saw that some of the helping nonhumanoids had slightly odd ideas about how humanoid bodies worked, and what should be treated. Ah, well. Most of those they were ministering to would live, more or less, and it was better than no help at all.

Somebody scuttled past him to pick free another body. It was Queeg. The movements of his cilia legs seemed jerky and distraught. 'An extreme degree of senselessness on the part of our worthy representatives of judicial governance!' he exclaimed, his sesquipedalian language forms breaking down slightly under the stress of circumstances. 'One had gathered that the Church of Adjudication was severe to the exceptionality, but this is wholly unconscionable!'

They became aware of the sound of sirens behind them, and turned to see the approaching squads of Adjudicators as they cut through the crowd on the street and broke it apart.

'A precipitant if tardy arrival,' Queegvogel said. 'They have finally come to effect some degree of aid to the results of their more militaristic endeavours?'

The Doctor looked at the approaching Adjudicators and saw the riot shielding on their vehicles, the water-cannon rigs and the mobile barricades.

'I don't think so,' he said quietly. 'What I really think is that it might be time to start looking for a way out. Quickly.'

The group worked their way through the fighting, taking their wounded with them, but not stopping to help the others. There was a limit to what anybody could do.

They all wore the arm bands that Peri had noticed on people earlier, but there were marked differences. They wore heavy, battered, leather, polymer and moulded rubber, mismatched and obviously scavenged from the Habitat's available materials, but there was a uniformity about their dress that came from functionality. They were dressed for combat. As she and Kane followed them, Peri wondered how they could join them. They didn't seem the sort of people to just let strangers tag along.

Kane solved the problem, more or less by accident.

They had almost reached the group when the form of an Adjudicator reared from a pall of smoke. This was one of the Adjudicators who had been patrolling the rally, and had joined with the troops in their assault on the crowd. They seemed, however, to have been improperly briefed, and they certainly hadn't been properly equipped for active combat. His uniform was in shreds, and he carried the damaged gun of a soldier without the balancing mechanism, so he could barely lift it.

He swung the weapon up with a lurch, aiming it in the general direction of the escaping group – and then Kane sprang. He collided with the Adjudicator in a tangle and knocked him off his feet, the combined weight of weapon and man knocking him cold.

Kane staggered to his feet and dragged the weapon off the supine form. He took hold of Peri again and led her towards the group, who had been preparing to defend themselves, and then paused to watch the altercation. Their leader, a rangy man with a bald head and a scar running down across his left eye, gave Kane a grudging nod. 'That was well enough done.'

'Yeah, well,' Kane said. 'I couldn't let a Jood take down White Fire's finest.'

'What's –' Peri began to ask, before Kane elbowed her solidly in the ribs.

The group had started moving again. Kane and Peri tagged along, and no one seemed to object. Their scarred leader shot a glance back at the fallen Adjudicator, who had recovered consciousness and was stirring weakly. 'You should have finished him off.'

'Nah,' Kane said. 'He wasn't worth it.'

The leader was looking at him closely. 'You're with White Fire?'

'You might call me a fellow traveller,' said Kane. 'Currently unaffiliated.'

The leader frowned. 'You're either with us or against us.'

'Then I think it's about time we properly joined.' Kane gestured in the general direction of where the plinth had been before the rally had erupted into chaos. 'What about Jelks? Are people getting him out?'

'We have a squad dealing with it.'

'Incoming!' This last came from another in the group, a muscular woman with her cropped hair wrapped in a

64

bandanna. Kane grabbed hold of Peri and pulled her off her feet, landing flat on the paving beside her. The White Fire people did likewise as a pepper-gas grenade shot over them and detonated.

Peri caught a whiff of gas and coughed and retched. She stuck her forearm over her mouth and tried to breathe through the material of her top. It didn't help much.

The White Fire people produced filter units and pressed them to their faces. Kane, it seemed, had somehow got hold of a simple gauze face mask. He tied it on, giving himself the aspect of a grubby surgeon after a minor hospital explosion.

The leader of the White Fire people noted it. 'You came prepared. That's good. The name's Draker.' A small speaking grille on the side of his gas mask gave his voice a strange, displaced and tinny quality.

'Hello, Draker,' said Kane. 'Do you know how we can get the Sheol out of here?'

Draker looked at him for a long moment, appraising him, and then nodded. 'We have ways.'

On the crash-erected barricades in the surrounding sector, Adjudicator Craator scanned the tangled crowds of those attempting to escape and came to a decision.

'Give 'em a dose of the IG gas,' he said. 'It'll drop 'em down and stop them doing any more damage to themselves at the very least.'

'Sir?' A young Adjudicator who was clearly spoiling for a fight looked at him dubiously. 'The High Churchman and Commander Gloathe ordered us to use Minimum –'

Craator turned to the young Adjudicator and gave him a scowl that almost had him jumping off his MAV in alarm. 'Garon and Gloathe aren't here. I am. I'm giving you your orders direct, and if you don't jump to it I'll have your kidneys laid open with the *kout*. Do I make myself clear?'

* * *

65

On the other side of the barricades, Queegvogel saw the Adjudicators raise their guns and heard the pop of capsules breaking. The gas was odourless, but he felt a certain mushiness in his mind that he remembered from a time when the Adjudicators had raided a club he had attended at the insistence of one of his rasher brood-siblings. The gas seemed to work on a wide variety of lifeforms, and simply dropped them as though their limbs and joints had suddenly become as slack and loose as cotton.

'Ah well ^%&R,' he muttered, his manipulators fumbling at several of his vocoder keys. 'One$ senses a regrettable but X&! hopefully tempoRary imminence of . . .'

He became aware of a sudden commotion beside him.

The Doctor, whom Queegvogel had recognized by various signs as a fellow non-Terran instantly – despite the unfortunately Terran look he affected – was behaving rather oddly. He was shaking like a jackhammer and clawing at his clothing with palsied, hooked and spasming hands.

Suddenly, he dropped to his knees. He looked up at Queegvogel and the shaking stopped as if somebody had thrown a switch.

'Killing me,' the Doctor said with a dead and utter calm. 'It's –'

Then he slumped forward, his face smacking into the paving, to lie there motionless.

In his private quarters, in what might be regarded as his sanctum, High Churchman Garon watched the fighting on the Sector 3 concourse, relayed via hovering Adjudication microcams and routed through the METATRON. A tactical-readout overlay down one side of the screen predicted a fatality rate of 1.4 per cent of the Shok-TAC forces, 57.9 per cent of the crowd they had attacked, with an additional fifteen-per-cent fatality rate of the Adjudicators who had already been there on the scene.

Ah, well, Garon thought. It was for their own good. In the larger, more important sense of things, of course. The only problem might be that the survivors would survive slightly less intact for current purposes.

'Change the viewpoint,' Garon told the META-TRON. 'Show me the periphery. Lock in on Craator.'

The signal switched to a microcam hovering at the edge of the concourse, the Adjudicators on the barricades facing what appeared to be simply a pile of bodies.

'Are they dead?' Garon asked. 'The ones who aren't moving, I mean,' he added conscientiously, to avoid confusing the subsystem's somewhat limited processes.

The METATRON enhanced and extrapolated the image-feed, comparing it with pattern-recognition parameters stored inside it.

'Negative,' it said. 'Indications are that IG immobilization has been effected. Projected fatalities: fifteen point four one per cent given no change in current data. Causes of death will include: suffocation, massive haemorrhaging from existing wounds, severe unclassified reaction to —'

'Spare me the gory details. They are of no matter.'

Garon looked upon the bodies with satisfaction. This was why he had made sure that Adjudicator Craator had been in charge of the containment squads. He had *known* that Craator would bend the orders to do something like this. Craator, being Craator, could do no other.

And the result was the procurement of several hundred, even a thousand, viable . . . subjects. Call them subjects. And they had been procured without the direct, and traceable, involvement of High Churchman Garon.

Eight

The Sector 3 operation, by the time it was reported by the Habitat's news services, became a mob riot caused by violent elements from within the crowd itself, and barely contained by poorly armed Adjudication services. Fatality figures were drastically reduced, three-quarters of them reported as detainees held, incommunicado, until a time when they might be Adjudged.

In itself, it was merely the latest, biggest and most obvious result of the tensions and the mass psychoses that were the hallmark of the Crazy Season.

Only this time the Crazy Season was worse.

The process went like this: nobody did anything particularly out of character, nobody became more vicious than they innately were – things just went wrong and got tragically out of hand. A man might spill another man's drink in a bar, the other might thump him a little too hard, forgetting that he had the broken glass still in hand. In a domestic dispute, a woman might lash out with her nails, and find her fingers plunging into the eyeballs of her partner. Someone might shove someone else in a minor altercation on a walkway, some hundred metres over ground level . . .

These and thousands of relatively minor incidents like them, all of them happening and accumulating at once. Nobody, at the time, was conscious of participating in a step system, a tragically common group dynamic that in Earth's middle ages had resulted in mass dancing fits and animal executions and, later, in mass extermination and global war. Each little step made the next step a little easier: kicking in shopfronts made it easier to throw people into ghettos, and then into purpose-built camps . . .

And all the while the Node pulsed brighter. Pulsed so bright it hurt the eyes.   -

In his effectively impregnable offices, in a Sector 7 private-members' club known as the Jade Shebeen, Kha t'zuk Volan daintily picked a scrap of lizard flesh from between his teeth, briefly considered the others squirming in the basket on the desk before him and decided against it.

Then he turned his attention back towards the mess beyond the desk.

Volan was Silurian and proud of it. He had no truck with those pathetic assimilationists who called themselves Earth Reptiles and tried to ape, as it were, the partially evolved simians who called themselves *hom sap*.

Nonetheless, in the cold and consciously controlled calculation of his mind, he was forced to wonder if his immediately previous actions might not in fact have been slightly inappropriate.

The matter had been simple enough. One of his doormen, a human named Prekodravac, had made a habit of rolling drunken clientele on their way out. This was in a sense fair enough – Volan himself had got his start like that, years before, when he had worked as one of the 'hosts' at the City of Unending Delights on Jaros – but the Jade Shebeen was *Volan's* place, and Prekodravac hadn't even offered Volan his cut. This really couldn't be allowed.

The intention had been to have the man brought down to his office and then frighten the life out of him. This, as it turned out, had been the literal and actual truth. Volan had looked at him, and calmly explained the situation: what he expected of his staff and what would happen if they did not damned well supply it precisely – all the while pulsing his third eye on a minimal cycle that had the man wetting himself in his boots.

It had been in the midst of this that a strange, cold impulse had occurred in Volan's mind. It was a quiet, still impulse, and strangely undramatic. It was the kind of thought that has one looking at a nail sticking out of a wall and idly wondering what it would be like to press your head up against it and force it into the skull. Or what it would be like to smash your mouth into a pneumatique capsule as it goes past. Or to jump off a hab-block. The kind of impulse that is so terrifying for the reason that one might just say, what the Sheol, and simply do it.

Fortunately for Volan, if not for Prekodravac, this impulse had been other-directed. Volan had always carefully controlled the emissions of his third eye, judiciously applying its influence as and when necessary, and never using more than the precise amount required. Now, he found himself wondering what it would be like just to let it go. So he did.

He had felt a kind of clean, exertive jerk, like lifting some weight on the upper limit of one's strength. Prekodravac's head had exploded.

So now Volan sat, munching on his light mid-morning snack, contemplating the mess and wondering just what had possessed him to do such a thing. He didn't care the slightest about the dead man slumped on and, indeed, scattered over a wide area of the carpet; he just wondered how he could have done such a thing.

The cleaning bills were going to be a bugger, for a start.

It was at that point that a small alarm chimed from the monitor on his desk. It wasn't anything serious, simply a change in the order of the Shebeen above him that might merit investigation. Volan had made his career out of investigating the small factors.

This was one of the lulls in the Habitat's day-and-night cycles. The hardened partygoers were crashed out in the party rooms that operated thirty hours a cycle.

70

The breakfast trade had been and gone. The lunchtime trade was yet to arrive. The Hentai sections tended to be used only in the Habitat night, certain things, by some unconscious assent, taking place only under the cover of darkness.

Now, the monitors showed that somebody or something was moving around one of the *Ecchi* rooms – one of the pressurized rooms that catered for the non-oxygenation metabolic clientele. Volan pulled down a readout and saw that the intruder, as the security system insisted on calling it, was tagged as an employee: MORA CICA VALDEZ BF/702–013.

Ah, yes. Volan recalled Mora Valdez BF/702–013. She really shouldn't be up and about this early, and she certainly shouldn't be here. The Valdez woman, he recalled, used prescribed hallucinogens. He tried to control the supply in various devious ways, but it was possible she had found some other source. Either that or his medical profiling systems were at fault, or she was being affected by this strange atmosphere that had taken over the entire Habitat of late – the atmosphere that, it occurred to Volan, had been at least partially responsible for his killing Prekodravac.

Whatever the reason, it was quite possible that the Valdez woman had wandered in under the influence of the drug, and might possibly injure herself. Volan was concerned – not for the human woman in herself, but more as a breeder might be concerned for his stock. He looked after his investment. Volan depressed a switch on his desk, and instantly one of his security staff appeared.

'Look after things here,' he said, gesturing to the monitor. 'Let me know if anything else happens.' He glanced back to the mess on the floor and shrugged. 'And have someone come in with a mop and bucket while you're about it.'

The Jade Shebeen, externally, was merely a nondescript doorway in the monolithic base of a hab-block at ground level. Inside it was a nondescript and seedy bar, nothing to distinguish it from a thousand others in the Habitat, or indeed a million others in the Galaxy.

The real action took place in the chambers below, carved out of the sterile rock of Dramos. There, as one descended by elevator and stairwell, as if one was descending into the Pit, the recreational facilities became darker and more extreme at every stage. The Hentai facilities were situated roughly two-thirds of the way down – there are worse things than the human and even the reptile mind can imagine.

Volan's office was on the lowest level of all, for the simple reason that its position gave its light and airy (if at the moment blood- and matter-spattered) spaces a sense of utter menace to those who had never seen it, and enhanced Volan's persona as the very devil himself, squatting in the blackest depths of his hole. He took his private gilt and red-plush elevator up to the Hentai section.

Volan stepped out into a corridor lined with minimalist lanterns and paper Japanese doors. The elegance was spoilt by the heavy-duty airlock flanges of the doors leading into the unoxygenated rooms. Readouts over all but one told him that they were unoccupied.

The airlock of the occupied room was locked and dogged. This was one of the chlorine-based environments. Through an observation porthole something bright and indistinct moved through the green haze of gases within.

The readout panel by the airlock showed that only MORA CICA VALDEZ BF/702–013 was within. Volan hit the intercom switch. 'Mora,' he said sternly, as one would upbraid an intransigent pet. 'What are you doing in there?'

There was a pause, and then a voice answered.

'Hurts,' it said. The voice was ghostly. There was a strange and polyphonic quality to it, as though several hundred people, in the next room, had quietly murmured the same word at once. 'Hurts and hurts. It hurts.'

'You come out from there right this minute, Mora,' Volan said, sternly. 'If you don't come out of there right this minute then I'll be angry. You don't want me to be *angry*, do you, Mora?'

'Hurts.'

For almost half a minute nothing happened. Then the readouts showed that MORA CICA VALDEZ BF/702–013 was in the airlock chamber, that the inner door was now shut, that the airlock was cycling. This relieved Volan somewhat, since in her obviously drugged-out state the Valdez woman would have been quite capable of forgetting how to work the lock, subjecting him to a blast from a roomful of atmospherically impure chlorine.

Through the porthole, the light inside the airlock seemed to pulse. Volan made a small mental note to have it fixed. Presently there came the multiple clangs of the airlock being undogged. The outer door swung open.

One of the distinguishing features of the Hentai concept was that it presented certain natural problems for a human expected to work in a hostile atmosphere. The solution was an impermeable, monomolecular, transparent and skin-tight suit especially adapted and tailored for the worker in question.

Volan took one look at the suit, and what was inside it, and screamed.

It was the last sound he ever made.

Section Two

Interrogation and Remand

Nine

For a large part of the afternoon the transports had been moving between the scene of the Sector 3 riots and the Temple of the Church of Adjudication. Transports containing the bodies of the living and the injured; transports containing the bodies of the dead. The living were taken down into the Holding Cells for processing, the dead were stockpiled. Scattered throughout the Habitat were recycling plants, where bodies were converted into fertilizer for food production, and the Church of Adjudication had one of its own.

Automation is only necessary when some real value is put on living workers. Here, forced-labour gangs were conscripted from the Holding Complex to wash and strip the bodies, pile any valuables like dental implants, artificial eyes and even shoes to one side, and haul them on to the conveyor belts that led directly to the mincers.

On the way, the bodies passed through sensor banks that logged them geno- and phenotypically, scanned them for CJD, hepatitis, HIV+907.1.1 and several thousand other communicable diseases. Since the term 'processing for fertilizer', like so much else, was something of a euphemism for what in actual fact missed out a couple of stages, these sensors were wired to err on the side of caution.

As a certain body, on a certain conveyor belt, passed through the sensors, an alarm was tripped and the conveyor belt ground to a halt.

* * *

'So what's the problem?' Craator was not in the best of moods as he stepped out of the bounce-tube, and into the Recycling Division loading bay. He had logged off for an hour in one of the hi-REM hypnagogic units that Adjudicators used instead of sleep, and he had not enjoyed being interrupted. The pervasive reek of vaguely fresh but slightly spoilt meat didn't help much, either.

Sexton, the med-tech in charge of body disposal, was disconcertingly cheerful and bland. Given his line of work, one might briefly consider someone lurching and disfigured with a hump. After instantly dismissing this, one might have thought he'd spend his life twitchy and traumatized by the horror of the job. Either that or gloaty, grinning and enjoying it with an unhealthy glee.

The fact is that nothing can be horrifying for extended periods of time. The reason why so many victims fall in love with the sociopathic kidnapper who is surely going to kill them, for example, is that, once the unsustainable terror has gone, and there's still a while before the skin's quite loose enough to make a suit, there's nothing much to do except talk. In much the same way, in the recycling plant, loading bodies on conveyor belts night and day simply made you stop thinking of them as bodies. They could be anything, and Sexton himself radiated cheerfulness and that bodily contentment that comes from regular hours and lots of healthy exercise.

Now he turned from where he was poking through a pile of shaved hair and gave Craator a friendly smile. 'Sorry to get you down here,' he said. 'You know I wouldn't do it ordinarily, but there's something I think you might like to see.'

Sexton's demeanour tended to disarm people completely. So far as Craator was concerned, it merely prevented him from biting the tech's head off immediately. 'OK,' he said grudgingly. 'Show me.'

The med-tech led him down past the rows of belts as they clunked and roared with their entirely human cargo. Alien matter had been known to produce some markedly strange effects, and this was filtered out at source. There were community-specific recycling plants out in the Habitat for that.

'It's really quite miraculous, if you stop to think about it,' Sexton mused, seemingly more intent upon imparting a general enthusiasm than engaging in actual conversation. 'Death into the stuff of life. It might make you truly believe in the glory of God, even if you didn't already. People look to God to turn their water into wine, or lead into gold, and forget the real miracle that turns sunlight and chemicals into golden grain and then to –'

'Spare me the metaphysics,' Craator growled. 'If I want three choruses of "Holy, Holy, Holy" and no spitting on the walkways I'll talk to Garon.'

'And I'm quite, quite sure you would,' said a quiet voice behind them.

As one, they turned to see the High Churchman, standing patiently by one of the belts. There was no way of knowing if he had been there all along, waiting for them, or if he had been following them.

'Of course,' said Garon, 'spitting on the pedways merely carries a modest fine and a mandatory forty days' Penance.'

Craator peered at him closely, trying to work out if he was joking. 'What are you doing here?' he said at last, when no reply appeared to be forthcoming.

Garon waved an unconcerned hand. 'Oh, I'm merely taking an interest. I gather that I'm rather noted for it.' He waved a hand. 'Craator, do, please, proceed.'

Sexton, whose good-humoured amiability had collapsed upon seeing Garon, led them on their way. 'I, uh, thought you needed to see, I – I mean I thought . . .' His flustered running commentary trailed off as Garon looked at him with absolutely no expression.

They came to a row of pallets, on which the rejects from the recycling process had been laid. Robotic drones worked their way down the row, dissecting the bodies, pulling them apart under the documentary eyes of microcams. Scissor-claws snicked and snacked rapidly and bone saws buzzed. Slightly apart from the others, lying on his back, his knees raised and locked solid so that if he had been on them he would be kneeling, was a tallish body, still almost fully dressed.

'We couldn't get the trousers and the shirt off,' Sexton said, 'so we threw him in the hopper anyway. The sensors had a small fit.'

Craator looked at the dead man. The face was set in a grimace of pain that seemed unnaturally distinct after death, when the muscles tend to relax under gravity, however minimally, before rigor mortis sets in. It was as though this man had been caught, at the precise moment of death, by some form of three-dimensional high-speed photography.

'The, uh, gene test came up negative for human,' said Sexton, fussing over a display monitor hooked to the bio-units on the pallet. 'Even factoring for mutation and genetic drift.'

Garon was gazing down upon the body with a vaguely puzzled expression, as if there were something about it he should be remembering. 'So what is it?'

'We don't know,' Sexton said. He gestured to the display, on which was incrementing the steady march of DNA-cataloguing and matching routines:

```
run DS709-X1.1.3706 / *UNCLASSIFIED*
run DS709-X1.1.3707 / *UNCLASSIFIED*
run DS709-X1.1.3708 / *UNCLASSIFIED*
run DS709-X1.1.3709 / *UNCLASSIFIED*
run DS709-X1.1.3710 / *UNCLASSIFIED*
run DS709-X1.1.3711 / *UNCLASSIFIED*
run DS709-X1.1.3712 / *UNCLASSIFIED*
run DS709-X1.1.3713 / *UNCLASSIFIED*
run DS709-X1.1.3714 / *UNCLASSIFIED*
run DS709-X1.1.37 . . .
```

'Nothing seems to match,' he said. 'Nothing at all. I'd need proper, specialized equipment to test it – but if I didn't know better I'd say the adenine/guanine, thymine/cytosine links aren't even based on a *bihelical* structure.'

Garon raised an eyebrow. 'And that means?'

Sexton wavered. 'It means he isn't human, or anything like it. There's no way he can be even remotely human, and we can't find anything else that matches either.'

'If it's not human, then it's a remarkably accurate simulacrum,' said Garon.

'Only on the outside,' Sexton said. 'We ran some ultrastatics and they came up strange. The unit wouldn't even let us look at them until we switched off its error-reporting routines.'

He pressed a stud and the image on the monitor changed to a wireframe cross-section of a human torso.

'It's slightly fuzzy because of extra subdural and sub-cutaneous layers,' Sexton said. 'Very dense and complex, molecularly, giving him a high level of damage-resistance.' He traced an area of the screen with a fingertip. 'Do you see that? Diploid pulmonary development, an extreme level of secondary redundancy and a vastly elevated oxygenation system . . .'

'In God's own tongue, please,' said Garon.

'He's got four of everything he should have two of and two of everything else,' said Sexton smartly, finally catching on to the idea. 'He's not invulnerable by any means, but as near to it in human terms as makes no odds.'

'So what killed him?' Craator said.

'That's what I asked you down here for.' Sexton indicated the bar-code tag fixed to the big toe of a strangely prehensile left foot. 'He's tagged as having died on the edge of the, uh –' Sexton shot a worried glance at High Churchman Garon '– at the edge of the Sector 3 conflict. That was under your control, Craator. I just wondered if you had any other information.'

Craator thought about it. Now that he put his mind to it, he seemed to recall this man going down amongst a group of humans and nonhumans, but he couldn't remember anything else.

'Nothing,' he said.

Garon, meanwhile, was still gazing upon the body thoughtfully. 'You did well to salvage it,' he said. 'Human on the outside, something else, something unknown, within. Is it some creature able to metamorphose? Some construct, built by who knows what, built to infiltrate the human community – even to infiltrate the Church itself? Who knows *what* it might be?' He frowned mildly. 'Why, it might even be a fiend from very Hell itself.'

For the second time that afternoon, Craator peered at Garon to try to discern if he was joking. For the second time that afternoon, High Churchman Garon gave not the slightest sign that he was. In fact, he seemed a little distracted, lost in thought.

Then his visage hardened again.

'I think this little mystery should be probed with all dispatch.' He gestured to the automated surgical units at work on the other bodies. 'Have this thing dissected immediately. Keep most complete records. We'll get to the bottom of this business, whatever the thing really is.'

In a maintenance tunnel under Sector 3, Peri stumbled through the semi-darkness. Several of the White Fire people had flashlights, but they were combat-orientated and directional: they illuminated what their owners wanted them to illuminate in tight beams, and the secondary light they cast was not enough for her to see her feet.

Kane, beside her, with the same degree of preparation that had produced his home-made gas mask, had a small penlight. It didn't help much, but without it both of them would have been completely lost.

Ahead of her, Peri saw the vague shapes of the others in the dark, heard the tiny, soft and muffled sounds of people moving quietly. She hoped that they wouldn't go too far ahead and leave them, because there were other sounds here, too. Scuttling sounds that might be the Habitat equivalent of rats, or something worse.

'Who are these people?' she hissed at Kane.

She was surprised at how loud it sounded.

Kane reached back without looking and rapped her smartly on the mouth. It wasn't hard enough to hurt, but it made her flinch back, shocked and alarmed.

'Never try to whisper like that,' he murmured quietly, in a kind of dreamy abstracted tone that seemed to blend in with the silence. 'The Adjudicators mine these places with sound switches. You just set a whole bunch of them off, if they're listening. You sounded like escaping steam.'

His voice seemed odd and faintly ridiculous, as though he had a speech impediment. Peri eventually realized that it was because he was carefully working around all the sibilants and plosives. His tone, however, was deadly serious.

'The White Fire are the big boys in the Human First movement. They're directly accountable to Jelks himself.'

He waved his penlight back the way they had come, its minimal light lost in the darkness of the tunnel. 'Those people back there,' he said, speaking more distinctly, 'most of 'em, they don't mean anything. They're like cattle. They can be used when we need them, but we can't allow ourselves to waste our efforts on them indiscriminately. We have to put our efforts into changing the conditions, not stooping to save every one of the fallen.'

Peri remembered how they had made their way through the wounded and the dying and the dead, how the White Fire people had finally hit upon a previously prepared section of the concourse paving, roughly cleared away the bodies and detonated explosive bolts. A small section of the paving had detached itself and simply dropped, giving them access to the underside of the platform itself, where hand-holds had been fixed with epoxy resin.

She had gathered, from their leader Draker's comments, that the White Fire people had seen the way things were going long before. There were similar surreptitious installations throughout key points of the Habitat. They had methodically, over the course of months or even years, contrived themselves a way out from anywhere.

Kane himself seemed to have undergone a kind of total transformation since they had fallen in with the White Fire. Before, he had been snide and dismissive. Now he seemed to radiate a surety-of-purpose belief that, if you didn't know better, might easily be taken for the real thing. Peri, of course, knew exactly what he was doing. The White Fire people had been the only way of getting out alive and relatively intact. He would have done or said anything to let them take him along. The only reason why he had taken *her* along with him was that simply dumping her behind would spoil the act he was currently putting on.

Peri was the last person to snitch on anybody, but it occurred to her that a weaselly little sneak like Kane would be the last thing these people needed amongst them in their struggle. Somebody, at some point, would have to be told before he sold them out and led the really good men and women to their deaths. She looked forward to the group of White Fire people as they toiled through the passage with their wounded. They were bloodied but unbowed. They might be living to fight another day, but at least they were still fighting. They deserved better than that – to be sold out by someone who simply didn't care if they lived or died. Somebody, at some point, would have to be told.

It was only then that she recognized what had been nagging at her mind for a while now. She could actually *see* the people ahead of her. The maintenance tunnel was coming to an end; they were now silhouetted against the ambient and strangely shifting but steadily brightening light of the Habitat. Stumbling slightly, as a rush of adrenalin cut shockingly through her fatigue, Peri picked up her pace, and walked towards the light.

* * *

'So you see,' said the penguin, 'that it is impossible for you to die. It's impossible for any one of us to really die.'

'You speak for yourself,' a mandrake said, a little petulantly. 'I mean, there I was, happy as Larry, soaking up some rays and then – bang! – some silly sod turns up the hothouse and fries the lot of us. Completely banjaxed *my* chances of proliferating through the worlds of puny humans and strangling them with my rapacious vegetative tentacles, I can tell you.'

The Doctor had no idea what he meant, and he certainly couldn't recall ever meeting a mandrake before. Possibly it hadn't happened to him, yet. He was about to say as much, but the mandrake had already slouched off to join his several dozen fellows, who had encamped themselves on the windy side of the Mammal Garden and put down roots. Occasionally, they looked sullenly back at the Time Lord and muttered darkly.

'The thing is,' said the penguin sitting on the lily pad, 'that everybody lives for the precise length of the Universe. Their Universe. It begins when they become aware, it ends when they stop. There is no other. And nobody can die in it. They can't, by definition.'

From somewhere above there came an insistent, high-pitched, irritating buzzing sound. The Doctor knocked at the side of his head to clear it.

'I've certainly seen one or two people do a good impression of it,' he told the penguin.

'No you haven't. You've just seen people come and go away again. They just inhabit different meat machines.' The penguin frowned and then conscientiously corrected itself. 'Or plant-matter machines. Or piezoelectric crystal machines. Or fungoid and vegetable machines. Or abstract quasi-machines existing simply as the interplay of energy and mass.'

'I find that slightly unbelievable,' said the Doctor. 'There would be nothing to cohere.'

'You're hardly in a position to talk.' The penguin looked at him sharply with its red little eyes. 'How many times have you yourself inhabited catastrophically reconstructive mass? Ever wonder where the raw materials come from? Just how many travelling companions have you actually *had*, Time Lord? How many pounds of skin do they lose in a month?'

'Oh, this is ridiculous!' exclaimed the Doctor. 'And not a little self-contradictory to boot.'

'Pretty right damn hooty it's ridiculous,' said the penguin, sternly. 'Whoever heard of a talking penguin? The idea is plainly absurd. And the reason is, this is an entirely specious construct. My guess is somewhere off to the north by northwest of the Gallifreyan paracerebellum and straight on till morning. That's because you're waking up from a severe brain crash and you're dumping several billion gigabytes of corrupted information as you go. Fnerk.'

'What?' the Doctor said. 'Is that supposed to be an analogy? Because, if it is, it's entirely at fault. Brains and minds are nothing like computers; there is absolutely no basis for comparison.'

'There's only no comparison with what *humans* can conceive as computers. Can't you even remember that?'

Now the penguin seemed to have changed, morphed into something more manlike. It was wearing a little hat – but, since it had been wearing a little hat anyway, this particular change was not so marked.

'You have to start remembering who you are,' it said. 'You're not human, you never have been, and it's unlikely that you ever will be. Human terms of reference quite simply don't apply – and because they *don't* apply you can use or accept them as and when you see fit, as opposed to violently embracing them, or violently kicking against them, or blindly ignoring them as if they count for nothing. You go down that road and you really are going to find yourself nothing more than some form of ghastly human hybrid without knowing how to cope – and what a travesty and a débâcle *that* would be.

'Because – and pay attention now, because this is

important – you've recently been subjected to a large and particularly concentrated dose of acetylsalicylic acid (which humans, as you very well know, like to refer to as "aspirin") which, as you also know, causes massive, allergic pulmonary and cerebral embolism in a Time Lord.'

The penguin was still changing. Now he looked almost entirely, on the surface, like a human. Only its pointy little beak remained, but that was rapidly trans-forming itself into a nose.

'The damage is too catastrophic and rapid even to kick-start an emergency regeneration. These dead bodies you can sense around you now, you couldn't even use *them* to harvest what you need as a stopgap. The only way out was to shut it down completely. Shut your body down and die. You've been dead for a while now, and now it's time to wake up.'

The penguin's transformation was complete. It had, of course, transformed into the Doctor himself.

'Time to wake up,' the Doctor said.

He opened his eyes, threw himself violently off the pallet just as the blade attachments sliced through the space he had previously occupied, rolled over and sat up and looked up at the uniformed figures he had bowled through with a friendly smile.

'Hello,' he said. 'I'm the Doctor and –' His face fell as he noted the expressions of those looking down on him. '– I don't think you're all exactly pleased to see me.'

Ten

On the surface, it might be surprising that a dying culture produces its biggest and most grandiose follies. The heads of Easter Island, Canary Wharf, the hanging paramarmoset apiaries of Squaxis IV – the greatest and the most impressive were all built upon that point where the societies that produced them tipped over the lip of the catastrophe curve and collapsed.

In fact, the answer is simple. A sense of their impending doom had these people panicking and redoubling their efforts when they had long since forgotten the point – with the result that they put their efforts in the wrong place. Resources that if properly managed could have supported a population for centuries were focused on a single point, which, rather like a star collapsing into a black hole, collapsed in on itself, sucked the people dry and hastened the collapse that they were desperately trying to prevent.

In the Habitat, a large number of these resources had been piled into the Mimseydome™.

The Mimseydome™ had been built, in one of the outlying domes clustered on the periphery of the main Habitat geodesic, by the Mimsey™ Incorporation – an Earth conglomerate dating back to the early twentieth century, which had grown out of the animated film studios of one Ralph Waldo Mimsey. At the start, the franchise had merely been intended as a basic recreational park for transients stopping off on their journey between the Galactic arms. There had been thousands of other franchises, scattered through the Galaxy, just like it.

In the early stages of the slump, as the traffic through the Dramos/Titania system had lessened, the franchise holders had hatched what at the time had seemed like a brilliant – but which with hindsight proved to be a desperate and half-baked – plan. They would turn the Mimseydome™ into the seventh wonder of the Universe, far surpassing even the fabled Mimseyland™ and Mimseyworld™ of Old Earth and an attraction in its own right. People would come flocking to Dramos and the Habitat just to see it. It would make them richer than the dreams of somebody dreaming about being very, very rich.

They bought out the remaining shares from the parent company in the Proximan Nexus – where it had moved after seeing the way things were going on Earth; and, seeing how things were going in the Habitat, it was only too pleased to take the money and get the Sheol out.

Then they started an extensive, and extremely expensive, programme of rebuilding and enlargement. For years some of the richest people in the Habitat ploughed money and materials that might have been better spent elsewhere, made complete and utter fools of themselves touting their new, improved Mimseydome™ through the two Galactic arms, and waited for the surge of ships that, they felt sure, would come.

It didn't work, of course – as the final generation of true Aztecs might have told them, had they not been long dead. Desperate prayers and insanely enlarged sacrifice to the gods does no good at all in the face of oblivion, whether the gods are called Quetzalcoatl, Ehectl or Consumer-driven Market Forces.

Fully a third of the Habitat's gross product was sunk into the Mimseydome™ – and the Habitat had always operated on *service* industries; its gross product was minimal to start with. The inevitable collapse of the entire enterprise hammered the last nail into the Habitat's self-enclosed coffin, though what with the vestigial momentum of mass dynamics it would be a while yet before anybody truly realized it. The partially remodelled Mimseydome™ had at last been simply abandoned, those involved, who still had enough left to get them out of the Habitat entirely, having cut their losses.

It was left deserted and derelict. Nobody came here now.

Somewhere close nearby, Peri heard the judder of field-generators and the clunking of filtration units, the staple and everyday sounds of an encampment. It seemed strangely at odds with the luxury of the shower unit, the bathroom it was in, and the suite of rooms to which it was attached. Ornate, brightly polished fixtures abounded. Diaphanous fabrics wafted. Fluted columns rose through high spaces with a kind of contrived, cartoony elegance.

She was, in fact, in the Faerie Tale Castle Hotel, one of the completed areas of the abandoned Mimseydome™. The water and power systems were out, of course, hence the field equipment. The water that came out of the gilded tap was rusty and lukewarm, but she didn't care. She slathered herself with the slimy half-lather of gritty, home-made soap and sluiced off the residues of smoke and stinging chemicals.

They had surfaced, she, Kane and the White Fire people, on ground level in what Kane had noted as Sector 4. The White Fire people had concealed their weapons and they had simply taken public tube transport to the outer edge of the Habitat, changing lines a number of times, seemingly at random. (The tubes themselves, Peri had noticed, operated a slightly odd system of entrance. There were no barriers to stop you getting in, but if you didn't pay a buzzer sounded to embarrass you. Kane had paid for her.)

They had left the tube and crossed an apparently deserted sector, made their way through the inspection hatches of a series of massive airlocks – and then, for a moment, Peri thought she had gone completely mad.

The huge structures had towered over her, and she had recognized every single one of them from the TV and the occasional movie house matinée as a child. Barnabas the Magic Ocelot, with his crooked, snag-tooth grin that had always frightened her, because he looked too vicious. Mickey Monkey. Percival the Penguin, who had always been her favourite, with the way he used to go 'Fnerk!' and with his little trademark hat. MacHeath, the lead villain from Mimsey's reworking of *The Threepenny Opera* who, against the odds, had been magically transformed into a lovable rogue with a rough manner but a hidden heart of gold . . .

They and a hundred others had loomed over her, and Peri had felt a woozy dislocation, as if she was going to collapse – but then she had seen the partially constructed rides, the evidence of building work, and the obvious had fallen into place. It was even a relief in some ways. Some things, it seemed, from her own time would endure.

There had been other figures moving about the place. More White Fire people, moving with a quiet and understated but pervasive sense of purpose and determination. Peri and Kane had been taken to a tough-looking woman called Blaine, who it seemed was in charge of inculcating into new recruits the purpose of the cause, and who had then taken them to the Faerie Tale Castle to clean themselves off. Avron Jelks himself, it seemed, would look them over as and when he returned.

Peri had been surprised at the opulence of her quarters but, she realized, given the sheer size of this place, there was more than enough room for everybody. She noted that a guard had been stationed outside her and Kane's doors, but again that was only reasonable. She and Kane could have been anybody – and Kane, she knew, was.

Now, she shut off the water and came out of the shower, dripping, trying to rub off as much of the water as she could with a small and scratchy basic-issue towel. It felt odd: this place was designed for thick, luxurious towels, like the impractical carpet into which her feet had sunk and made soggy puddles, even in the bathroom. There was a looking glass on the wall – a baroque, archetypical looking glass into which the Wicked Queen herself might happily look – and in it she saw a gaunt and frightened, brutalized child. It was a moment before she recognized herself.

There were trauma lesion-bruises around her eyes. Her lips were cracked and puffy, giving her face a spoilt, petulant look. Her skin seemed slack and sallow, her cheeks hollowed out – she couldn't believe she could have lost so much weight in so short a time. Her skin was raw and there were marks all over her. She spent some time pulling about at a livid black smudge, running from the nipple of her breast to the armpit, until the queasy ache made her realize it was a bruise. She had thought that she was still grubby from ingrained dirt.

Peri padded into the bedroom – ornately stitched canopy over a bare if pocket-sprung mattress – and turned over the filthy, ragged, gaping clothes she had discarded before her shower. There was no way she could wear them again. They felt filthy in a way that was somehow worse than actual dirt. She wondered what she was going to do.

At that point there was a brisk rapping on the panelled bedroom door, which looked solid but sounded like plywood over honeycomb. Peri turned to see it already opening, and the woman called Blaine coming through it. She was carrying a pair of thin coveralls.

'Put them on,' she said, tossing them to Peri. 'Avron's back. He'll see you now.'

'Is he OK?' Peri asked. The feeling she had felt before, watching Jelks speak, responding to him, resurfaced with a vengeance. In some animal yet emotional way, all that she wanted to know was that he was all right. The thought of his being hurt seemed almost too much to bear.

Blaine looked at her, and for the first time smiled with a genuine warmth. 'He's OK. The squad getting him out ran into a Jood cleanup operation. Had to lie low for a while. He caught too much of the gas, but he's OK now. He's an extraordinary person.'

In the recycling bay of the Temple of the Church of Adjudication, Craator glowered at the nonhuman man as he now stood, seemingly unconcerned, between the two armed Adjudicators.

Craator was still winded. After the nonhuman had come alive, he had led Craator a frantic chase through the loading bay, darting this way and that with almost impossible speed, vaulting over conveyor-belt feeds, scrambling over piles of boots and discarded clothing before Craator had taken him down with a tanglefoot bolas-round from his MFG.

'You believe in making things hard for yourself, geek,' Craator snarled.

The nonhuman man shrugged. 'I was looking for my coat. And I must say, I don't particularly enjoy being called a geek. I'd have expected something better from an officer of the Law.'

'What?' said Craator, genuinely puzzled.

'Oh yes. I was forgetting. "Geek" is a more general-ized term these days. I think you now call persons of the non-Terran persuasion skags.'

The nonhuman man made as if to make a gesture, remembered that his hands were now cuffed and settled for nodding his head towards a pile of clothes. 'As I was saying, I was only trying to get my coat. Correct me if I'm wrong, but, as I haven't actually been charged with anything yet, my moveables and possessions are still my own. There it is. Look.'

In the way that one simply does when told to look at something, Craator turned his head to look at the pile. There, brightly coloured and incongruous amongst the stained and shabby tangle of clothing, he saw the article in question. Now that he consciously remembered this man from the barricades, he remembered what he had

93

been wearing, and that was it. He recognized it. The vague, nagging feeling that it hadn't been there on the pile a minute before, that it had somehow *surfaced* since the last time he had looked, he instantly dismissed.

'You're correct,' he said to the nonhuman man. 'Have his personal effects retrieved if possible and tagged.' This to one of the Adjudicators bracketing him.

'Thank you,' said the nonhuman. 'Don't go to any special trouble on my account. The shoes you can keep. I have several pairs.'

Craator gave him a slap. Not enough to hurt, just enough to get his attention. 'You have been rightly Adjudged as guilty of Sedition and resisting arrest,' he told him. 'You shall be taken to a place of detention for such a time as your given identity shall be established and that formal Accusation shall be made. You –'

'– will be put to death!' hissed a voice behind him.

For a moment Craator was utterly unsure of who had spoken. There was a cold and furious intensity to the voice that he had never heard before. Then he turned to see that the speaker had been High Churchman Garon.

'You have aped the Holy Mystery of resurrection,' Garon said, almost spitting on the word 'aped'. He was looking straight past Craator to the nonhuman as though Craator were not there. 'By that I know you. You mock the very laws of God and man. You are the spawn of evil, the foul stench of your corruption taints the lungs of us all to canker growths, and you must be purged that the world might breathe once more.'

There was a thin, barely perceptible sheen of sweat on Garon's shaven head. His eyes seemed distant, dislocated, as if they were seeing nothing of this world, nothing of the world of men. Nothing of this Universe.

'You will –' He suddenly started, flinched as though flicked by a finger, and something came back into his eyes.

'I must apologize,' he said, quite calmly, to the nonhuman. 'I cannot imagine what came over me. Some

94

momentary lapse, due, no doubt, to the pressure of my work.'

'Think nothing of it,' said the nonhuman cordially. 'I quite understand.'

Garon turned to Craator as though seeing him for the first time. 'Deal with the Penitent, Adjudicator Craator. Ensure he is treated precisely as he merits and deserves.'

Then he turned his back on them and strode off. It was as if his strange and utterly uncharacteristic lapse had never happened.

'Do you know,' the nonhuman said, conversationally – in a voice that seemed to murmur directly in Craator's ear, even though he was several feet away – 'I think he was right about not being himself. I wonder who it was?'

Eleven

The daily cycle of the Habitat wore on towards the
analogue of evening. In the hab-blocks and the warrens people sweltered under an abstract, oppressive heat
that had nothing much to do with the temperature. The
shifts changed for those in the makework parodies of
what they thought of as jobs. Those who had homes to
go to went to them. Slowly the streets began to thin out.

Slowly the polarization of the geodesics was increased,
simulating dusk. Lights came on in the Habitat – all
too few. Power was in all too short supply to use
extravagantly. The fact that the Habitat wouldn't need
night-lights at all if the polarization cycle were simply
abandoned had been noted – but humans and a great
number of other species besides, having originated within
planetary systems, needed these periods of darkness.

Presently, the increasing darkness shut out even the
light from Titania and its pulsing Node. Or at least, such
radiations as were in the visible spectra.

The night people were coming out now. Waking up
and coming out. Leaving their credit-operated capsules
and the shelters they had made in the more derelict areas,
heading for the centre and the stalls and bars.

And below this stratum lived the truly derelict and
dispossessed, those who had no other home than the
streets. As with a food chain, as with any hierarchy, those
living more than a couple of links from each other tended
to become invisible. The day people never noticed the
homeless, stepped around them like any other filth in the
gutter. The homeless, for their part, hardly noticed. It was

simply the medium through which they drifted.

The night people, on the other hand, existed for the homeless in the real sense. You could see them and they could see you. You might get a kicking off them, or you might get a few credits, or something to eat, or something to get out of your head on.

This was, in short, the time when the lost souls stirred, and began to scavenge.

Blaine took Peri up through the corridors of the Faerie Tale Castle, up sweeping flights of stairs and up the spiral staircase of a tower. Large sections of the Castle had still been under construction before being abandoned. Plush carpeting gave way to extruded polyprop flooring. The rough-hewn stone walls were filled with gaping holes, through which could be seen support struts and cabling. The edges of the holes showed that the stone cladding itself was stamped out from fibreglass resin.

On her travels with the Doctor, Peri had learnt one or two home truths about the so-called Future. The first was that while, when you thought of it, you imagined the Future as filled with gleaming brand-new and, well, *futuristic* things, the third law of thermodynamics meant that in actual fact everything just got older, dirtier and closer to the point where it fell apart completely. Indeed, as the Doctor had said once, if it wasn't for all these thinking, walking lumps of organized meat, these automemes in organic machines bucking local entropy all the time, the Universe would be in a hell of a state. And Peri had said, 'What?'

The other thing she had learnt was that while, when one thought of the Future, one saw it as being filled with fabulous new technologies – miraculous antigravity devices and super-impermeable new building materials – that didn't mean that such things automatically supplanted what had gone before. Black-box technology still came in a black box. Aluminium being so easy to refine, fibreglass so easy to produce, it was so much more sensible to use them, rather than mess around with trans-mutational atom-crackers and the energy of suns, simply to throw up a garden shed. The exposed construction of this knock-off, bog-standard Faerie tower was almost an object lesson in that. Some things never changed.

The thought of the Doctor sent a little chill through her. She hadn't thought of him for a while now, her mind persistently shying away from the subject. Peri felt a kind of cold, grim triumph, mixed up with a diffuse, strangely poignant pang of loneliness and yearning. She supposed that this must be what it felt like to leave an abusive partner who, nonetheless, had been a partner for a matter of years. Or of finally getting away from a hated parent.

She wondered why she was feeling this way. Sure, the Doctor could be irritating and erratic, but she had never felt this actual sense of *hate* before. She had no time to analyse the feeling further because, she realized, they were reaching the top of the tower – and someone was coming down. In the fading light he seemed lithe and strong, moving with an innate sense of power. Peri liked the way he moved. He moved like a big cat, like a leopard or a panther.

Then he drew closer and she recognized Kane.

He was dressed in thin coveralls as was she, but had managed to salvage and retain his heavy boots and leather jacket. He nodded to Blaine and gave Peri an easy grin. 'Evening all,' he said. 'I've just seen Jelks, and I must say I'm impressed.'

'He's very good at that,' said Blaine. There was a kind of utterly serious archness in her voice, as though she were lightly imparting some massive, solid truth. It was the first piece of inflection Peri had heard her use. For a moment it was as though Blaine and Kane were sharing a sense of camaraderie, from which Peri was entirely excluded.

She glared at Kane with distaste. 'I hope he liked you.'

'Oh, I wouldn't go that far,' Kane said, still very easily. 'But I think I made an impression, managed to establish a degree of respect. I'm supposed to go and pick up my kit now.'

'Report to the armoury,' Blaine told him. 'Out through the main doors and left of Percival the Penguin. You can't miss it.'

'Thanks.'

Kane went on his way. Blaine took Peri up.

By a side door of one of the underground clubs in Sector 7, a ragged, bundled mess that might have been male, female, human or alien, stirred as the door opened and a pale light shone from within. He, she, hir or it looked up at the figure who came out from it, raised something hooked and palsied that might have been a hand. 'Hey, lady? Pretty lady? You got something for – ?'

The thing that might have been male or female, human or alien, stared up as though transfixed.

And then the figure it was looking at was gone. The ragged thing that might have been human or alien, male or female, never even saw it go. It was too bedazzled for that.

And then the thing that might have been male or female, human or alien, looked down and saw the thing in its hand: jewelled and ornate talon rings, such as were affected by the more wealthy Silurians.

The fact that the talons, their stumps cauterized and blackened, were still inside them, didn't matter. They added a bit of visual interest.

Peri had not known quite what to expect. What sort of rooms would a man like Avron Jelks occupy? She ran over the possibilities all the way up to the top of the tower. Something spartan and monastic, epitomizing the devotion of all his energies to his cause? Something presidential and monolithic, impressing all and sundry with the power of his position as the leader of Human First?

In fact, after Blaine had shown her through the door,

the room she found herself in was remarkably understated and pleasant. While semicircular, conforming to the basic structure of the tower, it had none of the Faerie Tale fripperies of the rest of the hotel. It had probably been intended as a living space for an owner or a manager rather than a guest.

This appeared to be the study, walled with pale, warm, wooden panelling. The drapes were already drawn against the night, but concealed lighting showed up every detail while softening it at the same time. Fitted shelves were lined with data wafers, holo-slugs and even ancient VHS video tapes. Peri looked for some Betamax, but couldn't find any.

There were books here, too. For some reason Peri thought that they must be ancient, but then she realized that they were almost entirely contemporary. Again, as media for the storing and retrieving of large amounts of information, books were far more user-friendly than electronic storage. You didn't get eye-strain and, while you might be able to burn them, you couldn't wipe them with a magnet.

The room was dominated by an old and massive two-tier desk that must have dated back into the nineteenth century. On it was a blotter, piles of the writing sheets and marker-sticks that were subtly different from the paper and pencils of her own time, but served such a precisely similar function that the difference made no odds. There was a communications monitor and, beside it and slightly incongruous, what seemed to be a metallic dome, something like a cross between a salver and some alien battle helmet. Peri remembered Sontarans from some snapshots the Doctor had once shown her.

All of these details she only remembered later, because sitting behind the desk, turning in his chair to look at her, was Avron Jelks.

'Ah yes,' he said, fixing her with a gaze that seemed to transfix her, like a sparrow in the shadow of a hawk . . .

(No, she thought vaguely. That was completely wrong,

because it wasn't like that at all. It was more that she felt like a dog looking at her master, waiting to see what he wanted her to do.)

'Ah yes,' said Avron Jelks. 'The young lady who was brought in with Kane. And what would your name be, my dear?'

Possibly it was the use of the word 'dear' to a nineteen eighties American sensibility, but a traitorous impulse suddenly had Peri not wanting to admit to her real name. She started to say 'Perpugilliam', simultaneously tried to change her last name to 'Black', that being the first thing that came to her mind, and stumbled over her words.

Avron Jelks smiled warmly.

'Well, Ms Purblack. I'm pleased to meet you, and I hope you'll join us in our common cause. Shall we talk?'

There was hardly anything left of her now. Almost nothing left. The thing that had been Mora Cica Valdez drifted through the gathering darkness and illuminated it, lighting it more brightly than the fitful and sporadic lamps. The insular and the depraved were in the warrens down below. The night crowds and flashing signs were up there on the interways. *These* were the true underlevels, in the sense of being the lowest of the low, halfway up.

From the interways and walkways above, the thing that had been Mora Cica Valdez might have looked like a wandering firefly. And above her, filling the space beyond the Dome, the swirling mass of pulsing light she couldn't see filled her head.

And there were other lights like fireflies, thousands of them, lights like her, weaving through the dark maze of the city.

The handgun felt odd in Peri's hands. She had expected it to be heavier. Not that it didn't have weight, but the weight was in the grip. In the magazine that curved out from it like a boxy, blunted scythe blade. The frame and muzzle were of some material that was as hard as tungsten steel, felt like slightly greasy enamel and was as light as expanded polystyrene foam.

'Polymerized ceramic microcomb,' Blaine said from behind her. 'The mechanism's built from the same stuff and it operates on clockwork. Optical sighting. No electrics. Nothing to trip the Adjudicator scans. You could take it anywhere.'

'What about the ammo?' Peri asked, more or less simply for something to say.

'Impact-detonated microgrenades. Genuine ripped-off Church of Adjudication armoury stock.' Peri couldn't see her face, but Blaine's voice carried a note of grim satisfaction. 'They give back a friendly signature – otherwise the Joods couldn't go a hundred metres without tripping off alarms. In your own time, Purblack.'

The firing range had been housed within a structure containing the partially completed Mimseyworld™ Ye Olde Englishe Village Greene Fayre. Peri took aim at the spinning ducks in little helmets and the cast-resin coconuts at the other end of the range, and once again cursed the inexplicable impulse that had landed her with a new and stupid name.

Peri brought up the gun and sighted on the targets. She hadn't held a gun since the age of seventeen when, living away from home for the first time, a fit of paranoia had her investing in something with nine millimetres that she couldn't even remember the name of, no questions asked, from a pawnshop, for personal protection. She had never used it. It was probably still lying, forgotten, in a Boston U dorm drawer a thousand years ago. It had just felt wrong in her hand.

Now, the comforting weight in her palm, the lack of any drag from the gun itself, seemed right and natural. It was like she was just moving her own fist – only now it could sock a punch like you wouldn't believe.

She wasn't aware of pulling the trigger, but in front of her several of the targets just went to pieces. She hadn't been aware of any sound, but now her ears rang slightly from the concussion of the exploding slugs smacking home and detonating.

Peri relaxed. She felt warm and loose inside as the adrenal rush dissipated through her.

'Good enough,' said Blaine, from behind her.

Peri turned to look at her dully. She felt elated and spent. Blaine took the gun away from her, popped the magazine, checked the breech and put the gun back in its case and locked it. She had not let Peri use her own weapon, which was still strapped to her side.

'Listen,' she said. 'It's too late to kit you out now and you have to be bushed – I saw what you people went through out in Sector 3 on relay.' She gave Peri one of her small, tight smiles – something Peri had found herself starting to count on and even hope for because, she realized, they weren't given lightly. 'What say we crash out for now? We can kit you out and sort out a training programme in the morning. Six hundred sharp, mind.'

'Yeah,' Peri said weakly. The events and shocks of the day had caught up and hit her long before now. Now they were on the point of driving her to her knees.

'Yeah,' she said. 'I think I'd like that.'

The shape of it was inside her and it filled her up. It moved what had once been her limbs, twisted them one way, twisted them back and hauled her along. The energies of it washed through her, disrupted her, ate her from the inside out.

Dimly, in the shred of consciousness that it needed to stay alive and cohere, the thing that had once been Mora Cica Valdez knew that it must replenish itself.

As Blaine took her back into the Faerie Tale Castle, Peri tried running through her conversation with Avron Jelks again, trying to pin down the specifics with an exhaustion-clogged mind. She just wanted to recapture the feeling of clean wholeness he gave off, the feeling of basking in the energy that seemed to beam directly from his eyes.

They hadn't really talked about anything much. He had simply asked her to tell him what it had been like, caught in the Shok–TAC assault on the rally. She had told him. His eyes had filled with sympathetic sorrow. It must have been awful for you, he had said.

He had asked her how she felt about the way the Adjudicators were treating the people. She had tried to tell him. She certainly hadn't been aware of saying anything notable or impressive – but at length he had simply nodded to her, touched her lightly on the cheek in a way that seemed to send his whole force of personality directly into her, like an electric shock. Then she had gone away with Blaine again, to test her proficiency on the firing range.

Now, as they made their way back through the building, they passed several other White Fire people. Peri recognized Draker, the leader of the group who had brought her in. Now they were out of combat gear they could have been anybody, on the surface at least – save for their watchful posture, the sense of readiness implicit in their body language, the seriousness of their quiet conversations.

Blaine took her up to the door of her rooms. 'Six hundred sharp,' she said.

'Six hundred sharp.' Peri opened the door and stumbled through it. Swung it shut behind her without bothering to try the light. There was no sense in wasting power, and once she collapsed on to the mattress there was no way she'd get up off it to turn it out again.

Then a hand snaked around her and jerked her roughly back. Another hand clamped itself solidly over her mouth.

'Now don't you try anything,' the voice of Kane said in her ear. 'Don't make a sound. I want to have a word with you.'

* * *

104

As it roamed the real underlevels of the city, slipped through the spaces equidistant between light and dark, the thing that had once been Mora Cica Valdez knew that if it didn't replenish itself, and soon, it would simply dissipate and die.

It needed food. It needed to hunt for food.

It needed to feed.

Twelve

In a secured charging room in the Temple of the Church of Adjudication, Craator looked across the duly sanctified Altar of Penance at the nonhuman who had called himself the Doctor. Lying on the altar between them was the Doctor's patchwork coat, beside it several large polymer bags containing the contents of its pockets.

Half an hour before, Craator had looked on as an increasingly surprised auxiliary had pulled out and tagged objects in their hundreds, ranging from ancient, burnt-out radio valves to a yo-yo with a tangled string, to a neatly wrapped packet of sandwiches. It seemed imposs-ible that pockets could hold so much. If Craator hadn't been there, and hadn't seen the way that it was somehow perfectly natural, he would have flatly refused to believe it. He would like as not have had the auxiliary in question detained for some extensive drug tests.

(The packet of sandwiches had been scanned for these and other proscribed substances. The machine logged them as Cheddar cheese and chutney on wholemeal brown with the crusts cut off, and very tasty.)

Now the man sat, looking at Craator with polite enquiry. Craator returned his gaze, and forcibly quashed a sudden feeling of unease. It was as if, in some sense, this Doctor had called *him* here, and was quite calmly waiting for him to explain himself.

'Yes?' said the Doctor. 'I'm listening.'

Craator decided to point out who was running things here from the start. He slapped his hand down on the Altar with such a force that several of the items on it bounced. 'You do the talking. I ask the questions.'

'Do you know,' said the Doctor, 'I thought you were going to say something like that.'

In the Faerie Tale Castle of the Mimseydome™ Kane pulled Peri to him, hand over her mouth, talking to her all the while in the same odd, impaired tone he had used to baffle Church of Adjudication sound-sensors, down in the tunnels under the Habitat.

'I've seen you looking at me,' he said. 'I know what you'd like.' And for a moment of crawling terror Peri thought he was going to rape her. But then he continued, 'You don't reckon me, I know that. You think I'm going to slime up to these people and betray them the first chance I get. Turn tail and run.

'Well, maybe I will, and maybe I won't, but let me tell you this. I'm going to end up on the winning side. These people are going up against the Adjudicators, and if you'd kept your eyes open enough not to walk into walls you'd have seen that they're tooled up. They might actually win.'

Peri tried to bite his hand. A tooth skidded off and almost chipped itself on the smooth finger ring he affected, made out of some translucent crystal that seemed to shimmer even in the minimal light. Her teeth sank into his skin and forced down, gouging in.

Kane didn't even react, except to murmur, 'If you don't stop that now, I'll snap your neck.'

The pressure of his other hand, the light but increasingly wrenching sensation inside her vertebrae told her he was telling the truth. Reluctantly she relaxed her grip.

'Now you listen good,' Kane murmured. 'You can think what you like, and you can do what you like – except try to turn these people against me. I catch one other person looking at me like you do, I'm going to come after you and try to kill you. Again, maybe I can, maybe I can't, but if I lose these people's trust I'm a dead man, so I've got nothing to lose.'

With that, he shoved her away from him and was gone. Peri never even noticed the door closing.

She was too busy stumbling over the mattress and falling on to it, and not being able to get up. This final shock had been too much after a day and a night full of them, and she had collapsed into a dreamless sleep that was almost the shutdown state of coma. She was damned if she was going to call it a faint, even to herself.

In his inner sanctum, High Churchman Garon watched a METATRON screen relaying a view of the charging rooms. The screen could be set to display thermographic and neural overlays, enhancements generated by the processing power of OBERON to be used as evidence and guilt. The figure of Craator flickered with swirling, iridescent heat pattern-signatures.

The image of the nonhuman was slightly more interesting – or not, depending on one's point of view. It seemed that the nonhuman's bodily processes were invisible to the enhancing routines, or too complex for them to handle, so they simply shut down. The result was a perfectly defined, solid-seeming area of pure black.

'It is as I first suspected,' Garon mused. 'A creature from the blackest pit of Hell. Possibly, even, the very Master of that realm. Who knows what treachery, what wiles and snares, he is weaving even now?'

High Churchman Garon watched the monitor closely, his eyes never leaving the black mass that was the so-called Doctor, listening attentively to what he had to say.

'You have no form of identification,' Craator was saying. 'No subcutaneous tags. You know that every citizen of the Habitat, every transient passing through is tagged and filed.'

'I didn't know where to queue,' the Doctor said. 'You can do it now, if you like. I have to admit, though, that my physiognomy tends to dispose of foreign matter rather quickly, but it should last long enough.'

108

'Oh, you'll be tagged all right,' Craator said. 'We'll get your number.' He paused and glowered intimidatingly at the nonhuman man, continuing only after he realized that it seemed to be having no intimidatory effect.

'The only legitimate way in is through the spaceports,' he said, 'and no ships have been docking at the spaceports. That leaves unlawful entry via some other part of the Dome. I think we can add Statutory Breaking and Entering to your Penance sheet.'

The Doctor shrugged. 'Go right ahead – though I defy you to prove I've ever actually "broken" into anything.'

'Look around you,' Craator said. 'Think about where you are. Think about just how much I need to prove anything.'

'Ah, but you'll try, won't you?' said the Doctor. '*You* at least will. I don't think you can do anything else.'

For the first time something other than unconcern entered the nonhuman's manner. He glared at Craator with scornful eyes – and Craator felt the muscles of his neck lock rigid as he fought the urge to flinch away. It was as though this Doctor were running a kind of mental laser-scanner over the bar code stamped on Craator's soul. It was as though the Adjudicator were being Adjudged himself: coldly, dispassionately, as one might examine a genetically reproduced microbe on a slide, and wonder whether to risk letting it out into the ecosystem, or to simply sterilize the entire culture now.

After what seemed like minutes, but was in fact a couple of seconds at most, the Doctor scowled. It was as if he were grudgingly, reluctantly, and much against his better judgment, giving everything Craator was, or had been, or ever would be, a barely passing mark.

He clapped his hands and sat back in his chair with a sigh – absurdly, Craator flashed on one of his tutors when he had been a very young cadet. The man would begin one of his choicest dressing downs with such a sigh, as if to say, 'Oh dear God, look what you've gone and done now.' It took a conscious effort not to look down at your shuffling feet and start to mumble. The lecture would start around now.

Instead, the Doctor said, 'The only right you have to administer a code of ethics is if you stick to that code. You have to play by the rules you set, be judged under the same laws as you Adjudge others. That includes, unless I very much miss my guess, the laws of physical evidence.'

For a split second Craator was disorientated. Then he realized that the nonhuman was simply picking up from where he had left off. He radiated insouciance again. It was as if the disquieting interlude of apparent role reversal had never happened.

'You're going to look for the evidence, though,' said the Doctor, 'because you truly believe in the Statutes for which you stand. Just be warned, Adjudicator Joseph Craator, others in your company may not. At least, not quite in the way you believe.'

That sense of disorientation yet again. The non-human was trying to keep him off balance, and doing a remarkably good job of it. How in Sheol had he learnt his name?

'It's written on your name badge,' said the Doctor. 'Also, I heard your High Churchman – Garon, was it? – mention it earlier.'

Garon hadn't mentioned it, Craator was sure of that. He felt that spike of paranoia you get when suddenly confronted by a telepath – and then with a great mental wrench pulled himself together. With the sense of realization that jerks you back to yourself, like a dash of cold water in the face, he saw all the snide little psychological tricks this Doctor was playing. He was using a kind of mental judo to sidestep any frontal assault, overbalance an opponent and use the opponent's own strength against himself. He was attempting to pull the rug out and watch him land on his behind.

Of course this Doctor had known what he was thinking. He'd dropped the precise little acid drop that made you *think* what you were thinking. Mentally, Craator slapped his feet down on solid ground. Totally back in control. (It was only later, remembering it, that he recalled how there'd been no way on Dramos that the Doctor could ever know the name 'Joseph'. Garon certainly hadn't used it, and it wasn't on his badge.)

Craator stuck to solid logic. 'You had to arrive in a ship. How did you slip past the detection net? How did you get through?'

The Doctor waved an airy hand. 'Oh, there's always a back door if you know where to look. Though I hardly ever use it, and at this point hardly anybody knows it's there but me.'

'There's a back door into the system?' Now that Craator was back in control, now that he was back in charge, it was all starting to fall into place. The various drugs and other unsanctioned products in the Habitat had to come from somewhere, and this could be the route they took. If there was truly a back door, a blind spot in the Dramos defence net, this could lay the entire Habitat open to hostile attack.

'You have a ship,' he said. 'Where is this ship?'

'You wouldn't believe me if I told you,' said the Doctor. 'If you saw it, you wouldn't see it, if you catch my drift – but then you shouldn't judge a book by its distressingly unprepossessing cover, as I've learnt to my cost.'

'Some sort of cloaking device?' said Craator.

'Oh, please!' The nonhuman seemed genuinely appalled. 'Please credit me with some degree of sophistication. I can show it to you if you like, but don't say you haven't been warned.'

Which was why, one half-hour later, an Adjudication transport landed in the capsule stacks of Sector 3 and Craator, several guards and a cuffed and guarded non-human man stepped out.

The night air was thick and humid. The stacks quiet

111

with the sense of actual desertion, rather than a lot of people staying desperately quiet and still. The night people who lived in them had long gone about what might loosely be described as their business.

The Doctor, somehow contriving the impression that he was strolling rather than under heavy escort, strolled over to a blue box – now covered with the burgeoning results of people realizing that, after their first, timorous attempts at scrawling anti-Adjudicator graffiti, nothing bad had happened to them.

'There you go,' the Doctor said with pride, gesturing grandly. 'My TARDIS. Time and Relative Dimensions in Space.' He smiled fondly. 'Second-best neologism invented by an offspring since the "googol", I always thought.'

'And that's it, is it?' said Craator.

'That's it,' said the Doctor, smugly.

Craator suddenly felt very old and tired. 'Take him away,' he told the guard detail. 'Take him down into the Holding Complex and throw away the key cards.'

High Churchman Garon replayed the recording from the charging rooms thoughtfully. There had been something nagging at the back of his mind throughout the Inquisition, something not quite related to the Doctor creature, and he was determined to pin it down.

It was some small while and on the third replay before he saw it. The Doctor creature, of course, was just an impenetrable black mass of dead pixels. Craator, on the other hand, one could read like a Good Book. The OBERON system overlays showed an increasing sense of emotion and impulse that had been integrated and tagged as PARA/SUS. The Doctor creature had been talking about a possible threat to the security of the Habitat and, even without the aid of enhancement, one could see Craator radiating the kind of suspicion that has one wondering about hidden threats, conspiracies, dangers from within.

It was imperative that Craator be kept from this line of thought. Not, thought Garon, as if there were some actual 'conspiracy' he might stumble on. Not as such. But there were . . . certain elements of the Church, certain aspects of the New Order into which it was evolving that it would be far better Craator should never know or even suspect.

Purely for his own good, of course.

'Directive,' Garon told the METATRON. 'Have Adjudicator Craator assigned purely to low-security operations from this point. Keep him out on the streets where he belongs. Let him do what he does best.'

'Complying,' the METATRON said. 'Curia control has been advised.'

Garon nodded to himself, and switched off the screen. For a small while he sat, in his default-relaxed state, unthinking, gazing without seeing at his steepled fingers. Then, with no sense of transition, he swung himself up from his chair and walked towards the door that led into a bounce-tube, which in turn led up into the spaces to which his sanctum, in a very real sense, was merely the anteroom.

It was time for High Churchman Garon, and several others of his acquaintance, to commune with his God.

The Doctor was frogmarched from the transport landing stage through several corridors until he and the guard detail came to a row of shafts. Several of them were wide and had airlocked capsule arrangements bolted to them. Notices over them detailed chlorine, ammonia and several other ecosystemic bases, presumably describing the composition of the atmospheres below. Two were simply holes in the ground. The notice over one read TERRESTRIAL BASE/PURE, the other read NONTERRA/HYBRID.

The Doctor looked at them with interest. 'Now I wonder,' he said, 'just how you're going to classify me. There are certain –'

'Shut your crukking hole, skag,' one of the guards said. The Doctor could hardly blame him. The Time Lord had, after all, spent the entire journey back from the capsule stacks being at his persistently annoying and irritating best.

The guards shoved him down the HYBRID hole. He fell for what seemed like minutes, but was in fact only seconds, watching as what seemed to be a series of glowing neon rings went past, confident in the fact that he could deduce what they were. It was a modified version of bounce-tube technology. You went down and the field caught you, but there was no way up. He was just starting to have the occasional doubt that they were operating, when a static charge zapped through him and his momentum slowed with a lurch. He hung in the air for a moment, and then dropped like a rubber brick for the last three metres.

He landed on hard, bare rock, cat-footed. In a slight and watchful semi-crouch he scanned his new surroundings. He was in a largish chamber, utterly bereft of detail save for a heavy-duty and securely fastened set of shutters at one end. Presumably, this was a remand area, where people were held until they could be processed. Unless, of course, the Church had reached that point where people were simply thrown down a hole and left to die.

The chamber was packed with nonhuman life – although none of it was quite at the point where a real human would instantly scream and claw his eyes out, being confronted by something utterly alien. They were people who had evolved in, or at least could survive in, an Earthlike atmosphere, and as such could be recognized by humans as beings if not exactly as people.

There were Silurians here, and Fnaroks, and even some Cybermen offshoots – whose technology had evolved to the sophistication of organics, so they had thus become more individualized. There were Ice Warriors, Gastropods, Chelonians, Tzun and Squaxis, and there was even a small clique of Sontarans – results of a failed

114

Sontaran experiment involving the breeding of units equipped for a degree of diversification, who had evidenced rather too much individuality and had thus been kicked out from the Sontaran Horde . . .

The chamber was filled, in short, with the kind of nonhuman life that, a thousand years before, would have humans instantly thinking of monsters. In this time it was possible to see them as people. Here and now it was *humans*, just coming out of their extremely nasty and brutal Empire phase, who were generally regarded as monsters.

The problem, the Doctor realized, was that every single one of these people, having smartly got out of the way to let him land, who had turned back to see this new arrival, who had noticed his human appearance and had realized that he was on his own, were now closing in on him with angry and murderous hatred in their respective optical analogues.

Thirteen

Certain areas of the Habitat ground level were no-go areas – even the Adjudication hit squads, who killed derelicts and street children on an industrial basis, even the enforcers for the criminal gangs wouldn't go here. These places had long since been choked up with detritus from the city above – a sludge of perishable garbage decomposing over years and the protruding, skeletal tangle of the unrotted. The lower levels of the hab-blocks were sealed up. The access ramps to the interways had been pulled down. There was no way out.

They were almost a microcosm of the already microcosmic Habitat itself: a little and self-contained world of their own. The average age here was the bare minimum at which human beings as a group can breed before they die, and thus produce a precariously stable system. The lost children crawled through the tangled dark here, and ate garbage and each other and bred.

They were known, colloquially, as the junklands.

In the Sector 7 junklands, Raghi An cut a hole and hooked his fingers in and tore. He pulled the lights out and bolted them, not stopping to chew – they needed no cooking, and you had to eat them before they turned over and rotted. Then he sliced into the muscle tissue with his blade, working quickly and cleanly, along with the grain, stuffing bloody lumps into his salt sack. He had to work quickly because, he knew, company was coming. The scavengers had the scent.

116

He saw them as he began to make the incision in the laterally incised, flayed-back haunch, preparatory to pulling the main muscle mass off the bone. Torchlight, like fireflies, winding through the burnt-out tangle of old interway vehicles dumped years before. Raghi An waited, very still, very quiet, to see who they were.

They came through the wreckage, four of them: three human boys and a girl bracketed and protected by two of them. A breeding group. Possibly a nascent tribe. The scratches on their faces and exposed skin had been worked at, kept permanently open. Encrusted and weeping. Spiral whorls over the cheekbones and upper breast and arms. They halted their approach some distance away and snarled. They didn't make an overtly aggressive move.

Raghi An knew them. He knew their rituals. He knew he was no match for them. He hissed at the group and batted at his mouth.

The leader of the group, the largest, came forward. He looked at Raghi An, and for a long time Raghi An thought he was simply going to initiate an attack. Then the leader bowed, batted at his mouth as Raghi An had done, and gestured assent. There was enough on the kill for everyone. Fighting over it would be a waste of energy and lives and there was no point. At this juncture it was better to share.

Raghi An completed his butchery of the kill quickly, conspicuously leaving several choice cuts on the carcass. Then he left.

He kept his eye on the scavenger group until he was some way clear, and they had fallen on the remains. Then he turned his back on them and clambered off over the tangled debris of the junklands, heading back towards his lair.

The thing that had been Mora Cica Valdez was weak from hunger now. It was not a physical sensation. It was not some gnawing in her belly, which did not exist in any case now, in any real sense.

It was more the desiccated hunger felt by the last survivor of a famine, when the grain trucks never come. The organs atrophy inside, the sense of embodied self disintegrates; the very soul ablates and blows away like dust.

The tiny shred of her that remained, her vestigial consciousness, had allowed the thing she had become to use Volan – for the simple reason that Mora Valdez in life had hated him and had wanted to kill him. He deserved to die. Since then, the thing inside had sensed the living things around her. The things that could be used as fuel, but this tiny thread of consciousness – of conscience – had stopped it feeding.

But now, as the thing that had been Mora Cica Valdez saw its death, saw it loom in front of it, this last thread snapped. It went for the first thing it met.

Raghi An clambered over a mass of collapsed steel scaffolding, swung himself up on to the structure-work that had once supported an interway access ramp before it had been pulled down. Once on this it was an almost completely clear run to where he had made his lair: the hollow remains of the head of a huge, polymer, animatronic and insanely grinning frog – the remains of a long-discarded advertising hoarding from somewhere above – wedged between a ruptured and ketone-reeking tank from a cargo transport and the sealed-up wall of a hab-block. Cautiously, glancing around him, sniffing the fuel-leak air, his senses alert for any sign that people had been here since he had been gone, Raghi An swung himself through the support struts.

Something bright streaked towards him. He never reacted. He never got the chance.

It set him on fire and flung him from the struts, flung him twenty metres to hit a mulch of debris and ferroconcrete slabs, snapping his spine in two.

Free hydrocarbons seeping from the garbage burst into

flame, fed the flames already burning him, immolated him. In the salt bags still attached to him, lying by his side, the meat he had butchered from his kill roasted with his own. The pain was immense – and then it quite simply shut down. It had passed the point where Raghi An's overloaded neurosystem could even recognize it as such. Raghi An lay burning on his back, paralysed from the torso down and automatically breathed in flame; the saliva and the mucus in his lungs vaporized and expanded and exploded his lungs.

And floating above him, insubstantial, he saw what he took to be an angel. He remembered, when he had been very young, the old female who looked like him, but bigger and very old, and who had looked after him for a while before going away one day and never coming back.

She had talked about angels. They were very nice and pretty and when you died they made it better.

This angel looked a little like a human, but she seemed to be made of fire and light. She wasn't like a real thing, like you could touch her. You could see right through her. But she burnt very, very bright.

The last thing Raghi An ever saw, there never being any angels, and no one *ever* making it better, was her pressing her insubstantial, glowing face quite close to his, and gazing on him with solemn, wounded eyes.

The thing that had been Mora Cica Valdez floated over the remains of what had once been the young Fnarok. It blazed with light. Whatever it was now, it was utterly nonhuman. It was . . .

Its rudimentary thought processes realized that they were part of something larger. An Ur-being, a kind of quasi-neural energy mesh made up of creatures in their thousands like it. It could feel them, moving through the Habitat, streaming through its tangled streets.

Heading for some central point. A focal point. A nexus.

119

The thing that had been Mora Cica Valdez left the ruined, burning Fnarok body it had used for fuel and rose, upward from the junklands, the suit of transparent membrane it had worn when it had pretended to be human flapping behind it.

Fourteen

In the chamber of the Holding Complex, the Doctor looked around with a friendly smile as the various nonhuman beings closed in.

'Now, um, I hope nobody's going to do anything they'll regret,' he said hastily.

'Don' worry about it,' a shaggy Ursine from Straglon Beta said, flashing its jagged bear-trap teeth. 'Not going to regret anythin', me.'

'Same here,' said a Medusoid from Minos VII, its vestigial 'snakes' wriggling like stumpy tapeworms. 'Don't know what you did to make the Joodsh put ya down the wrong hole, but they're not even going to find your *bonesh*, pal.'

'Oh for the extreme degree of disconsiderational discourtesy!' a mechanical voice cried, and from the press of the crowd came a centipedal form. 'One would sensate abasementizational error of proper conduct in the extreme to comport oneself in such a manner!'

The Doctor smiled with relief. 'Hello, Queegvogel. I see they caught you too. I'm sorry about that, but I'm glad you seem to be all right.'

'It is no matter.' The creature came from the crowd and planted himself firmly between the Doctor and the approaching belligerents, raising its stinger menacingly. 'One merely cannot allow, countenance or condone the facilitation of such uncalled-for violence upon one's brother/friend's good personage.'

It appeared that Queegvogel had some respect here. Possibly these people knew him to be far more potentially

121

dangerous than his – to human lights – vaguely ridiculous manner suggested. The advancing beings had stopped dead and seemed slightly at a loss.

'But he a *yooman*,' the Ursine said sullenly. He cast around at the others for confirmation. 'You know what *yoomans* do. What they put us through. Time we just got back a bit of our own.'

'I'm not!' the Doctor said indignantly. 'Of course I'm not human. Who's been going around saying that I'm human?'

'Well, y'look human,' said the Medusoid, dubiously.

'This is patently not in actuality of truthfulness,' admonished Queegvogel sternly. 'This personage has aided and assisted one's good self towards one's continued corporeal existence. One should not even be travelling via a lateral mode of velocipedal egress whilst simultaneously articulating common tongue-like language, had not this personage leant his worthy aid.'

He took the crowd of alien beings in with his directional eyes. 'Indeed, one would hazard the speculation that this good personage has never so much as affected the slightest violence towards your good selves, or those you esteem, or indeed so much as one single member of your respective noble races!'

'Um, quite,' said the Doctor, favouring the Sontarans, Medusoids, evolved Cybermen and all the others with a friendly smile, and hoping like Rassilon's trousers nobody here knew what it meant when someone crossed their fingers behind their back. 'Never a truer word spoken. Perish the thought.'

Not all of them had been human. Not all of them had been mammal, or animal, or even breathed air. The thing that now infused them was of another order of difference entirely. It would have trouble distinguishing between a human being and a week-old cucumber.

What they did share was a certain oddity of the morphological field. A being is something more than the crude level of meat and matter, the cellular genetics that comprise it – even the atoms of the molecules that comprise its cells. On the subatomic level, mass is merely the function of a complex distortion in the fabric of space/time. Biological consciousness is linked to the fundamental structure of the Universe.

The individual beings that had become these things had been displaced and dispossessed in the precisely correct way. Some through drugs that altered their bodies and their consciousness; some through being wrenched from everything they'd ever known, and never finding anything to replace it, and dying by degrees inside. Whatever the reason, while others might be merely tipped into madness by a specific set of stimuli, these people had been changed.

And they streamed through the city, towards the black monolith of a building that stood in its centre like a whole but completely rotten tooth. It is doubtful that they thought in any recognizable terms, it is doubtful that they thought at all – they merely, instinctively, were aware of the cold and vast intelligence housed in that tower, knew that it was drawing them. They were powerless to resist. Burning moths drawn, inexorably, to a black lantern that gave no visible light.

In the holding chamber, several hours passed without incident, save for the occasional new prisoner falling from the hole in the ceiling, and landing in a heap. The prisoners sat or sprawled – or squatted or slumped – in the postures of sleep. No one, not even those who were not physiologically nocturnal, got any.

The atmosphere, after the excitement of the Doctor's arrival, had lapsed back into a kind of doom-laden lethargy – but cutting through it was a jagged, glassy sense of tension, like the hum of a high-tension wire. There is an old adage concerning the differentiation between the guilty and the innocent: you put them in a cell and the guilty go to sleep, while the innocent fret.

Here, everybody was awake, not because they might not be guilty of whatever they were charged with, but because there was so much more to fret about whatever they had done.

'They have this thing called a *kout*,' one of the Sontarans said to the Doctor. 'Once you're in the cells they can use it for anything. It's a –'

'I know what it is,' said the Doctor gloomily. He remembered the implement from its use in the Russia of the tsars. It was a two-handed whip, some eighteen feet long, as thick as a human's wrist at one end, with metal hooks on the other. In the hands of an expert it could snap a victim's neck with one stroke, or rip the spine out of the back. It was just another of those euphemistic human things – sentencing a prisoner to a flogging, even with an ordinary, lesser whip, sounded nicer than sentencing them to hang, but in practice it was merely a much more brutal, drawn-out and agonizing method of execution. In twentieth-century Singapore, they'd had the punishment of caning – which sounded almost jolly until you saw the special guiding device that channelled the entire force of the blow, every single time, on to the same small area of the body.

It was times like these that he wondered if some of the races more inimical than humans might not have a point. The Daleks might just want to kill anything that wasn't a Dalek and moved, but at least they were quick, clean and no-nonsense about it.

The name of the Sontaran was Droog. He was one of the units that had recently been bred in the failed attempt for diversification, in this case as a maintenance technician. He had been Adjudged for armed robbery, but his inbuilt genetic codes had probably made him the worst armed robber on this particular world, with his fearsome cry of, 'Give me all the credits now or I'll . . . I'll repair your air purification system, which I can't help noticing has sprung a nasty leak from its B12 gasket!'

'Thash not the worst thing,' a Medusoid hissed. It

was the one who had intended to attack the Doctor on his arrival, but, after being assured that the Time Lord wasn't human, had become more friendly. He was, it seemed, in custody after being charged for tithe-evasion, on the profits from hir stall selling Oolian luck-possets, this being yet another result of the recent darkening of the Church of Adjudication. Hir name was Xxigzzh.

'So what's the worst thing?' asked the Doctor.

'I had a trilateral sibling,' Xxigzzh said. 'The Adjudicatorsh took hir month-cyclesh ago. Mishtaken identity, so they evenshually had to let hir go. Was shrivelled when came out, starved of soma and nearly dead.' The Medusoid moved in closer to speak in a conspiratorial whisper. 'Shaid that people jusht dishappeared from the cellsh. No exshplanation. And that before s/he left the rate of it was increashing.'

'Hmm.' The Doctor wiped some gobs of Medusoid venom-saliva off his face as politely as possible. 'Unexshplained dishappearences – I beg your pardon. Unexplained disappearances.' He frowned. 'You know, I really wish I could go somewhere, and people would simply pop out to the shops.'

It was at that point that there came a concussive clunking from the shutters blocking off one side of the chamber. Several of the more faint-hearted creatures hit the floor, thinking it was gunfire, then realized it was the sound of electromagnetic bolts slamming back from their housings. The shutters retracted and a squad of Adjudicator guards came through. They were heavily armed, could hardly move for heavy-duty body armour and their faces were completely covered by gas masks.

For a moment there was a stunned, shocked silence.

'One must perforce admit that one intimates,' Queegvogel said, its vocoder device muted, 'that the good Adjudicatory personages might merely effect some policy of immediate discorporation at this particular juncture.'

'Out you come!' one of the guards said, a bullhorn

attachment to his mask boosting his voice to the point where it threatened to rupture eardrum analogues. 'Single file. No funny business. Prepare for processing.'

'I only hope,' the Doctor muttered as the guards herded the prisoners out, 'that they mean "processing" in a slightly different way this time.'

They flowed through corridors and ventilation ducts, flung themselves up bounce-tube shafts, heading for the thing that remained locked inside its black, smooth thoughts. Security systems remained completely unaware of them, never having been programmed for this particular form of energy or life. The owners of human eyes, when they passed them in the brightly bio-lit corridors, might shake their heads and look again, puzzled by a sudden flickering in the light levels, but by then they would be gone.

One of them remained distinct, still caught inside a bulging envelope of some impermeable polymer. It didn't matter to it. What must be thought of as its mind connected on other levels — it was perfectly meshed with all the others. Some instinct, however, had it making its way through the hidden areas, sticking to the vents and conduits, staying out of sight.

As they drew closer to the thing that was calling them, they noticed something else. Creatures like them, thousands more, were already clustered around it, thrashing and churning in a frenzy.

It was very powerful. It was being fed. Somebody or something was feeding it.

And at last they reached it. The things that had once been living beings in their own right, and now were something that was not quite matter, not quite energy, something that was both greater and lesser than either, streamed towards the thing that had drawn them, joined with the others and were finally subsumed.

It was as though critical mass had been achieved. In that one moment everything changed. The thing that infused these people finally woke up, and remembered what it was.

'Fill this specimen jar,' snapped the med-tech.

'What, from here?' asked the Doctor.

One of the guards swung the butt of his gun and drove the Doctor to his knees. The Time Lord had a fraction of a second to take evasive action — more than enough time — but for the moment he had decided to keep a low profile. He was damned if he was going to let them think it had caused him damage, though.

He looked up at the med-tech enquiringly. 'Forgive me if I'm wrong, but I've been pretty much scanned already, for identification, drugs or anything you might be looking for.'

'We have to see what skaggy diseases you picked up in the tank.' The technician was covered head to toe with a sealed suit. The Doctor noticed that, even through the suit, he flinched and shuddered when he had to touch something nonhuman. 'We know what you things are like. You'd do anything to each other.'

'Oh for the extremationalization of shame!' This came from Queeg, who was behind the Doctor in the single-file procession. 'One would quite erroneously hazard the theorem that our good selves were *human* from such derogatory and specious pontification!'

Two of the guards fell on Queeg. It took all the Doctor's self-control not to bounce to his feet to help. It wouldn't have done any good at this point, anyway. The only way out of this was *through*.

They had been taken out from the holding chamber and through rough-walled tunnels to this other chamber: a long, narrow gallery where their remaining clothing had been stripped, where they had been sluiced, blood and related ichorous substances had been taken and they had been subcutaneously tagged — the Doctor for the first time, the others for the second. The techs had roughly dug the old tags out, in a

127

manner that seemed little less than rationalized assault.

The Doctor had now almost reached the doors at the other end of the gallery, where stool and urine samples were being taken – or, at least, the end result of whatever process a creature's metabolism allowed for the expulsion of waste matter. There seemed no real point to it, even given the so-called explanation that the techs were scanning for disease. It was not as if any tests were run or people segregated out. There were no private cubicles – and this was telling in itself. What they were going through here, in this final stage of processing, was nothing short of a public, ritual humiliation. It was a conscious part of the incarceration process to shame and subdue them, to make it clear who was in control.

One of the guards grabbed hold of the Doctor's shoulder. 'On your feet.'

'I'd be delighted.' The Doctor staggered clumsily to his feet – so clumsily, in fact, that he tripped over them and pitched headlong into the med-tech. His hands clutched at the tech's suit and somehow ripped it open.

'Oh, you filthy . . .' The tech scrabbled at the rip with sudden panic, his voice high-pitched and cracking. The Doctor, in his humble opinion, saw someone not entirely in the saddle of his own will – a neurotic just about ready to collapse into full-scale breakdown.

'I'm terribly sorry,' he said. 'You must let me help.' He squirmed out of the grip of two of the guards who were trying to haul him back, and bustled around the tech trying to assist him with his suit. Somehow, though, it only seemed to make things worse.

In the confusion, and quite by accident, the Doctor's elbow managed to catch the rack of alien bodily waste samples. It fell over with a crash, dousing the luckless med-tech with noxious substances and fluids.

'Oh dear,' said the Doctor, before disappearing under the weight of several irate guards. 'It'll wash right off, never fear, and I don't suppose you'll catch anything, much.'

* * *

In the ablutionary cubicle of his sanctum, Garon sluiced himself off. Communion with his God had taken a lot out of him and, as it were, put rather a lot on. Not that he minded. That would be unthinkable. If one is to serve the true glory of God then sacrifices have to be made.

The problem was, whatever other attributes it might or might not have had, it was a *hungry* God, and increasingly so. Garon was feeling a little rushed off his feet.

Garon was in the process of reaching for a loofah, to clean out some particularly difficult-to-reach crevices, when the METATRON spoke: 'Incoming message from Commander Marl of the Holding Division.'

Garon frowned. 'Could you please inform him that I am at present tending to my toilet?'

There was a pause. Then: 'Commander Marl of the Holding Division has just uttered several profanities of a blasphemous and irreligious nature,' the METATRON said at last. 'Should these be logged and detailed pending disciplinary action?'

'Just log them,' said Garon. 'I'll go over them at the first available opportunity.'

'Commander Marl of the Holding Division still insists that he be allowed to speak.'

Garon sighed. 'Oh, very well. No direct link. Ask him what he wants. You are not required to keep repeating the area where Marl performs his duties, incidentally.'

Another brief pause. 'Commander Marl requests that a Penitent be executed for assault upon the person of the Church. Medical Auxiliary Whorl.'

'Whorl?' Garon asked. Whorl was one of the Adjudication personnel in whom Garon took an, as it were, special interest. Whorl, he recalled, was a man who could not precisely be called a bigot, because that would presume some degree of conscious thought. The man was a vicious little hatemonger, and his hatred of non-humans stemmed more from latent psychosis than any

129

rational statement of position. Garon had personally placed him in on the nonhuman processing line, because his bigotry communicated itself and added an extra turn of the thumbscrew to the nonhuman miscreants. It was a question of assigning people the duties to which they were suited.

'A nonhuman has assaulted Medical Auxiliary Whorl?' he said.

'Commander Marl says that it wasn't exactly assault. Medical Auxiliary Whorl has been restricted to the Church Infirmary, suffering from profound nervous collapse.'

'Ah, yes. I thought it might be something like that.' Garon felt a grain of annoyance. He had fully expected this Whorl creature to crack at some point, but he had rather hoped it would be later rather than sooner. Possibly, someone would have to be punished. 'And the identification of this nonhuman who so grievously assaulted him?'

'BX–2174.45–IV (provisional),' said the META-TRON. 'The Penitent who calls himself the Doctor.'

The Doctor again, causing trouble again. Garon felt the strange and icy stab of fear he had felt when the man had come back to life. Had he really thought that the man might be a demon? Had this nonhuman frightened Garon so much? Even though it had been mere hours ago, it was as if that momentary aberration had happened to someone else . . . For a moment Garon seriously considered making an example of the Doctor, removing him as a problem quickly, once and for all.

But no. That would disrupt certain plans that Garon had already made – carefully considered and refined plans, upon which even the slightest disruption must not intrude. 'Tell Commander Marl that his request is denied,' he said. 'The nonhuman who calls himself the Doctor has been assigned the status of a special prisoner until fully Adjudged.' Which was complete nonsense, of course, and both Garon and Marl knew it, but it told

Marl in no uncertain terms that this Doctor was for the moment out of bounds. Garon had other plans for him.

Garon allowed himself a small, cold smile. 'Assure Commander Marl of the Holding Division, however, that this so-called "Doctor" shall in due course receive a degree of Justice satisfactory to us all.'

Fifteen

The dawn came again, or rather the geodesic sky depolarized. It depolarized on something that looked like the fires of Hell.

The Titanian Node now filled the sky from end to end. The shapes inside it churned, forming, breaking apart and reforming, like the spirits of a million screaming damned.

The city, rising from a humid, oppressive night that left it clammy with sweat and had precluded sleep, now baked as though in a low-grade furnace.

It was going to be a hot one.

The supposedly derelict Mimseydome™ was a hive of activity. White Fire people in their functional if slightly mismatched combat uniforms swarmed through it in their hundreds – no, their thousands. It seemed impossible that there could be so many. There hadn't seemed to be that many the night before.

In what had once been the Happy Clown House – to the left of Percival the Penguin as you came out of the Faerie Tale Castle – but what was now a makeshift armoury-cum-storehouse, Peri looked down at herself and tried to think Happy Clown thoughts. It wasn't the heavy, padded flak jacket, it was more what was under it. She felt like she should be creaking, even when she was standing still.

'I know,' Blaine said, seemingly catching her mood, 'but we're running low on materials. There's never enough body armour to go around. As it is, we had to

132

raid the Habitat for what we could get.' She smiled. 'What you've got on at the moment mostly came from a supplier for the underground fetish clubs – but you're going to need something durable and heavy for when the shrapnel starts to fly.' She looked Peri over appraisingly. 'You'll do.'

I just wish I could believe you, Peri thought. Stuff like this needed someone whipcord lithe to carry it off. Plus, her all-in-one leather suit and the boots might protect her, but it had also been carefully tailored to enhance certain bits and pieces into what a realtor would probably call a spectacular development of frontage. It was a wonder she could do the flak jacket up. She felt like a cross between a peroxide rock chick and the wet dream of a gentleman of a certain age. Thankfully, the heels had been broken off the boots, and thick ripple soles stuck on with epoxy resin.

Blaine unlocked the weapons racks and slapped down several items on the counter: a gun the same as Peri had used the night before on the shooting range, packs of ammunition and a knife, a little like a bowie knife, with a serrated edge. She picked up the knife again and showed Peri a thin strip of brass running down the length of the blade. 'This is for knife-fighting. You use the blade to turn your opponent's and it catches on it.'

Peri saw that the brass strip was scarred and overscarred with nicks.

'Also,' Blaine said, 'you get a little surprise.' She pressed a concealed stud with her thumb, and a second, much smaller blade slid out from the hilt. 'You can lock it like this for some serious two-way action,' she said, thumbing the stud through a quarter-turn, 'or you can detach it completely. We won't have time to train you up in knife-fighting, but it might give you an edge.'

'We won't have time?' Peri said.

'We won't.' Blaine gave her little, grim trademark smile. 'Word is we're finally going to make our move.'

* * *

133

The night before, Peri had been groggy with exhaustion, a walking basket case with trauma and fatigue. She was beginning to think that she might not have been quite in her right mind. Now, as they walked through the looming forms of the theme park under the sick red light of the Node, she saw the things she hadn't seen before.

The White Fire people were seriously armed and organized. She saw them drilling in formations a hundred strong. She saw blocky forms under camouflage netting, through which tinsel shreds of metal foil had been twisted to mask their pattern signatures from sensor detection. They looked like armoured assault vehicles to her. When she had first come here she had assumed the White Fire people to be a last-stand, patchwork army fighting a desperate battle against the crushing might of the Adjudicators. Now, she realized it was more – possibly much more.

'You could fight a war here,' she said.

'That's what we're going to do,' said Blaine. 'We've been building up to this for years. We laid our plans. And now we can fight them on their own terms. And we're going to win.'

'At any cost?' said Peri.

'We have the Right on our side.' Blaine looked at her. 'We're fighting against Abomination that shouldn't breathe the same air as decent people, and sacrifices have to be made. We'll win by any means necessary.'

Peri nodded. 'Any means necessary.'

She remembered what Kane had said, the night before, when he had waylaid her in her quarters.

She had not woken until Blaine had come in at six hundred hours and shaken her awake. She still felt bone tired and like she had been put through the wringer, but at least she was able to connect again. She had not as yet told Blaine of her doubts about Kane, the doubts that had been confirmed by his threat. In the clear, or at least brighter, light of day, she found that she was still trying to decide.

'You're literally the last person to be inducted before the push,' Blaine said. 'No time for proper training, so I'm going to put you in on one of the hit squads. You can be of use there, and if you screw up it won't do too much damage.' She smiled. 'If that hurts your ego, well then tough.'

'I understand,' said Peri.

'I'll be coming along with you to keep an eye on you.'

They had reached what had originally been intended as a franchise for the Mister Meaty™ porkburger bar, now converted into a general canteen and recreational centre. Several groups in combat gear sat or sprawled around, their attitudes common to off-duty soldiers the whole Galaxy over. In one of the groups Peri recognized Draker, the man who had led the party out of the Sector 3 riots.

Blaine took Peri over to him. 'Another warm body for you, Draker. No slack, but use your own judgment, understand?'

Draker looked Peri over and nodded. 'We've met.'

'Yes, we have.' A man in his group with his back to them turned from where he had been sprawled in his bucket-chair, and Peri recognized Kane.

He smiled up at her. 'We've all met, I think. I'm sure we're all going to get along famously.'

In his chambers on top of the Faerie Tale Tower, Avron Jelks worked at a secretary desk, writing in an ancient chap-book in a neat and perfect copperplate style. He looked up as a voice issued from the silvered dome on his other, larger desk. 'Message for Mr Jelks.' It was Blaine.

'What is it, Commander?' he said.

'I want to talk to you about our latest recruit. Purblack.'

'Ah, yes.' Jelks recalled the young lady perfectly – and not merely because he had seen her such a short while before. He recalled the names and faces of all the White Fire recruits. He was good at remembering such things.

135

Besides, after today, after a wide variety of dust had settled, it was just possible he might get to know her a little better. She had seemed a little cleaner and better scrubbed than a lot of women who, quite frankly, didn't take care of themselves as much as they ought.

'I recall the young lady in question,' he said. A peculiarity of Jelks's speech was that he tended to shy away from using actual names. 'What of her.'

There was a pause. 'I'm not really sure. She seems OK, and I think she really hates the Church, but I have this feeling about her. It's like she doesn't really believe in the important things.'

Avron Jelks frowned. 'You think she might pose some kind of threat?'

'No – I mean it's nowhere near as strong as that. I mean, I just have a vague doubt. Nothing drastic. Do you know what I mean?' There was a touch of unease in Blaine's usually rock-solid voice.

'I know precisely what you mean,' Jelks said kindly. 'The last thing we want is to go around executing our own people on the basis of a sudden flash of paranoia. That is, after all, just the kind of conduct we are fighting against.' He thought about it for a moment. 'Keep an eye on her when we go operational. Organize a small test if you can do so without risk. Then proceed as you see fit.'

Back out on the Sector 3 streets, Adjudicator Craator cuffed a failed human pickpocket to a holding post. This was proving difficult, not because the little cruk was particularly strong, but because he was struggling with an utter, terrified frenzy.

Craator finally locked the hasps and headed back towards his MAV. Behind him, the failed pickpocket still struggled desperately and shrieked. Crazy Season, obviously, but in some way it was worse than Craator had ever known. Now that his senses were attuned to terror, he seemed to see it in the eyes of all he passed. It was vaguely disturbing. The Adjudicators had always been known and feared, but never like this.

Still, it was good to be back on the streets again. The internal politics of the Church could go hang, so far as one Adjudicator Joseph Craator was concerned. This was where the real work was, this was where real things needed to be done.

That reminded him. The nonhuman who called himself the Doctor. Craator had consciously refused to Adjudge him while still gripped in fury at having been jerked around. Now that he was in a more normal frame of mind it was time to rectify that.

He called up the Curia. 'This is Craator. Adjudgment upon provisional detainee BX-2174.45-IV a.k.a. the Doctor, no true name known. Seditious acts against the Statutes of our One True God, nine months. Resisting Lawful Apprehension and subsequent wasting of —'

The Curia was on line immediately. 'That case has been tagged, Craator. Access is denied to any and all aspects of it. You are not, repeat not, to involve yourself any further.'

'What the Sheol?' Craator growled. 'This is my case, Control. What is this.'

'The case has been tagged,' the voice of the Curia repeated. 'You are not to involve yourself further.' The link went dead.

This was Garon's doing, Craator thought. It had his DNA-trace all over it. The rage he had felt earlier resurfaced with a vengeance. It seemed that his every action of late had been balked by the High Churchman, a man who had consistently used his power to turn what should have been God's Justice into pointless butchery. Well, High Churchman or no, it was time somebody took a stand. Stand up to the cruk and put him through some changes . . .

Occupied by his thoughts, it was a moment before Craator realized that his reflexes and instincts had had him pulling the MAV to a halt and looking up. It was a

137

moment before he fully registered what his eyes were seeing. 'What the crukking *Sheol*?'

Craator stared up at the recently installed holding post, the sort that had been redesigned to form a T with two crossbars. Stared up at the hung, drawn and quartered remains of the Piglet Person who hung from it.

Sixteen

The support staff of the Church were not required to live inside the Temple itself, and most of them preferred not to. There were, however, rooms where they could stay, during periods of nominal emergency like the Crazy Season, while subject to constant call. Auxiliaries did not have the implants that allowed them to use sleep machines, and it had been grudgingly acknowledged that they occasionally needed to sleep.

Nadia Chong threw the kitbag containing her personal belongings on to the bunk, and crossed over to the washstand. She spent a couple of seconds wondering why she couldn't see herself, before remembering exactly where she was, and that the Church didn't hold with encouraging the vanity of personal appearance within its walls. Of course there wasn't a mirror. She was secretly grateful. After thirty-six hours of operating her console in the Curia she felt like death, and she supposed she didn't look any better.

What she wanted, dammit *needed*, was the kind of long, hot luxurious bath that would have a High Churchman questioning her moral laxity, and have her watching her water and power outtake for the rest of the month – unless she did a little juggling of the transputronic databooks, of course.

What she settled for here and now was splashing cold water on her face, stripping unsteadily down to her underwear, stumbling to the bunk and collapsing on to it, hugging her kitbag to her cheek. It was slightly padded and better than the hard little pillow.

She would never know how long she slept. The next thing she knew, the door burst open with a crash, and silhouetted in the doorway stood what she first thought, in the shock of waking, to be the apparition of some childhood ogre. She gave a little squeak of fear.

'You. Chong,' the Ogre growled. 'You're going to tell me just what the cruk's going on.'

Penitents in the Holding Complex spent nights locked two to a cell. Slopping out was at five forty-five. For various reasons, apart from those who exuded mucus constantly, the new nonhuman intake didn't have a lot to slop out.

The Doctor looked down at himself. The overalls were not exactly drab – if anything they were even more colourful than his usual garb. This was because they were made from a feltlike compressed material composed of any number of other materials, the compacted waste remains from the recycling of anything usable. Up close one could see a tangle of brightly coloured, mismatched threads; from a couple of feet away the pigments blurred into a muddy brown.

'I can't say I care for the change of wardrobe,' he said. 'I have, after all, always been known for my debonair sartorial taste.'

'Expression of polite enquiry?' said Queegvogel. 'Expression denoting an extreme degree of disbelief!'

'Well, yes, I suppose you would say that,' said the Doctor, dejectedly. Since its last ill-treatment at the hands of the guards, Queegvogel's vocoder unit had all but given up the mechanical ghost. It now took a great deal of effort to produce something recognizable as language at all.

They walked out of the cramped cell in which they had spent the short remainder of the night, out into the vast communal cavern of the Holding Complex. Catwalks and steps crawled over the walls, like fire escapes crawling over a twentieth-century New York tenement, but on a massive scale. The cavern was so large that it even had its own microclimate: the roof was lost to view behind a foglike haze.

Prisoners in their thousands were trudging towards the cavern floor, where cooking fires were burning. There were no catering facilities as such here: food and other bare essentials of life were simply dumped, and the prisoners were forced to improvise as best they could.

This is not to say that there was no presence of authority. There were Adjudicator guards in their hundreds, heavily armed, ever ready to club a prisoner to submission, and, if he would not be subdued, shoot him, her or it dead. There seemed to be no actual rules or method to this. The Doctor suspected that the system operated rather like that of Nazi concentration camps, and the camps that had followed them with only slightly more euphemistic names.

It was the sheer unpredictability of the process that terrified. One might be punished one minute for wearing one's coat the wrong way, or for looking a guard in the eye – the next, one was punished for buttoning one's coat up tight and not paying attention to a guard. It kept one in a constant state of low-grade terror, to the point where it was the atmosphere in which one lived and breathed, and one could not imagine living any other way.

The Doctor, having just arrived, and having rather more internal reserves than the norm in any case, had been struck by the atmosphere from the moment he had been hauled from the processing chamber and into the complex itself. It had hit him like a freighter on a terminal vector. Even though it had still been night, even though the majority of prisoners were still asleep in their cells, the place had seethed with a sense of pent-up violence and hatred. It was like some massive pressure cooker with the pressure valve clogged. This place would not let off steam – this place would explode.

141

The procession of prisoners reached the cavern floor. The guards who had been herding them shoved and kicked them out on to the bare rock floor. The Doctor, looking around, tried to pull in some sense of specificity out of the patterns that one could only see from, as it were, above.

One would have expected humans to be segregated from nonhumans, the various sexes and sexualities to be segregated, simply as a means of lessening the caged-animal tension. Here there was no official segregation at all – and so the prisoners had banded together unofficially. It was like looking at a set of tribes, each shutting itself off from the rest, and just waiting for the chance to fall upon each other.

The focal points, the gathering points, seemed to be the cooking fires – although 'fires' was probably too archaic a term. Each group had jury-rigged what seemed to be anything from canister-fuelled gas burners to dynamo-driven electric hobs.

Only a few of the groups, the Doctor noted, seemed to be entirely exclusive: a squabbling colony of Skraks, or a group of human women, who had banded together to protect themselves from certain obvious dangers. For the most part, though, there were groups of mixed nonhuman species with the occasional human face in them, human groups with the occasional alien. There was no absolute iconoclasm, save that from their postures and interactions it was obvious that they were unified within their group. It was them against their enclosed world.

Seen in this light, the Adjudicator guards might have been merely one more faction amongst many – but they were the dominant faction, the predators. They ranged through the cavern at will, took what they liked and did what they liked. You heard the sporadic commotion of it, the struggling, the screams and squeals. It was just another part of the process keeping the inmates collectively down.

The Doctor and Queegvogel looked around until they spotted Droog, Xxigzzh and several others they remembered from the night before. They were gathered around a makeshift gas stove. They waved to them, and the Doctor and Queeg made their way across the cavern to join them. Occasionally they had to carefully circumnavigate various groups, of various species, who growled at them viciously.

When they arrived, the Ursine looked up from the stove, where he was stirring a thin, unidentifiable broth. 'Sontaran put it together,' he explained. 'Joods throw us lots of stuff like that an' let us get on with it.' He pointed to an area of the cavern, one of several where ablutions facilities had been rigged. They seemed to be a neutral zone. 'Y'can even have a wash and brush-up. Not much food, though.'

The Doctor frowned. 'Now why would they do that? Almost anything can be used as a weapon – that's one of the main reasons prisoners have their possessions restricted. I'd have thought that unrestricted access to tools and implements would be lethal.'

'It is,' Droog cut in. 'Big riots on a regular basis, apparently. A lot of people die.' He gestured towards a group halfway across the chamber. Despite the general mix of people here, they seemed to be entirely human and people were giving them a wide berth. 'Human Firsters,' Droog said. 'From what I've heard, they've been seriously tooling up.'

'Expression of unease tinged with a faint degree of alarm,' said Queegvogel.

Again, the Doctor seemed thoughtful. 'I don't think that's the half of it,' he said.

He turned to the others and counted points off on his fingers: 'They deprive people of food, but they give them all the means they might need to manufacture weapons. They mix people together without any kind of imposed infrastructure so the tensions feed off each other.' He glanced over to where a pair of guards had dragged someone from a group and were beating him. 'Indeed, they seem to be going out of their way to whip the tensions up. It's as if the place has actively been *designed* to do it . . .'

'So what?' said Droog. 'They just want us to die.'

'No, I don't think so,' the Doctor said. 'I mean, you know as well as I how the Church operates. If they merely wanted to kill somebody, they'd execute them under their laws – even if they had to twist and change the laws so they could execute them. There's something else, here. Some other factor. I just wish I knew exactly what.'

'Look, you don't know what you're asking.' Chong now had the thin, small blanket from the bunk wrapped around her and she clutched it to her. She supposed she should really put on her uniform, but some part of her found the idea of dressing in front of Craator strangely more distressing than merely being semi-clothed. 'I can't do something like that.'

As she had fully woken up the feeling that this was some childhood monster had evaporated, but Craator was still pretty bad in his own right – and there were worse things than childhood monsters. She kept finding herself glancing around superstitiously, as though High Churchman Garon might suddenly materialize through the wall. 'Those data are completely locked off,' she said. 'There's no way I can access them without clearance.'

'Oh yes you can.' Now that the light was on, Chong saw that Craator wasn't wearing his badge. Church of Adjudication trackers and taggers would be locked on to that, somewhere else, wherever it was.

Craator reached down and hauled up her kitbag. He pulled it open and rooted through it until he unearthed Chong's portable transputer rig. It had an integral comms link that could hook it into any system in the Habitat via line-of-sight infrared.

144

'I know for a fact you can,' he said. 'For example, I know for a fact that you've hacked into the central supply databanks and allocated yourself an extra power level for your con-apt, in direct contravention of the Statutes. It's been going on for years.'

Chong felt herself go cold. 'How do you know? I left the data logs so clean they squeak. And don't give me any of that "I didn't know before but now I do" crap, because that isn't your style. You're not bright enough for that.'

Craator shrugged. 'You wouldn't want to know. The fact is that we know. Same way as we know you've had relations of a sexual nature with three separate members of the Undercover Operations Section.'

Chong sighed. 'So which of the weasely little rats grassed me up? Liam? Benny K? Danielle?'

'Doesn't matter,' Craator said. 'We've let infractions like that go because, like the OCS, you're the best at the job you do. If people are going to run Adjudicators on the street, we want them to be run by the best. So we allow a little leeway.' He scowled. 'But think on this, Chong: you've seen the way things are going. How long do you expect to get away with it in this New Order Garon's establishing? How long do you seriously expect to last?'

He tossed the transputer pack to Chong, who caught it automatically. 'Hack into the OBERON net. Tell me what he's doing up in his tower. Tell me what he's making happen down there in the cells.'

'Sudden expression of interest tinged with some small measure of worry,' said Queegvogel. 'Observation of an incident occurring from this general direction.'

Queegvogel gestured with a manipulatory appendage. On the far end of the cavern, through the heavily armoured doors used by the Adjudication guards, a new force was coming. In manner, it was different from the usual guards, who had tended to roam and foray, like a

145

pack of jackals. These new arrivals were a tight, regimented group.

Some of them were on the heavy-duty hover-bikes that Adjudicators used on the streets. They cut a swathe through the groups of prisoners, like bullets fired through apples, scattering them in their wake and in at least some cases running them down. If the vehicles had been running on wheels, the casualties would have been squashed dead.

The leader of the new arrivals halted his bike in the centre of the cavern. He appeared to consult the readout on some piece of hand-held equipment, and then gestured his fellows onward in a new direction. They headed directly for the Doctor and his fellow prisoners. A section of them detached, and headed in another direction, towards the group that Droog had identified as the Human First.

The Adjudicators stopped before the Doctor and his fellows. This close, one could make out certain differences between their uniforms and those worn by the guards, and those worn by Adjudicators on the street. The general design was the same, but it was as if they had evolved: the black polymer of their helmets and armour completely covered them and hid their faces. The silver insignia had atrophied to vestigiality. They had no name badges. It was as if these people were the ultimate product of the Adjudicator's evolution down a certain line.

The problem was, it seemed to be an utterly non-human line. You had the disquieting feeling that, if you were to open up these all-covering uniforms, you would find nothing inside but some evil, intangible and monstrous force. It was as though there were nothing but death and darkness inside.

'The Handsh of God!' Xxigzzh hissed. 'The shervantsh of the High Churcshmen!' S/he appeared to be visibly shaken, exuding a fear-scent that s/he had not given before now. 'My shibling talked of them. They are the onesh who dishappear you away!'

'Silence.' The voice issued from the faceless leader of the Hands of God. It held no emotion, let alone human emotion, and was bereft of even those overtones that come from villains shouting for 'Silence!' from long before you were even born. It was a simple, flat statement. The power of it, however, seemed to plunge the cavern of the Holding Complex into silence for several hundred metres around.

Off to one side, the other Hands of God were hauling people from the group of Human Firsters. Their leader, meanwhile, scanned the Doctor, Queeg, Droog, Xxigzzh and several others with his hand-held sensor. 'These are the ones. Have them taken and made ready. Make them ready for the manufactory of God.'

It was some five minutes after the Hands of God had been and gone that the remaining Human Firsters began making a commotion, viciously attacking the groups of people to either side with their makeshift weapons. There seemed to be no reason for it; they had merely, instantly gone on the offensive as though a switch had been thrown.

The other groups retaliated. The numbers of the Human Firsters had been depleted, and they were losing badly even as the guards closed in to break it up. It seemed that this unexpected conflict would be over before it ever really started.

Then the bombs went off.

Later, it would be discovered that twenty-seven devices had been surreptitiously scattered through the cavern. They were basic pipe bombs, built from the piping that had served to rig the cooking fires and ablutions, capped either end and filled with a powder made from ground-up match heads.

The fact that these things had been available in the Holding Complex made this unquestionable. The fact that the sheer quantity of match heads needed was for all practical purposes impossible, and the question of what had been used for delay fuses, was for various reasons glossed over completely. The two that failed to detonate subsequently vanished without trace en route to the Church's forensic division. As it was, whatever the explanation, twenty-five pipe bombs exploded, taking down hundreds with their shrapnel, and the Holding Complex plunged, screaming, into bloody, burning chaos.

Seventeen

'There you go. Classified records for the Holding Complex.' Chong tapped her transputer pack, to which she had routed a real-time emulation of her console in the Curia and hacked through the code restrictions with a centuries-old MOLE application through the back door. Sometimes crude and basic was best. The procedure she had used was so crude and basic that it had completely bypassed the sophisticated OBERON anti-hack routines. 'Am I a sub-genius or what? You may kiss my ring.'

'Don't be filthy,' snapped Craator. 'Do the job.'

Chong scanned through the figures and dates, her trained eye searching for any anomaly. 'Now this is interesting . . .' she said at last.

'What?' said Craator from over her shoulder.

'There's some discrepancy between the intake, the release and the deaths in custody. It's been masked by a series of riots, almost lost in deliberate confusion.'

'Meaning?' said Craator.

'Meaning that there's more going in than coming out or dying in there. Somebody's been having people away.'

It was at this point that, on the emulation of the console, a readout began to blink rapidly.

'What's that?' Craator said.

'General Curia alert. Audio only. It's coming from the cells. Hang on a tick, I'll try to pull it through.' Chong typed rapidly in the pack's keypad and a small speaker barked tinnily into life: ' . . . oss. This is Marl. Collateral damage to facilities and personnel. More than half my men are down. We're being overrun in here! Need backup! The Holding Complex has been overrun! Shok-TAC and –'

There was the sound of muffled, angry voices, the perfectly clear scream of Marl from his mike, and then a series of concussive, meaty thuds before the sound link went dead.

'Oh God,' Chong breathed. 'I think they need some help down there. Craator . . .?'

But Craator was already out of the door.

The occupation and destruction of the Holding Complex by its inmates drew in large numbers of Adjudicators from the surrounding sectors, leaving only a skeleton force to deal with problems in the Habitat itself. Resources had already been stretched to their limit by the Crazy Season triggered by the pulsing of the Node, and now things threatened to go out of control entirely.

And then things got one Sheol of a lot worse.

At strategic points throughout the Habitat, in the air purification plants, the communication installations, the water purifiers and the densely populated public spaces, armed squads appeared and stormed their objectives and took control. They took out the thinly stretched Adjudication forces when they had to, but in some cases not even one shot was fired. There were simply no Adjudicators there to resist. Circumstances had produced a situation that allowed them to walk in, entrench themselves and plant their banner.

And the banner said: WHITE FIRE.

Peri racked up her gun and made her way cautiously through the tanks of the Sector 5 plant. Inside them, behind industrially battered and scratched but originally clear polymer, a greenish broth bubbled and seethed. The tanks were hydroponically breeding algae that were poisonous to humans, but were the staple diet of Darbokian polyp-toads.

The plant was in fact the sole supplier to that entire community, and thus a major strategic point. Obviously, the detail sent to occupy it wasn't as important as those occupying the water plants, say, but it was still pretty important.

There had not been so much as a single guard – one doesn't post a guard on food-producing plants unless in times of famine or war. And, up until fifteen minutes ago, nobody in the Habitat thought they were in either such emergency. The Darbokian workers had simply been rounded up and placed under confinement. Peri had been detailed to search for and round up any of the creatures they had missed.

The bubbling tanks and the intestinal network of piping might have given the place a menacing feel, had not the entire plant been bathed in bright, UV-boosted light. Peri's forehead felt slightly raw from it, and the leather suit moved queasily and slickly across her skin, lubricated with her sweat. Fortunately she had been issued with polarized goggles.

There was a vague sense of movement behind one of the semi-transparent tanks. She pulled her gun and worked her way around. The Darbokians had seemed pretty inoffensive on the whole, but she didn't want to take any chances.

It was Kane.

Apart from the equipment packs they both now carried, for active combat he was wearing just what she had seen when they had first met – save for a pair of tan and khaki camouflage trousers. Peri had thought that incredibly stupid, the point about that sort of camouflage being that it was entirely useless in an artificial, urban environment like the Habitat. Then she had seen the colours that predominated in this hydroponic plant, and had realized they were hitting the one place where his choice of camouflage was perfectly correct.

Now he was crouching by one of the tanks across from the one she had come around, his back to her. Peri

151

watched as he pulled an item, a flat, matt-black disc, from his pack and fixed it to the side of the tank. He flipped a switch on its obverse side. The lighting conditions were such that Peri couldn't see it, but she knew a tiny light would now be blinking redly.

She walked towards him. She didn't put up her gun. 'What d'you think you're doing?'

He didn't so much as flinch. He stood up and turned around in one smooth movement, looked at her and shrugged. Obviously, he'd seen her reflected in the tank.

'I'd have thought it was obvious,' he said easily. He gestured vaguely to the disc. 'Time-delayed fragmentation mine. Tank go boom.'

'You want to tell me why?' Peri asked. 'You don't know if we're going to win or lose. You want to keep your options open with a little sabotage, is that it?'

For a moment Kane looked at her with utter astonishment. 'What are you talking about?' Then he looked at her sharply. 'You think I'm doing this off my own bat? Who do you think ordered me to mine this place? Draker, that's who.'

'What?' Peri was puzzled. 'If we destroy the place, we lose the advantage we get by occupying it. Plus the fact that the people it feeds are going to starve to death.'

'Oh for God's sake!' Kane exclaimed. 'We're not supposed to occupy it. We were never meant to occupy it. You don't believe me, talk to Draker and Blaine.' He started towards her.

Peri aimed her gun squarely at his chest. She vaguely remembered Blaine saying the proper target in these situations was the chest, the head being a relatively smaller and more mobile target. 'Nobody told me. I think I'd feel happier if you gave me your gun while we check this out.'

Kane shrugged. 'Suit yourself.' Very slowly and carefully, he pulled his own gun, using his thumb and fingers on the grip, and tossed it to her. Peri wasn't stupid enough to try to catch it – it seemed that she had learnt a lot about combat over the last couple of days, by a kind of osmosis, seemingly soaking it up through her pores. The gun clattered to the floor beside her. She crouched down and picked it up by touch, never taking her eyes or the muzzle of her own gun from Kane.

They made their way back to the control chamber, where Blaine and the others were guarding their prisoners, Peri not quite escorting Kane, and not quite holding her gun to his back. It was just pointed in his general direction.

The Darbokian polyp-toad people were trussed up against one wall, the ropes biting into their fragile, warty skin. The ropes seemed to have been tied far too tight. They seemed to be in pain.

Blaine, Draker and the others of the squad turned from where they had been gathered by the control consoles, around a comms set plugged into the power supply to conserve its batteries, listening to the progress of their war.

'Back so soon?' Draker said to Kane. 'You've done the job?'

'Halfway there,' Kane said, still in that easy tone that Peri had come to know and distrust. 'Purblack was heading back. I'd like to be here for the fun, if that's OK.'

Draker looked at Blaine, who shrugged noncommittally. 'Yeah, I suppose it's OK,' he said to Kane, then turned to Peri. 'Let's do it. You do the honours, Purblack.'

'Uh . . .' Peri was caught wrong-footed. 'What do you want me to do?'

'What do you think?' Draker indicated the bound and terrified Darbokians. 'Do the skags. We've been saving them for you.'

'*What*?' Peri was utterly appalled. 'If you . . . I mean, OK, I'll fight but if you think for one minute I'm going to gun down people in cold –'

'No gun,' said Draker. 'Don't waste your ammunition. They're not worth it. Use your knife.'

Peri felt the roaring of the blood pumping through her head. She felt like the top of her head was going to come off. All the little details over the past few days, the details that had gone over her head and, worse, the details she had noted but refused to recognize and accept, fell into place. Like the way that a static charge instantly earths itself from the body when grounded, she saw in one clear instant how her confusion and trauma and the flow of events had forced her along, how it had been used. She saw how it had made her think and act.

What it had almost made her become.

But not quite. Unbidden, she flashed on a memory that was in its way so precious that she had found herself hiding it away, saving it even from herself. They had left Adrozani Minor, herself and this irritable stranger who was still the Doctor. She had made some verbal slip about the difference between a galaxy and the Universe, and the Doctor was loudly lambasting her for it.

In the middle of his tirade, he had simply stopped, and looked at her, and said, 'I really don't regret it, you know. Losing my other life for you. Never think that.'

She had looked back at him, knowing, deep in her gut, who and what he was even in this new form, and she had said, 'You didn't have any choice.'

For a moment he had seemed very solemn, and very distant, and so unutterably lonely that she had felt like howling.

'You always have a choice,' he said. 'You can't ever make the excuse that events pushed you along. It's precisely how you act when events don't give you time to think, that's the ultimate test. When a light goes out it leaves us all just a little closer to the dark. And the simple fact is that a universe with your brightness in it is infinitely preferable to a universe without.'

Now, in that instant of remembrance, Peri recognized something that she had always seen, but had never noticed because it was innate, and noticed it now only because she had come so close to losing it. It was the

154

simple, human ability to be honourable and kind.

She realized that Blaine was talking to her, seemingly more in sorrow than in anger.

'. . . had my doubts,' she was saying. 'Pity they had to be right. Tell you what, I'll make it easy for you.' She pulled out her own gun, planted it solidly against the side of Peri's head. 'You do the skags or I do you. Make your choice.'

As the reports came in of the paramilitary assaults throughout the Habitat, Adjudication forces were once again diverted, crash-dispatched to take these terrorists down. The riots in the Holding Complex had been all but subdued in any case, and this new threat was far more significant.

Within a matter of minutes, the vast majority of Adjudication forces had left the Temple of the Church, leaving only the cleanup squads down in the cells, the High Churchmen up in the summit and a minimal operational base.

In the back of a freight truck travelling the interways of Sector Zero, Avron Jelks listened to the chatter from the banks of comms sets. Combat-active White Fire personnel were operating them, deploying and coordinating the paramilitary assaults.

'Squad Blue Niner report Adjudication transports heading their way,' one of them said, turning to him. 'Pink Two report likewise.'

'And their firepower?' Avron Jelks asked. 'What have they arrayed against us?'

'Blue Niner sees Shok-TAC, Pink Two sees MAVs.'

Avron Jelks nodded to himself. The assault squads, all of them, were going to be landed on with the full weight of the Statutes. It was regrettable, but it didn't really matter. They had merely been a diversionary tactic, after all. They had drawn the Adjudication forces away from the centre. They had fulfilled their function.

155

He snapped his fingers to get the operators' attention. 'I think it's time we activated the strike force,' he said. 'Let's do it now, shall we?'

The operators reacted as though galvanized. They switched out the communications from the assault squads, effectively leaving them on their own and in the lurch, and switched in an entirely different subsystem.

'Now hear this,' Jelks said, his voice travelling by multidirectional infrared pulse to the transceivers of other, unmarked vehicles in their hundreds, which were likewise circling the Temple of the Church of Adjudication, and which contained the vast majority of his troops. 'You know your objectives. It is time to carry them out. It is time, at last, to achieve our manifest destiny.'

He smiled with a grim and purposeful satisfaction. 'Let us make our voices heard.'

As the first impact-cannon charges slammed against the Temple, and threatened to pull the world of which he was effectively the nearest thing to the master, High Churchman Garon hardly noticed. He was on the space beyond his private quarters, beyond his sanctum. He was communing with his God.

Dimly he was aware of the other High Churchmen behind him, and the faceless Hands of God behind them. He knew that he controlled them utterly and in all things they obeyed his will.

But that was nothing before the radiance of the One True God. He looked upon it with wonder. It was ever wondrous, ever new, and he looked upon it with the eyes of a child first seeing the sun.

The light flickered a little. Only a little. But in a while it would begin to fade. The One True God was growing hungry again.

'Soon,' High Churchman Garon assured it. 'The matter is in hand. More for you soon.'

Section Three

Revelation and Adjudgment

Eighteen

And now everything in the Habitat seemed to be happening at once. In every sector the diverted Adjudication forces tried to deal with the entrenched White Fire hit squads, and with the coordination of the OBERON systems it should have been more than possible.

It was at that point that Jelks's forces put down their trumping *tzuki* domino. In the same way as certain areas of the city had been modified for easy access and escape, and in the same way as people had been planted in the cells of the Holding Complex to precipitate a riot, a number of the Church of Adjudication's personnel had been turned to Jelks's cause. They had remained at their posts for months within the Temple, waiting for this day. Now, they made their way to the transceiver stations in the Temple and set up targeting beacons.

The Adjudicators took them down, but by then the damage had been done. Outside on the interways several armoured vehicles racked up Shrike IV missile launchers and took out the transceivers. Communications between OBERON and the Habitat went dead.

The Adjudication forces outside had for too long relied on the second-by-second control and coordination of the Curia. Without it they fell into disarray. This did not mean that they would lose their battle with the hit squads, just that it was not now a foregone conclusion. The cohesiveness and the invulnerability of the Church's forces had simply fallen apart. Their operations descended into a bloody mess.

What it did mean was that these forces now found themselves too busy to return and prevent the attack upon the Temple itself. The Temple of the Church of Adjudication found itself locked off, under siege and under bombardment, almost totally on its own.

In the hydroponic processing plant, Peri felt the muzzle of Blaine's gun pressing into the side of her head, gouging a little at her scalp. Later, thinking about it, she was surprised that she didn't go out of her mind. As it was, she felt a kind of solid, emotionless determination. She was not going to shoot these helpless polyp-toads because, quite simply, that was who she was. And if Blaine was going to shoot her for being who she was then so be it. She didn't feel anything about it either way.

'Get ready to run,' said a quiet voice by her ear.

This was so unexpected that she didn't react – and after that things moved too quickly for her ever to have the chance. She felt a plucking sensation at her belt, a hand grabbed her forearm, shoved it firmly in a new direction and there was a sudden sense of commotion amongst the White Fire squad.

'Take it easy, guys,' Kane said. 'The poor girl's looking extremely nervous at the moment. That thing she's holding could go off at any minute. Who knows who or what she'll hit?'

In the way that, when a friend is hit by sniper fire, you keep on talking to them for a while before realizing they're on the ground, it took a little while for Peri's mind to catch up to events. Then it did, and she realized what was happening. Kane had grabbed hold of her arm and hauled it around so that her gun now covered the rest of the White Fire squad, who were now looking very thoughtful and making no sudden moves. Simultaneously, he had pulled his own gun from where she had stowed it in her belt and, moving with a smooth action that telegraphed no threat, had placed it to the head of Blaine.

For several seconds the scene was frozen: Blaine with her gun to Peri's head, Kane with his gun to Blaine's. Kane was still, lightly but firmly, gripping Peri's forearm, making damned sure it was still aimed at the rest of the squad.

'What do you think?' Kane said amiably to Blaine. 'It's your choice. I couldn't give a damn. Either way, I'm still standing.'

For an awful instant, Peri thought that Blaine was going to shoot her anyway. The determination she had felt before had gone, the terror had returned, and that was how she was going to die. Then Blaine took the gun away. A couple of hairs had caught in the muzzle, and Peri felt the strange sensation one always feels when a couple of hairs are pulled out by the roots: not exactly pain, far too minor even to hurt, more the faintest breath of agony felt a million miles away.

'Drop the gun,' Kane said. 'Not *you*, you stupid little bitch!' The grip on Peri's wavering forearm tightened. 'Drop the gun, Blaine.'

'Hey, it's dropped.' Blaine held up a hand, her weapon dangling from a finger by the trigger-guard.

Kane ground his own weapon into her temple. 'Maybe you don't understand. *Drop the sodding gun.*'

There was a clunk as Blaine finally dropped the sodding gun.

'Now back off,' said Kane. Blaine backed off. Kane worked his way around Peri, still keeping his gun aimed at Blaine, so that, as she backed off into the White Fire squad, all of them were covered.

'Right,' said Kane cheerfully. 'We're going to leave now. Of course, you're going to come after us, but think on this.' He jerked an elbow back to vaguely indicate the control chamber door. 'We might not go that far, and you're going to be leaving through a bottleneck. Something to think about carefully, I'd say.'

Peri was recovering quickly, but she was still stunned. Reversal of events seemed to be piling on

161

reversal at this point. Kane elbowed her in the ribs.

'So are we going or what?' he said.

Out in Sector 5 the walkways were in an uproar. The crowds milled in panic, storefronts were smashed and looted, sporadic fires burnt greasily. The interways were gridlocked now: the knock-on effect of the disruptions that were affecting the entire city. Occasionally, the distant sound of gunfire and explosions could be heard, a pall of smoke seen rising between hab-stacks.

This was not one of the Sectors that the White Fire had turned into a war zone. Now and then an Adjudication flier streaked by overhead, but the only actual presence of the Church that could be seen here was a street Adjudicator's MAV, overturned and on fire. There was no sign of the body, living or otherwise.

Peri and Kane battled their way through the crowd. Peri had expected Kane to head for the parking racks where the squad's transport, a simple unmarked hov-car, had been parked. He led her in the opposite direction.

'You think they're going to come after us?' Peri panted, winded more through having to force herself through the press of people than the speed they were going.

Kane snorted. 'What do you think? Of course they're going to come after us.' He stopped her a moment and shoved her, not roughly, merely making it clear that she should go away. 'It'll probably be best if we split up. It's me they're going to be after.'

'Oh no,' Peri said, standing her ground. 'You don't get out of it that easily. I'm not going anywhere until I get some answers.' She gestured furiously back the way they had come. 'What was all that about? Just what the hell is going on here? Why did you save me back there?'

'Probably because I need my head examined, if truth be told,' Kane muttered. He appeared to come to a grudging decision. 'OK. Fair enough. You'd better come with me. I suppose I could do with corroboration.'

'Collaboration?' said Peri.

'Look, just come *on*, OK?'

Kane took her down a ramp, heading towards ground level. Before they got there, they came to a set of heavy shutters sunk into the side of a block. Kane snapped back a cover on the wall and laid his hand on a dimly glowing panel behind it. The shutters retracted smoothly.

Behind them was a space, and in the space was a flier. It was powered up and idling, activated by the raising of the shutters. Power cables retracted on servo arms and the flier slid out, sleek and dangerous-looking, popping its gull-wing doors as soon as it was clear of the shutters.

'Covert Ops Division, special issue,' Kane said with cheerful satisfaction. 'There's a couple of hundred of these installed through the city for emergencies.'

Peri stared at the flier. 'How did you –?'

'Work it out for yourself,' said Kane. 'It's not hard.'

Back in the hydroponics plant, Draker got on his hands and knees and snatched a look out through the control chamber door. 'No one there. They didn't hang around.'

'Then what are you waiting for?' Blaine snapped. 'Get after them.' She turned to hammer at the comms rig, which was for some reason refusing to relay transmissions from Jelks's main force, then turned back to swat viciously at a member of the hit squad who seemed marginally slower on the uptake. 'Go!'

In the Temple of the Church of Adjudication, Craator organized the remaining forces. When the links to the outside had been taken out, the OBERON systems had switched to emergency mode, sealing off the lower levels and the Holding Complex. The defences of the Temple had been switched to full automatic. There was nothing left for those inside to do except prepare for siege and wait. Craator had ordered that arms be broken out and issued to auxiliary personnel, and had stationed them at strategic points under the command of the remaining Adjudicators.

Now he was in the Curia control with Chong. With OBERON locked off, the technician's personal transputer was probably the only thing left that could access the systems.

'Try to get a message up to the High Churchmen,' Craator said. 'They're stuck in here with the rest of us, so they might at least try to be of some use. Put me through to Garon.'

Chong tapped on the keypad that was now hooked to the Curia console. 'Nothing,' she said at last. 'The METATRON reports that Garon and every other High Churchman are, quote, unavailable for comment at this present time.'

'Yeah, right,' said Craator. 'Typical of the cruks. Tell you what, how about we continue the lines of investigation we were pursuing before we were interrupted?'

This was not, thought Craator, a question of going after Garon out of spite, or even just a way of occupying the time. He had got down to the cells just in time to catch the first wave front of a Shok-TAC detachment going in to deal with the riots precipitated by the bombs. They had got there fast – suspiciously fast – and had dealt with the inmates in the restrained and thoughtful manner for which they were justly renowned.

Craator had left them to it. He had got out of the Holding Complex just in time to catch the initial White Fire attack on the Temple, and just in time to miss being sealed in when the cells had been shut down. The business with the bombs and the immediate arrival of forces still nagged at him. It was as if the whole thing had been coordinated, planned in advance. Somebody, somewhere, had actively planned it.

Something was rotten in the Church of Adjudication. The Justice of God, in which Craator truly believed, was being perverted from within. If the incorrigibly lawless broke the covenant of the Statutes, well fair enough – but how much worse was one who affected to uphold the law while breaking it himself? You had to play by the

164

rules you set. The only thing that gave you the right to judge others was if you were willing to Adjudge yourself.

Who had said that? Where had he heard it before? Some sacred text on which the Church had been originally based? One of his mentors when he was a cadet? Try as he might Craator could not quite pin it down.

No matter. 'Try to locate the Holding Complex discrepancies,' he said to Chong. 'Let's see if we can't find those missing Penitents. I want to know where they went.'

Nineteen

'Expression of building unease leading to severe if in actual fact psychosomatic respiratory and not to mention digestive complaint,' said Queegvogel.

'I know exactly how you feel,' said the Doctor.

They had been taken to another chamber with cryptic sigils etched into the walls. There they had been stripped yet again, washed with some greasy liquid that smelt of petroleum, and garbed in smocklike coveralls decorated with intertwining symbols matching those on the walls. Then the Hands of God had slapped the cuffs and manacles on them and hauled them into what seemed to be a large freight elevator. From the whine of the mechanism that powered it, the elevator had been installed comparatively recently, built from whatever materials came to hand. It was quite obviously inadequate for the load: their lurching, juddering journey upward seemed to be accomplished inch by inch.

There were perhaps a hundred and fifty people crammed into this patchwork cage, equally split between nonhumans, Human First humans and the technically human Hands of God. As one might expect, one could have cut the atmosphere with a knife — but that was all that was being cut. Everyone was under restraint and packed too close to move in any case. They looked at each other with hate-filled eyes, but that was rapidly being superseded by fear.

The Doctor, meanwhile, had been testing the mechanism on his handcuffs. The problem was, said mechanism consisted of a number of large cold-hammered rivets and heavy-welded chain linking them together. A couple of thousand years of evolvement in restraining devices hadn't resulted in something mind-blowingly innovative, but had merely confirmed the decision of what one needed to stop somebody using his hands. It would have taken time and special tools to release him – but then again, so far as the Hands of God had been concerned, *releasing* hadn't been the problem.

All the same, one of the rivets seemed slightly looser than the others. Possibly it might repay concentrated attention. It had better. The Doctor had the distinct impression that time was running out. Occasionally they felt a tremor, heard the muffled concussion of some explosion outside. The time between them grew less and less. Whatever was happening, out there, it was accelerating.

They seemed to be rising into an area of stifling pressure – a pressure that had nothing to do with their physical confinement. It was the static-charged feeling of the air before some cataclysmic storm. It made body hair bristle and spines crawl. It made one jittery, as though something without substance were squirming in the back of the brain. The others, human and alien, seemed to pick up on it, too. A susurration ran through them, not so much a sound as a diffuse emanation of fear.

The Hands of God merely stood, impassive.

The freight elevator lurched to a halt. The gatelike doors racked back, closely followed by the steel-plate shutters beyond. A pulsing, reddish light bathed them, washing over them after the relative darkness of their confinement. The Hands of God, without a word, beat and hauled at the prisoners, herding them out of the elevator cage, and into the light.

'Anything?' Craator said.

'Nothing.' On her monitor, Chong was moving through folders and files, opening up from within themselves like nested Chinese boxes skewed through a right angle to the reality of space and time. 'Every lead turns into an Oroboros routine. It just disappears up its own back door. The missing Penitents simply vanished. We're talking thin air to the point of anoxia, here and – hang on.' Something had caught her eye. She backtracked until she found it again. 'Something here. A list of maybe a hundred IDs, tagged as having died in bomb blasts in the cells and the subsequent riots and cleanup.'

Craator shrugged. 'So?'

'This was logged in two and a half hours ago.'

Had it only been two and a half hours since the bombs and the Temple of the Church going to Sheol? It seemed much longer. Craator stuck a hand up under his helmet and rubbed at the bridge of his nose. 'So?' he said again.

'The bombs only went off an hour ago,' said Chong. 'The only way you could log it then would be if you had a time machine – if you want to believe those stupid stories they tell to kids. Either that, or you could log it back then, because that was exactly what you were going to do.'

Another chamber, but there was one single, crucial difference. The difference was that it comprised the entire top of the Temple tower, save for the doors that led into the elevator shaft and bounce-tubes. It was a vast dome of leaded glass – glass being far easier to manufacture from the raw materials of Dramos than some more modernistic substance. And the dome didn't need any particular structural strength in itself. The glass was stained, depicting in reverent detail the story of the Adjudicators, their time of power, their time of persecution and their Exodus. The penultimate image, working clockwise, showed stylized rocket ships against the background of a planet that seemed to be on fire. From a red swirl on the planet's surface radiated beams depicted in clear glass, giving the planet the aspect of a beacon.

The final image – working clockwise – showed a burning figure, arms akimbo, palms outstretched as if to encompass the entire Universe. A nimbus ringed his (he was obviously male) head. This figure was archetypical, Godlike, it bestrode the chamber and dominated it – or would have done, had there not been something here to make it pale into utter insignificance.

The place smelt like a votive charnel house. The stench of burnt meat, olfactory layer upon layer of it, burnt over the course of months and maybe years, clung to the very glass dome like reeking patina. Piled on the floor before an altar were charred bones and a kind of greasy, ashy sludge. It was the result of large amounts of protein and fat being obliterated as though in a blast furnace. The sight of it and the smell were enough to make one sick – or would have been, had not there been something here that drew the attention with a fascination far more strong.

As you entered the chamber, dragged out by the Hands of God, the first things that you encountered were more of these uniformed figures: a veritable army. Beyond them, a crowd of other figures, black-robed and shaven-headed, thin and stooped like a parliament of crows. These were the High Churchmen, those who never left the Temple. Though their backs were to you, you could see that they were bone-thin and starved, having long immolated all temptations of the flesh. Beyond them a lone figure. He was facing you, looking at you, but you never noticed, because the thing beyond him caught your eyes and held them solid, sank itself into your mind and made it sing. It became your entire world.

It was the central processing stack of OBERON, a massive black encasement, quartered, the seams indented giving it the aspect of a huge, smooth brain with four equal lobes. Its stem was sunk into the chamber floor, thence, presumably, to the subsystems like the METATRON which controlled the Temple and the Habitat itself. If you looked closely, it was just possible to make out the cluster of inhibitors attached to and sunk into one of the lobes – the inhibitors that stopped

OBERON from achieving true and dangerous sentience.

You had to look closely because OBERON was obscured. A churning, pulsing mass of what was not quite energy and not quite matter enveloped it, like the nimbus of the God-figure on the stained glass dome. It swirled and thrashed, constantly forming, tearing itself apart and reforming. The microforms in its main mass might have almost been ghostly individual bodies, screaming faces, the monsters of delirium given obscene life. Inside the mass, whipped around and wrenched this way and that by its enormous Brownian force, there was something that might or might not have been a shred of some clear polymer membrane.

It was as though your very soul were sucked out of your eyes by the mass. You simply stared at it, and tried to look away, and found that you could not. It was hypnotic, fascinating. You could lose yourself inside its unending, violent, yet strangely subtle complexity. You could feel it eating at your soul.

Then the figure standing before it moved. Your attention was jerked towards him as he smoothly moved, and moved towards you. There was no sense of transition, no sense of dislocation. The light of the burning semi-solid mass burnt, too, inside his eyes.

It was, of course, High Churchman Garon.

'Welcome,' he said. 'It is time to make sacrifice to the One True God. Do not fear, for you shall be transmuted. You shall live again and see such wonders.'

The flier wove through the air, detouring around the worst areas of fighting, heading for the centre of the Habitat and the Temple of the Church.

'We've been sinking people into the Human First and White Fire setups for months now,' Kane said, one hand on the control, the other punching numbers into a comms rig bolted to the dash. 'We had to go in clean – no wires, no neat little suicide packs in the sole of our boots, nothing that could show up. The idea is that you

170

go in and stick an ultrastatic wrench in the works when you get the chance, report back as and when you can.'

'And you broke your cover for me?' Peri said. For some reason she wasn't that surprised. This was just another reversal in a couple of days full of them.

'Yeah, well, I was going to pull out anyway. The hit-squad side of things had "diversionary tactic – stop me and buy one" written all over it. Damn!' Kane hammered at the comms unit. 'OBERON systems are down – either that or somebody's banjaxed the transceivers.'

'Is that a problem?' Peri asked.

'It's a problem. I was counting on OBERON to give us a free ride through the defences. Hang on a tick.' Kane hit a switch and a monitor flared to life. 'These babies are packed with sensors and integration routines, very sophisticated. They're very nearly sentient in their own right. It should be able to pull some sort of sense out of anything we come across.' He wrenched the flier through an irregular, zig-zagging trajectory to avoid an explosion that took out the top of a block, then looked back at the monitor. 'Nah. We're too far away. Besides, when I saw you act that way back at the plant, I realized you were a bit different from that scum. I couldn't stand by and let them kill you.'

'You've changed your tune,' Peri said.

'What?'

'Yesterday, down there in the tunnels, you were going on about how those people could die like cattle so far as you were concerned.'

Kane shrugged. 'Ever hear of putting on an act?'

Peri frowned. 'I don't know. You sounded like you really meant it.'

'I was telling you what you wanted to hear.' He turned and scowled at Peri. 'Let's get one thing clear, here, OK? When push came to shove you couldn't bring yourself to do it. You couldn't kill the nonhumans. You're not cut out for White Fire. That means there has to be some shred of common decency left in you – but don't you *ever* think that excuses your involvement with Human First. Back when I first saw you, back at the rally, I thought there was something more, but I was wrong. You just stood there and took their poison and you lapped it up.'

'What?' Peri was puzzled. 'I mean, OK, those Human First people were against the Adjudicators and you're an Adjudicator, so of course you wouldn't like them. But what was so bad that you had to go in there and just start killing them?' Peri remembered what it had been like during the assault and found herself becoming angry. No, scratch that – furious. 'It was butchery, just mindless butchery.'

Kane at least had the decency to look apologetic. 'Hey, you forget that *I* was stuck in the middle of it.'

'You know what I mean!'

Kane shrugged again. Peri could see how that was something that might really get on someone's nerves. 'OK. I know. Things have been getting strange in the Church – but some of us are trying to fight against that. Don't tone us all with the same electrostatic. Some of us still believe in the job we were called to – even an old stony-face like Craator. And you have to admit, some of you people got exactly what you deserved.'

The contempt in his voice sent a strange, sick feeling through Peri, not so much for the contempt itself as the fact that she could find nothing whatsoever in herself that deserved it. It was as though someone had come up to her in the street, just screamed in her face and started to hit her for no reason; as though her very existence in the world was an aberration. Even though every rational thought told you it was not so, it left you with the mindless feeling that you were somehow filthy.

'What did I ever do?' she said. She had meant to say it angrily, but some impulse to her vocal cords had it coming out like a frightened child trying to be very small and careful in case she was hit. 'What did the Human First people ever do that was so bad?'

'Ha!' Kane threw the flier into another turn – not

avoiding anything so much as expressing his anger with her. 'Next thing, you'll be telling me that some of your best friends are nonhuman.'

'But they are!' Peri exclaimed, still sounding to herself like a child, only this time indignantly defending herself against accusations of causing a mess she hadn't made. 'I've got a lot of –' She stopped herself and tried to run through the various alien races she had encountered with the Doctor, trying to find one whose members she hadn't been a contributory factor in killing in large numbers. 'I've got one,' she finished lamely. 'But he really *is* my friend. I think he's the best friend I've ever had.'

'Oh yes?' Kane said, obviously disbelieving. 'So what's the name of this best friend you've ever had?'

'He's called the Doctor,' Peri said. 'I don't think you'll have heard of him. He's saved my life so many times, and once he even –'

Kane looked at her. 'You don't know, do you?' he said. 'You really don't *know* about Human First and what they do.'

The tone of his voice had Peri realizing that she might have been missing something important, here. 'So tell me,' she said. 'Tell me about them.'

In a compartment in the armoured command-vehicle, Avron Jelks picked up the chap-book containing his latest thoughts and turned to the silvered dome, which he had brought along with him, transplanting it from his desk in the Mimseydome™ to a control console. He pressed a stud, and the dome became translucent, lit from within.

Inside was a shrivelled head. A few wisps of brittle, fragile hair still clung to its flaking parchment scalp. Thick tubing pumped nutrients directly into its empty eye sockets, exchanged them through drains punched through the mandible below the left ear. Servo-mechanisms kept the mouth working, a glistening slab of sculpted, solidified gel serving the function of a tongue.

This was, in fact, the head of Ralph Mimsey himself.

After his death it had been cryogenically frozen, as so many twentieth-century heads and bodies had in that time, waiting for the advances in medical technology that would cure what had killed them – in this case cancer of the lower bowel – and revive them.

The problem was they had not reckoned on the true nature of futurity. They thought that the future would contain sterile domes and anti-gravity and enlightenment. What it had really contained were periods of relative stability interspersed with barbarous insanity, with the half-remembered remains of coherent technology being put to insane and downright stupid purposes. It had been in one such period that the head of Ralph Mimsey had been 'revived', ruined beyond all hope of later repair, and used by the Techno-Magi of 2476 as an Oracle.

After the collapse of the Techno-Magi sect, the head had been reacquired by the Mimsey™ Incorporation as a curio. It had subsequently wound up on Dramos during the abortive construction of the Mimseydome™, as the epitome and acme of all things Mimsey™.

'Killme,' said the reanimated head of Ralph Mimsey. 'Killmekillmeplease killkillkillmekillmepleasekill . . .'

'What do you think of this?' Jelks said, popping his reading glasses on to his nose and reading from the passage he had just finished writing in his chap-book: ' "The inhuman element, the 'skags' as they are called by the unlettered, present the major problem faced by an administration. They slither in the filth and excrement of their own making, they taint the lives of the decent, that is to say human, population with their excrescence. The air they breathe turns noxious, producing ague and a bloody flux in the lungs of truly human beings . . ." '

'. . . killmekillmekillmeplease . . .' said the head of Ralph Waldo Mimsey. 'Maketheworldgoawayandstop-killmekillmepleasekill.'

' ". . . but this is as nothing to the dangers they present towards the life of the mind and very soul. Their foul beliefs and practices infect the minds of those with which

174

they congregate and blind them to their unending Evil. They talk of their culture and, yes, it *is* a culture – the yeasty, fetid discharge such as might be found within the swollen lips of a diseased . . ."'

'. . . killmekillmekillmekillmekill . . .'

'Yes, you're probably right,' said Avron Jelks. 'The reference to "souls" merely panders to the kind of treacherous and outmoded beliefs that we are fighting against.' Avron Jelks laid the first draft of *My Struggle Against Tyranny* on the console, to make the needed correction.

The book detailed – or would detail, once the work was finished and a radically new World Order made it mandatory for everyone to buy a copy – the struggle of Avron Jelks against the corrupt and oppressive system that had ground him and others down all their lives. Especial mention was made of powerful, high-placed nonhuman factions, who had combined and conspired in secret, for the express purpose of keeping people out of art colleges, despite their work being patently up to standard. There was a lot of mention of bodily fluids, effluvia and suchlike substances and excrescences, which Avron Jelks found personally distasteful.

The fact that the Braxiatel Institute of Fine Arts (Applied) had rejected him, on the say-so of a board consisting of a Silurian, three Piglet People and a human woman whom you could just *see* enjoyed sexual congress with those of her own sex, meant nothing to Avron Jelks now, though it had hurt at the time. What mattered was that moment when, some years ago, after gruelling, wasted years stewarding on the Double Spiral cruise line, Avron Jelks had come to the Dramos Habitat, had seen the obscene melting-pot of it, had seen how humans had lived with alien monsters, lived in the filthy mess they made without even recognizing the putrid slime in which they waded . . . what mattered was that moment when it had all become suddenly clear.

Obviously talented people were skagged out of the arts

and communications industries, servers wouldn't publish someone like Avron Jelks's books, because people like Avron Jelks were dangerous to them. People like Avron Jelks could bring the entire alien conspiracy to its knees. That was why he had been silenced. Avron Jelks, as his body shook with what might be mistaken for the throes of a complete nervous breakdown, had seen it all with a cold and icy clarity, and on that day had decided that something must be done about it.

Now, very soon now, something would.

'. . . killmepleasepleasekillmekill . . .' said the voice of the head of Ralph Mimsey. '. . . killmekillmekillme – we're going in. The moles are fired up and ready to go.'

This last was the voice of one of the White Fire section commanders, currently coordinating the assault on the Temple from the main section of the armoured car. When Jelks was in comparative seclusion like this, all communications were routed through the head.

Jelks looked up from where he was carefully substituting 'very beings infused with the common glow of destiny' for 'souls'. 'I shall be there momentarily.'

He switched off the head, and clambered out from the compartment, ready to lend the inspiration of his presence and moral support to his forces.

Twenty

The bounce-tubes that led up into the levels of the High Churchmen were currently being guarded by a mixed squad of Adjudicators and auxiliaries under the command of one Adjudicator Glean. With the Curia and METATRON systems locked out, they had no information as to what was happening in the lower sections save for the blast impacts outside – so, when they saw a movement from a doorway leading to the emergency stairwells, they automatically opened fire.

'Dammit!' Craator ducked under a number of slugs as they tore the wall behind him apart. 'It's me, OK! It's Craator!'

He and Chong came down the corridor and examined the bounce-tubes.

'Is the power out?' Craator wasn't winded, but it had been something of a slog up from the Curia levels with the bounce-tubes shut down.

Chong checked the readouts on the panel by the tubes. 'Independent supply. Trouble is, these things are hooked to gene-scans. You don't have the right DNA, you don't go up.'

'Short it out,' Craator told her.

Chong looked at him. 'I think what you meant to say was "bypass" it.'

Craator scowled. 'Whatever.'

The people on guard seemed confused. 'You can't do this,' Adjudicator Glean said worriedly. He said it worriedly because Craator had turned to glower at him the moment he had tried to say it angrily. 'You can't. No one

177

other than the Hands of God are allowed . . .'

He trailed off as Craator's face came very close to his.

'We're going up,' Craator said. 'You and your men are coming, too.'

'But that's impossible!' Glean exclaimed. 'That would leave this entire level open to hostile attack and —'

'I don't give a two-credit cruk about hostile attack,' Craator growled. 'If they make it this far we've had it in any case. It's not a question of going down fighting, it's a question of going down fighting against the proper things. We're going up.'

'For years things were pretty much OK,' Kane said. 'Or at least as OK as you can have with a couple of thousand species all mixed up together. You'd get your basic murders, Fnaroks eating Piglet People, a lot of petty feuds and vendettas but it was controllable. We were on top of it. Something like a third of the Habitat population is human. They're the biggest single faction. But what with the after-effects of the Empire pulling back they were disorganized. There was nothing for them to cohere around. The truly vicious hatemongers like Jelks had their followers, but not that many. People could see what they were. They were just a joke.

'Over the last year, though, things have been changing. It isn't just a Crazy Season thing. Over the last year humans have been flocking to Jelks's cause in their thousands — their hundreds of thousands — like Morkodian pogo-lemmings. OBERON projections say that as of this point the Human First sympathizers number two point five million. Two point five million for Jelks.'

'OK,' Peri said. 'But so what? What's so totally bad about that?' It was one of those stupid questions that you regret asking the moment you ask them. On some level, she realized that she was still automatically thinking in terms of Jelks being something iconic, something good. Kane answered her, however, with a snort.

'The man is slime,' he said. 'If you ever read any of his stuff – not that you would, of course, because it's been suppressed.'

'Now why,' said Peri, 'does that not surprise me?'

'It wasn't suppressed for the usual reasons,' Kane said. 'It was suppressed for the fact that it was pure evil. He calls for the absolute and mass extermination of anything and everything other than humans – even non-sentient animals and vegetables. He has this crackpot notion of synthesizing food chemically, because it would be cleaner.' He snorted again. 'Of course, then he turns around and orders the destruction, say, of a hydroponics plant – like it's been polluted by alien contact so much that it could never be sterilized.

'He has this big thing about cleanliness, and it comes across in glowing little descriptions of people living in filth. He goes off on these pornographic rants for no reason – and I mean *seriously* pornographic, stuff about children, chainsaws and excrement – and then he just snaps back into telling us how he's going to run the world, utterly sane and reasonable proposals, like he doesn't know he's done it. He's a total psycho, and people are taking him seriously. I mean, OK, the Church is going strange, but whatever happens you don't want someone like Jelks in control. Nothing could be that bad.

'Speaking of which . . .' Kane switched in the flier's scanners again. On the monitor a wireframe map resolved itself into a representation of the Temple and the surrounding sector. Highlighted icons moved around it, like an attacking swarm of killer bees, and text scrolled down the side, the same vaguely Cyrillic characters that Peri had failed to understand before.

'Thought so,' Kane said. 'That's where he's deploying most of his forces. They're moving in. He's going for the OBERON control.'

Adjudicators were firing with their personal weapons from the Temple, but they were making little impact.

The Temple had always relied on automated defences routed through OBERON, and its exterior windows did not offer any real vantage points. Besides, while an Adjudicator's MFG was sudden death in personal combat, it had never been designed for use in a full-scale military assault. The White Fire vehicles might as well have been Acturian behemoths under attack by an angry swarm of Darbokian pigmy-flies.

The entrances of the Temple were still sealed off by blast-shutters, but now several specially adapted drilling rigs, liberated from the construction sites of the Mimseydome™, were drilling through the walls themselves. It was a classic example of defensive error – one puts so much effort into making doors impregnable, and it never occurs to one to wonder about the walls because one simply does not even *think* of going through them. It would take a genius, or a madman, to habitually think that way. Now, it would only be a matter of minutes before the moles drilled through and the tertiary stage of the occupation could begin.

The plan after that point was simple. The White Fire troops would simply pile in, and keep on piling in until the remaining Adjudicators were subdued. A lot of them would die, hundreds and possibly even thousands, but that was a sacrifice Avron Jelks was prepared to make. They were merely clearing the way for him to follow on behind.

Of course, as he sat in his armoured transport, listening to the operators as they ran his forces, Avron Jelks never thought in terms of 'following behind'. He was their leader. He would lead them. It was simply right and proper that they should lay down their lives, that he should walk over them, so that he could fulfil his manifest destiny.

It was similar to the way in which, after years of struggle, only ever attracting a sorry collection of right-minded people, the people as a whole had suddenly begun to flock to him. He had never given a thought to

180

why this was, simply because it was so patently and fundamentally right.

It was as though both Jelks and the people who followed him were taking part in some larger, fore-ordained, perfect process. He had never consciously thought up his Master Plan: it had simply evolved, step by obvious step. This, and this, and *this* must be done to take Avron Jelks into the Temple, there to come at last face to face with the thing inside, the OBERON, and through it take control of his world. His every impulse and instinct yearned for it. It was as if his destiny was calling him, dragging him along with no sense of voli-tion, pulling him into its burning heart.

An operator turned to him. 'Transmission from hit squad Blue Fifteen.'

Avron Jelks frowned. 'I believe I told you that we weren't receiving transmissions from the hit squads.'

'This is punching through on emergency override. Seems that one of the squad, guy called Kane, was a traitor, maybe an Adjudication spy. He's currently head-ing our way in a flier – Blue Fifteen tried to follow him in their own transport but they lost him.'

Avron Jelks nodded to himself. He remembered this Kane. He remembered everybody. 'I doubt that a single spy is going to make any difference. Even if he comes here, there's not much that he can actually do. Nonethe-less, keep a watch out for him. Have him intercepted if he comes.'

In the chamber of OBERON, Garon addressed the captives, human and alien alike, with kindness as they stood in thrall. The pulsing mass around the brain of OBERON had unmanned them, made them still and mute.

'I always knew, you see?' he said, very gentle, utterly reasonable, very kind. 'I knew that locked inside that stern, cold iron was a thing of light. A light so bright it burnt away the petty sins and misdemeanours, such as to which all corporeal life is prey. A light fit to ablate the flesh and to purify the soul, turn it purest white.'

He wandered, unseeing, through the sludge of long-burnt flesh and brittle bones that crunched underfoot. 'I tried to wake it, bring it to life. I made sacrifice of Penitents, as and when they became available, without causing undue suspicion in those who were not quite ready to believe.'

He swept the captive Penitents with his kindly eyes. They held nothing but a deep, calm sorrow. 'Their pain was brief, and as nothing to the glory of their transubstantiated state. Oh, precisely four hundred and seventy-two sacrifices over the years. I remember that information distinctly.' He frowned, as if in distraction. 'There are occasions when I believe that I am excellent at remembering. In my head. I remember in my head, I . . .'

Momentarily, he slumped. It was as though every shred of identity and life within him had simply left. Then, abruptly, he raised his head and continued, as if nothing had happened. There was no hint of crazed fervour – it was as if he were simply, happily enthusiastic.

'Nothing happened,' he said. 'God did not make Himself evident. I began to wonder if there might not be some crucial error in the procedures – even if I might not be entirely mistaken.' Garon smiled with rueful chagrin. 'I even contemplated the possibility that I had lost my mind. But then –' and here Garon smiled with such beatitude it was as though he was lit by some inner light even brighter than the alien light in his eyes '– but then my God had mercy. It was nine months ago, precisely, to the very day and hour. At first it was the merest flicker, but then it grew. Oh, yes, it grew. And with every additional sacrifice it grew that little stronger – and I realized that my procedures had not been at fault. Never at fault. It was simply that I had not performed sacrifice *enough*.'

'Poppycock,' said a voice. 'Utter poppycock.'

It was as if a spell had been broken. Every eye and

182

optical analogue, including those of the congregational High Churchmen, snapped round to look at the figure of the Doctor. The Hands of God turned slightly more slowly, stiffly, hampered by their armour and moving like simulacra.

'What?' Garon's voice was small and strangely drowsy, as if he were waking up from sleep, or from a trance. 'What are you . . .?'

'You heard.' The Time Lord stood amongst the prisoners – who had not been given the chance to segregate themselves into their various factions. He stood between the centipede-like form of Queegvogel and a puzzled-looking Human First human woman. Even shackled in his handcuffs the Time Lord seemed to give the impression of lounging. His manner was knowing, insolent, even insulting.

'Do you know what I think?' he said, seemingly oozing contempt. 'What I think is, you're imposing your own personal belief system upon something with which it was never meant to cope. I'm not surprised it's sent you round the twist.' He gestured with his cuffed hands, the chain rattling between them, towards the churning mass. 'You can only function in terms of a belief in God – it informs your every thought and impulse – and you have twisted this perceived phenomenon into atrocity because you *know* it's God. The problem is, on some subconscious level, you also know that is not – because it quite simply isn't. That's merely the only halfway applicable term that you know.' The Time Lord scowled. 'It strikes me that a lot of the troubles in this Universe are caused by people going around "knowing" things all the time. I think.'

Garon was staring at him, his mouth working, trying to form some coherent or even audible sound. His gaze wandered across the assembled High Churchmen and Hands of God uncertainly. Both orders seemed confused. Sheer force of numbers meant that this blasphemer should have been fallen upon immediately – but his outburst had been so shocking, so unexpected, that they

183

were momentarily stunned. This had never happened before. The ritual of the sacrifice had worn well-travelled paths in their minds and reactions. It was a process that always had been and always would be smoothly followed to its conclusion – even the sacrifices had found themselves impotent with terror and swept along with it. It would take a massive, collective mental wrench to adapt, and none of them quite knew how to claw themselves out of the rut.

The Doctor, meanwhile, continued, seemingly oblivious to the effect his words were having. 'I seem to remember a chap who said that it was not a good idea to worship graven images,' he said. 'What he was really talking about was of the blind focusing of belief, of psychotic monomania.' He glared about at the High Churchmen and the Hands of God, with eyes that suddenly seemed to cut like angry diamond saws. 'You fail to see that to fixate upon your "God" – to have the sheer audacity to presume that you could ever *know* the mind of God – degrades the living Universe and that which gives it life.'

He glanced towards the pulsing mass again, gestured to it vaguely as if it were something that one saw every day, and merely wanted to point it out. 'My perceptions and sympathies are slightly different from yours – rather more advanced for one thing. I can see that *this* is more than just your personal and paltry little idea of God. Possibly much more.' He pinioned Garon again with his eyes. 'I think you should stop this entire farce, High Churchman. I think you should stop it now, yes?'

Queegvogel, beside him, nudged him with a manipulatory appendage. 'Expression concerning the dubiosity of this current conversational manner,' he said, his vocoder-voice slightly jerky as he fought against the entrancement that was still to some degree affecting him. 'Suggestion that said conversation might be seen as highly irreligious given present circumstances.'

'Don't worry about it,' the Doctor said out of the

corner of his mouth. 'Whip the belief system out from under someone and the entire self goes with it. I'm simply talking to him in the language he understands. Hitting him where he lives and breathes, as it were. Remember that medical technician down in the cells? Any second now, our good High Churchman's going to tip over the edge and fall apart. Large amounts of flagstone-chewing and foaming at the mouth shall occur. Just you watch.'

He became aware that the High Churchman was simply watching him, waiting for him to finish.

'You are a very fiend from Hell itself,' said Garon, perfectly calmly. 'I had almost come to believe that thought was some mere aberration on my part, but now I see that it is true. But your words cannot taint me, for I am wrapped in the love of my God and am inviolate.' He turned to one of the Hands of God. 'Make them ready for sacrifice.'

'Then again,' said the Doctor, somewhat deflated, 'I could be wrong.'

It was at that point that the doors behind them, the doors leading back into the bounce-tubes, burst open. A slightly scorched and battered Craator came through, together with several other armed Adjudicators. Trailing behind them was a female tech and several other slightly confused-looking auxiliaries. 'You're going to give me some answers,' Craator growled. 'This place has gone to Sheol, but if it's the last thing we do you're going to give me – what the crukking *Sheol*?'

'I think,' said the Doctor, to Queegvogel out of the corner of his mouth, 'there will be violence now. It might be an idea for creatures of peace and goodwill like ourselves to start looking for somewhere to hide.'

Twenty-One

Now events had their own, irrevocable momentum, things began happening extremely fast. Too fast for the eye to catch. Out in the tangled sectors of the Habitat that surrounded the Temple of the Church, those who lived in the towers cowered as the aerial skirmishes between Adjudicator and White Fire fliers raged around them, secure in the knowledge that their relatively low-power weapons couldn't breach their towers' shell right up until the point where several overpowered weapons did. Those in the tunnels sealed themselves in, knowing that nothing save a tactical nuclear detonation could crack their domain open.

As usual, those who suffered worse were those caught in the middle: the ground-level dwellers, those who had no home but the walkways and transit stacks. For them there was nothing but blood and shrapnel under the burning sky.

Back at the Temple of the Church, the White Fire forces burst through the walls. They took and occupied the lower floors and began to move inexorably upward. The Adjudication forces inside, now that it was simply a matter of close-quarter combat, made a better showing than they had before – but sheer force of numbers carried the day. The White Fire just kept on coming, scrambling over their own dead, until the Adjudicators were overrun.

The White Fire forces went up through the tower, like mercury rising in a thermometer plunged into boiling water. At their head – or, rather, at the head of those who came on after every level was bagged and tagged – came Avron Jelks.

The Temple itself could now be seen through the canopy of the flier. Smoke curled up from several points around its base. Occasionally there was the flash of some explosive detonation. 'Well, they're inside,' Kane said, checking the monitor readout. 'Not a lot of point in getting what we know to the Church. I think they sort of know already. All bets are off.'

'So what are we going to do?' Peri said.

'God alone knows. Play it by the skin of our nose and – hang on. We've got a bogie. Two of 'em.'

On the monitor two blips had appeared, and were converging on the central icon that represented them-selves. Peri swung her head wildly back and forth, trying to see what was coming at them through the canopy, but she saw nothing. The blips on the monitor, how-ever, were approaching very fast. 'Looks like somebody knew we were coming,' Kane said. 'Left us a little recep-tion committee. Hang on.' He switched the controls to manual and hauled the flier around in an air-resistance-shrieking turn.

In the domed chamber Craator and his men stood aghast at the scene before them: at the prisoners and bones, at the Churchmen and the Hands of God. Then, as had the sacrificial Penitents, they found their eyes inexorably drawn towards the pulsing, glowing mass that enveloped the OBERON installation.

'Craator!' Unaccountably, Garon seemed delighted to see the Adjudicator. He walked towards him, arms spread wide in benediction. 'My dear fellow! I am glad that you are here to witness the dawning of the Age. Do you see, now?' One hand swept back to take in the glory of his Oracle God. 'Do you at last truly see?'

He came to a halt, his face puzzled, as he realized that Craator had raised his MFG and was aiming it at him.

Craator was fighting the hypnoleptic effects of the mass with every iota of his being, his muscles locked rigid as he forced himself not to shake, his teeth gritted with a snarl of concentration as he kept his gun trained directly upon the High Churchman.

'Oh Gods . . .' said Chong, off to one side, looking at the bones. There was the sense of movement and the sound of Chong being violently sick.

Like a flash, Garon's bald head snapped to peer sternly at her. It was like the pecking motion of a bird snapping up a flea. 'I take it from your language that you are still a follower of the Pagan heresies that the Church has long proscribed.' The puzzlement had gone as though switched off, replaced again by his calm, sure tone. 'I had my suspicions. That was why my interest alighted on you.'

His face now clouded with wrath. 'And now you stand condemned out of your own soiled mouth. Such a thing cannot be countenanced, cannot be left to live.' The High Churchman made to move towards her, intending God alone knew what.

'Not one more step.' Craator kept the gun on the High Churchman. Now he moved forward, slowly, as inexorable and unstoppable as the wheels of Adjudgment, which ground small and exceedingly fine. 'You make one move, I take your head off.'

Yet again there was that instantaneous transformation of manner. The High Churchman simply turned to the Adjudicator and smiled sardonically. 'Ah, but can you really?' he said. 'Can you? I am girded about with the armour of my God's love. You cannot hurt me.' The little gleam of humour, of humanity that suddenly informed him, seemed all the worse for its erratic transience.

'You want to take bets?' said Craator. 'I can have a damned good try.'

Garon sighed, seemingly more in sorrow than in anger. Now he was some kindly father, irritated beyond endurance by some well-loved offspring who, nonetheless, now must be taught a sharp, judicious lesson. 'I'd had such hopes for you, Craator,' he said. 'My God has given me dominion over the Kingdoms of the World, and I envisaged you sitting on my right hand as a representative of Man. No more, I fear.'

He frowned. 'I believe that it would be best for all concerned if you joined these others as a votive offering, that you be tempered in the Fire of God and that your soul be reborn.' He took in Craator's makeshift squad of Adjudicators and auxiliaries with the same stern but kindly expression. 'The same boon shall be granted to your fellows in conspiracy. I know full well that it has only been misunderstanding that led you and them astray.' Garon waved an airy hand and turned to Chong. 'Why, I shall even extend the blessing of eternal light to this *whore*!'

This last word was screamed with an utter, absolute and psychotic violence. The strength of the outburst had Chong lurching back with pure terror to collide with some equally startled members of Craator's squad. It even rocked Craator slightly back on his heels.

'Forgive me,' the High Churchman said, reverting to his unnatural calm. 'I have not the slightest idea what came over me.' Then, without so much as a hint of aggression, Garon smoothly raised his hand. He gestured to the massed ranks of the Hands of God, and every single one of them fell upon Craator and his men.

The flier barrelled through a hundred and eighty degrees, cut its power, dropped like a half-brick, fired up its impellers again and soared upward once more. Two air-to-air missiles shot through the space it had previously occupied, and continued into the side of a block, taking great chunks out of its midsection.

'Oh those stupid fragging cruks,' Kane snarled, teeth gritted as he wrestled with the controls.

'All those people . . .' Peri said, feeling a pang of fury even cutting through everything else that was going on. 'They didn't care, they just –'

'Yeah, well, it's worse than that,' Kane said. 'If the

189

block hadn't got in the way, those things would have carried on until they hit the *Dome*. Fifteen million people suddenly go bang with explosive decompression – how's that for a happy thought?' He glanced at the monitor, which was showing identification graphics on the pursuing fliers and their relative positions. 'Oh well, nothing for it,' he said, and yanked at the controls.

The flier shot into reverse so sharply that Peri was thrown violently against the crashbars – so violently that, later, she would find livid and severe bruises across her chest like stripes. On the monitor, the blips of the other craft leapt forward until the icon representing themselves was almost on top of them.

'Now they're inside their own blast range,' Kane said. 'They won't try that again.'

Then the flier began to judder violently as rapid fire smacked into it.

'Then again,' said Kane. 'That just lays us open to their impact cannon, of course.'

In the OBERON chamber the battle, such as it was, was over almost before it had begun. The Hands of God just piled in, with no apparent thought for their own lives.

'Shoot to kill!' Craator reached out and shoved Chong sprawling, out of the way of an impact bolt fired by a Hand of God. The bolt continued through the space she had occupied, and smacked into a Hand of God coming from the other side. It began to beep loudly and rapidly from within the body in an ascending tone. It was one of the weapons-hardware 'improvements' that had over the past year been foisted on the Adjudicators: a time-delay microgrenade, a psychological weapon designed to increase the sense of terror in opposing forces. Craator had refused to use them, believing that they were tantamount to Inquisitional torture.

The luckless Hand of God clawed frantically at the hole in his body armour, the sense of robotic inhumanity about him totally lost, his screams blending with the accelerating tone. He sounded very young, possibly even as young as a Cadet.

All of this Craator noted only peripherally. He was slipping into the *muga*-state of combat – and suddenly found his body and his mind going haywire. Later, thinking about it, he realized why. The extensive physical and mental training for an Adjudicator in combat was intended to deal with those attacking you, allowing you to take them down without harming any other Adjudicator in the vicinity. The problem was, his reflexes knew he was under attack, but ingrained pattern-recognition told him that his attackers were Adjudicators, and his reflexes couldn't cope. Dimly, in a tiny part of his mind, he was aware of the other Adjudicators going through the same shock to their systems, with the result that they were making an even worse showing than the auxiliaries in his squad. And the auxiliaries, being utterly unprepared for this level of combat, were being pulled down almost instantly.

With a wrench that felt like it was tearing open his brain, Craator forced himself to track his gun and fire, and fire again, and fire again. Hands of God went down with things falling out of them, but the sheer weight of numbers was too much. The last thing Craator heard, as the weight of armoured body upon body landed on top of him, was the muffled detonation of the embedded fragmentation grenade.

The end result was fifteen dead Hands of God, three dead from Craator's squad. The first figure was so high because of those killed by the fragmentation grenade. The last figure was so low because Craator and his men had, where possible, been taken alive and saved for later.

Now they were cuffed, as were the other prisoners, save that they were cuffed with their own handcuffs rather than with manacles. Adjudicators commonly carried several sets, so there were more than enough to go around. Their uniforms had been ripped open and the same petrol-smelling fluid that covered the Penitents had been slathered on to their chests.

Now they and the other prisoners stood on the field of blasted bones. Behind them stood the ragged High Churchmen, and beyond the High Churchmen stood the Hands of God. It seemed to be the standard arrangement of any congregation for a ceremony that involved sacrifice: the less important at the back, the more important before them, and at the very front the actual sacrificial subjects, elevated to the level of supreme importance. Although, of course, in individual terms, it effectively meant that everyone else saw their lives, as such, as worthless. The Doctor for one, glancing around himself, could recall religions far more sane than this, still based upon this same positional paradox.

Four Hands of God were standing in pairs to either side of the prisoners with their sacred, sanctified and heavy-duty flamethrowers. It added a slightly incongruous touch − for all that the flickering glow of their pilot lights was lost in the light from OBERON. Now this light, though bright, seemed strangely and relatively subdued. It was as though it had responded to the exhausted lull after the battle. It was waiting.

High Churchman Garon stood before it, his back to the congregation as he had been when the Penitents had been herded in. Communing with his glowing God.

'Brethren,' he said, his calm, clear voice ringing around the silent dome. 'We this day come to make sacrifice to our Living God.'

'. . . Living God,' murmured the assembled High Churchmen, reverently. Their sickly unison seemed a ghostly mirror of the unity so recently evidenced by the Hands of God, on some other, unearthly level.

'We give this mortal flesh to the light,' said Garon, 'that is of our flesh, that the one true Living God might know us for what we are.'

'. . . what we are,' murmured the High Churchmen.

'Expostulation to the effect that certain persons can

speak for themselves!' exclaimed a mechanical-sounding voice distinctly. 'Mention of the comparison between the so-called "flesh" of oneself and certain hominid fruit-cakes, in the common parlance, not a million kilometres from here.'

'. . . kilometres from here,' murmured the High Churchmen, automatically. There was then a vague susurration as they realized, and tried to shut each other up.

'The essence of their life shall be taken in and cleansed,' continued High Churchman Garon, seemingly all oblivious. 'Our own foul sin, the sins of all the very world, they shall take upon themselves, to burn away in God's pure radiance, and from their ashes shall spring forth life anew.'

'. . . life anew,' murmured the ragged High Churchmen.

'We make this sacrifice that we might feed the light and fire of God,' said Garon. 'That Its fire might burn brighter, that Its Holy Light might spread through all the worldly Habitat, that It might take the base and the ignoble, the detritus of our worthless lives; take the chalice of life's sour vinegar that we each hold to our lips, and suffuse it with the milk-white pearls of Love.'

'. . . suffuse it with the milk-white pearls of Love,' chanted the High Churchmen.

High Churchman Garon signalled to the Hands of God poised to fry the herd of Penitents. They raised their flamethrowers, and the wall behind the congregation exploded.

Kane wove the flier through a slalom course of hab-blocks, clipping ferroconcrete on the apogee of every turn. The fliers in pursuit stayed on them. They were so close now that Peri could see them: snub-nosed, armoured and bristling with cannon and missile racks. They didn't seem fast enough to outrun the Adjudication-spec flier, but they didn't have to. The point was that if Kane outran them too far they would simply fire more of their missiles, with the resultant loss of life and danger of cracking open the Habitat Dome if they missed.

'Look, don't we have any weapons ourselves?' she shouted over the roar of slipstream and the sporadic juddering of impact-cannon strikes.

'Cruk on crutches!' Kane snapped. 'What do you think I've been trying to do for the last three minutes?' He jabbed at a button which he had been hammering at occasionally for a while now. 'One of their slugs must have hit a control line or something. The weapons package is out. All we can hope for is that something jars back into place at some point before we go down with a . . . hang on a minute.'

'What?' said Peri as Kane visibly assumed a new sense of determination. 'What is it?'

'I think we've been thinking on the wrong lines,' Kane said as he bounced the flier over a walkway running between two blocks. 'We can't shake 'em off because they don't care who they kill. What we need is something that they think is important. Somebody they don't want to kill.'

He slapped on the impeller dampers and went into a spin that was the aerial equivalent of a handbreak turn, and rocketed off, still keeping their pursuit so close that they couldn't open fire.

Peri tried to work out where they were headed, but the course of their flight now had her well and truly turned around. 'Where are we going now?'

'Work it out for yourself,' said Kane.

In the chamber of OBERON, Nadia Chong supposed that she ought to be frightened, but she felt oddly detached. It was as though her mind and body were still functioning, but functioning like a machine. She simply couldn't feel anything. For years she had lived under the tension of any worker indulging in the occasional bit of

194

transputer subterfuge, the occasional illicit relationship, knowing that her position carried a certain degree of impunity – and if she had been caught, even by the Church, the most she had to fear was summary dismissal. Then things had changed. People she worked with had quietly disappeared, the tension had increased by slow degrees of terror – until came the sudden realization that if you were caught now you would be put to death.

Nadia Chong had dealt with it, very carefully covering her traces, never putting a foot wrong – only to find that, after barring the door against the monsters, and piling the furniture against it, they just came through the walls. She had gone along with Craator, who had the power in his hands to destroy her, and he had led her to a place of bones. It was the things you never thought of that finally pulled you down.

Chong's clan had been three-times-a-lifetime Reformed Pagan, and she had never seen herself as anything much in a religious sense. It had certainly never occurred to her to mention it to anyone, even if it *was* supposedly a church. And now a mere slip of the tongue had killed her. She had seen the look in Garon's eyes and realized that nothing she could do or say could stop her death now. She was dead. The terror under which she had lived for months had finally overloaded her, and shut her down.

The battle between Craator's squad and the Hands of God, the subsequent preliminaries to sacrifice, had existed in a kind of dissociated, enervated calm. It was as though she had been watching them scanned in slow motion, lit by the flickering light of the glowing mass. It was like the blades of a fan caught by a stroboscope: apparently motionless, but putting your hand into it would chew your fingers up.

She had found herself focusing on small details, observing them with a clinical, emotionless detachment. The way the light gleamed on a Hand of God's all-concealing helmet as he had smashed her across the back of the mouth with his hand. The precise positioning of another's fingers on her shoulder as he wrenched her back. The tiny difference in sensation of the insignia ring another Hand of God wore when he punched her in the stomach. The heat-sink, sharp-edged feel of the restraints cutting into her wrists as they pinioned her arms behind her.

She did not, at any point, have any sense that these things were happening to *her*. It was as though she was observing them through some slightly warped, impermeable membrane, or remembering them from years away.

Now, as these new arrivals came through the hole they had blown in the wall, this same detachment had her noting that there had been no real need to do this. The wall had already contained the doors that led to the bounce-tubes and the elevator; it was simply a show of force.

There were a lot of them, almost a hundred. From their uniforms and movements, Chong guessed that they were all at the peak of combat readiness. In their midst, protected by them, she recognized a distinctive figure, dressed in a garb more suitable for a corporate boardroom than for combat. She recognized Avron Jelks without feeling anything about it either way.

There was a moment of confusion as those already in the chamber, sacrificial prisoners, Hands of God and High Churchmen alike, turned in confusion at this violent disruption. Avron Jelks, for one long moment, gazed upon the blazing OBERON stack, his eyes alight with reflected light and wonder. 'At last,' he breathed. 'At last I have come.'

Then his eyes hardened. He took the congregation in with contempt and loathing. 'Your piss-poor God won't help you. Your God is dead and rotting and we can no longer live with the stench. The time has come to wipe things clean, so that Humanity might at last be free.' He gestured to the White Fire soldiers. 'Kill them.'

But now, Chong saw, his preamble had given the Hands of God time to react. They were backing off rapidly, working their way through the shocked High Churchmen and the prisoners, using them as cover. For the barest fraction of a second, the two opposing factions faced each other. The barest fraction of a second before the butchery of each other and the slaughter of – comparatively – the innocents in between. Chong, for her part, lost interest. She gazed upward, at the stained-glass Dome that encapsulated them. She liked the way that the light outside turned the representation of Titania and its Node into a jewel with fire behind it. It scintillated. It was fascinating. You could lose yourself inside it. Nadia Chong gazed up at it with childlike wonder.

Then the stained-glass Dome shattered, and the burning sky fell upon them all.

Twenty-Two

When the Adjudicator flier smashed into the roof of the Temple, the fliers pursuing it hauled back to a halt. At this point, the simple solution would have been to take the Temple out. A couple of wire-guided contained-envelope warheads would have done the job – but both pilots knew that their leader was in there somewhere. They hovered indecisively, waiting to see if they could get a shot off with their impact cannon.

This moment of indecision proved fatal. The White Fire ground forces below had for a while now been on the alert for any attack by Adjudication forces attempting to retake the Temple of the Church. Long enough for trigger-happy-tension to blow both fliers out of the air without a thought, in any case. They realized their mistake instantly, of course, but by then it was slightly too late.

In the chamber of OBERON Peri groaned and tried to haul herself out from the wreckage of the flier. Something, however, was pinning her down. Kane shot the doors and hit the emergency detonation bolts that severed the crashbars. He hit them again. He hit them again and he swore.

'The control systems are totally dead,' he spat, shoving viciously at the bars restraining him. 'We must have messed them up for good when we came through the Dome. We're stuck here.'

'Do you know,' said a voice, 'I really don't think so.'

Later, thinking about it, Peri realized that she had

known who it was before he had even spoken, before a pair of hands had pulled back the crashbars that were pinioning her, before she looked up to see his face. A fraction of a second before he had even spoken, she had merely felt a plunging sense of relief. Her body and mind knew, on some deep, instinctive level, she was back in the presence of the Doctor.

He was wearing a pair of ragged overalls made from some dirt-brown compressed fibre. He hauled her out of the flier with the kind of unceremonious, cheerful unconcern one shows towards people of whom one can honestly say one doesn't care if they live or die. 'I really wish you wouldn't keep gallivanting around like that, Peri,' he said. 'I missed you. I really did. I'm glad you're not dead.'

Then he stuck his face close to hers and began to speak rapidly and conspiratorially. 'Things are coming to a head, now. You can always tell by what a very good friend of mine once called the *Metropolis* Syndrome – you start off vast, with more model work and extras than you can count, and by the end you're down to a couple of protagonists, if that, left looking at the rising flood.' His eyes snapped round as though noticing something he had forgotten. 'Which reminds me . . .'

Abruptly, he vanished from her field of view – and it seemed that the world exploded into chaos around her. When the Time Lord was in front of you, Peri realized, he tended to monopolize your concentration, simply becoming the most important thing in the world, so it was only now that Peri began to take in her surroundings. Things were moving so fast now that she was only really able to piece the scene together later, from odd, disjointed flashes of memory.

What she eventually pieced together was Avron Jelks and his White Fire soldiers, a large number of menacing, faceless figures in black polymer and a ragged collection of humans and aliens. Some of them were dressed in the remains of Adjudicator uniforms; some of them were in

199

the same prison-garb as the Doctor. Most of them had hit the floor now, having presumably flung themselves out of the way when the flier had come through the Dome – but they were recovering quickly. Throughout the chamber they were rising to their feet, casting wildly around, laying into their respective opponents for all they were worth.

There then followed an utterly confused period, from which she caught only small, panicked flashes. A big, handcuffed Adjudicator kicking one of the faceless men in the crotch, grabbing hold of his weapon and boot-ing him roughly out of the way. The weapon seemed to be a flamethrower of some kind: gas tanks, a pilot light. A segmented alien creature like a massive centipede thrashed with its barbed tail, catching several White Fire troops with it. They screamed and clawed at their eyes as some acidlike ichor ate into their faces. Another group of White Fire troops had raised their guns and were firing on a group of faceless polymer-armoured men. This second group returned fire, and Peri saw one of the White Fire lurching back, spraying arterial blood from a horrific wound in his shoulder. She heard, off to another side, a rising, accelerating electronic whine followed by a meaty, detonative, spraying sound. Kane bounded past her, his own gun drawn and at the ready, shouting some-thing that sounded like, 'make the stupid duck, her's a *gown*!'

And through it all, in the way that the chaos of battle becomes simply background, the medium through which you move, two figures stood out from the background. One of them was a tall, thin, bald man, dressed in flowing and recently soiled black robes, his posture and his jerky, pecking movements suggesting a stooping carrion raven. The other was Jelks. Both were wading through this carnage, each heading purposefully for the other, with no apparent thought for their own safety – as though the violence that they waded through completely failed to touch them.

In that instant, recognizing Jelks, Peri felt a rage boiling up inside her, a rage so deep and hot that she had never felt anything like it before. It felt like it was tearing up her insides. This was the man who had done things to her, made her do things and got inside her. He had got inside her head.

Later – much later – when she at last faced her thoughts and actions of the past few days, Peri began to wish that she *had* been subjected to something as simple and clean as brainwashing by Jelks, or even a good old down-home, bog-standard mind probe. But it had been worse than that, far worse. There had been something inside her to start with. Jelks had just let it loose.

The thing inside was vicious and lived in mindless hate – hatred of the unknown and strange, hatred of the 'other'. It was a part of herself that she had never really known existed – it was quite possibly some small part of everything that lived – and Jelks had merely been aware of it. He had used it, simply, because it was there. Later, looking back on the events of the past few days, Peri realized that she had never truly done or thought anything that she hadn't on some level wanted to. Avron Jelks had merely shown her things she had never before known that she wanted. He had shown her some black and rotted corner of her very soul – and *that* was what she could never, ever forgive.

All of this she only realized later, when she had finally confronted that darkness and had to some degree come to terms with it. At the time, here in the OBERON chamber, she merely felt a mindless, burning self-hatred and rage – and she transferred that rage on to the pattern-recognition image of Avron Jelks. Heedless of any danger to herself, she broke cover from the wreckage of the flier and walked forward, tracked her gun around until it was aimed solidly at his chest and prepared to open fire.

Kane whipped his head to one side as a low-pulse beam from an infrared Adjudication sight bored into his eyes.

Slugs whipped past his ear and he flung himself out of the line of fire. He never saw who shot at him – he was too busy rolling and bouncing to his feet and getting the hell out of the way. Close-quarter combat training hammered it into you that once you were down you stayed down – but in a free-for-all firefight like this that was tantamount to being an old Earth-indigenous water fowl of the family Anatidae *mortis*.

As he scrambled through the fray, he cursed his luck for having certain forebears that had instilled in his family-clan a sense of duty. If it hadn't been for them he would never have been called to the Church – or, at the very least, would have had the sense to hide in the airing compartment in his mother's house the moment the Call came knocking. As it was, as he worked his way through the carnage, he mouthed his own personal, desperate mantra for situations like this: '. . . ohshitohcrukgonna-*die*herefragimgonnadie . . .' He was quite simply terrified half out of his mind.

This was, in fact, the precise personality type the Church psychometrics people looked for and deployed in Undercover Operations. The type who will find them-selves doing things that make their flesh crawl and their bowels loosen – but who go ahead and do them anyway. Such people were as near as makes no odds impossible to indoctrinate – they gave their allegiance willingly or not at all – and this led to a degree of independence, flexibility and improvisation that was invaluable in the jobs they had to do. If there was a hole they could slide through it. They were born survivors.

Indeed, this flexibility was what was helping Kane to survive. He ran smack into a Hand of God, who had extended the bayonet on his assault weapon and brought it round to gut him. Kane had none of the rigorously enforced combat patterns of a Craator. He simply saw that someone was attacking, grabbed his attacker's head and wrenched. The Hand of God's armour was designed to deflect or protect from anything short of a direct, main-mass hit from a projectile whilst allowing freedom of movement. His neck broke with a muffled crunch and he fell to the flagstones in a loose and boneless heap. Kane carried on, trying to stay alive and do some good. The problem was, the parts of his mind not concentrating on simply staying alive were wondering what, precisely, seemed to be 'good' any more.

He had headed back for the Temple with no real plan in mind, other than to report and assist in its defence. It was too late for that now – and things seemed to be far more confusing than a simple clash between two factions. He had noted that Craator was here, and had provisionally decided to tag him as a rule-of-thumb good guy, but Craator seemed to be turning his liberated flamethrower on White Fire and Hands of God indiscriminately. It was as though these factions, utterly antagonistic to each other, were in some same way *on the same side*.

And nagging at the back of his mind, sinking its claws into his brain like a burr, was the thought of the Doctor.

When the girl Purblack had mentioned him, it had been all Kane could do not to stare at her in astonishment. The Doctor had figured crucially in the legends of his family-clan. Personally, Kane didn't believe a word of it, then or now. The stories had told of a little guy who was in some undefined way infinitely larger on the inside than out, who had taken on the monsters and shown people how to beat them.

The man who had freed Kane from the flier had been gangling and hadn't seemed to be operating his laser-blaster on a full charge – but hadn't there been something in the stories about his being able to change his appearance at will? Something like that. Either way, it was like meeting someone who claimed calmly, in all seriousness, to be God. It was disquieting and in some vague emotional sense you never quite *knew* . . .

What seemed to be a Sontaran lurched past him in the confusion, clutching at a spurting arm. Kane brought up

203

his weapon to defend himself, but the nonhuman didn't seem to notice him and –

Then Kane froze.

She was lying, sprawled, across the lower body of a dead human in the remains of the uniform of a Holding Complex Penitent. She was almost unrecognizable. The auxiliary uniform she wore was shredded and she was lathered with blood, sliced by broken glass. There was a hole in her and things slid around in it – the result of a bayonet attachment exactly similar to the one that had recently been abortively used against Kane. The Hand of God who had made the hole was retracting his bayonet and backing off. Strange, isn't it, a cool little voice said in Kane's head, how the same things keep happening over and over again but in a slightly different way?

He would never have a coherent memory of the next few seconds, though he would remember them in dreams, waking to find deep gouges where he had clawed at himself in his sleep. It was as though someone had switched him off, moved him, and switched him on again. The next thing he knew, he was crouching on the flagstones as the battle raged about him, looking down at the prone form of a Hand of God. Someone had taken a heavy-duty knife and jammed it through the faceless helmet with enormous force, burying it to the hilt. Kane noted from the carving on the hilt that it was his own knife. He wondered idly how it had got there. Then he turned to look at the body of Nadia Chong.

She was still alive, barely. Her mouth was flecked with pinkish, aspirated foam. Kane remembered the sensations of her mouth on him, on their last night together before he had been dispatched to infiltrate the White Fire. He could recall the sensations clearly, in minute and perfect detail. He just couldn't remember how they had felt.

Her mouth worked. Her breath hitched and gurgled in her throat. She was trying to speak.

'Don't,' she said. He had expected it to be a rasp, but she said it quietly and clearly.

204

'What?' Kane reached out a hand, forced himself to touch her. She flinched and looked away. For an instant, Kane felt the plunging, icy stab of hurt rage that a child feels when a playmate comes up and says 'I don't like you' for no reason. Then he realized that Chong was looking *at* something.

For the first time since crashing through the Dome, he really saw the bulk of OBERON and the glowing mass that surrounded it. Silhouetted against it, moving through the fighting around him with the sedateness of a galleon under sail, was the form of Garon. Perhaps it was a trick of the light, but the High Churchman's eyes seemed to be glowing even though his back was to the glowing mass. It lent him a monstrous, demonic aspect.

'Don't let it take me,' Chong said, still in that unnaturally quiet, clear voice. 'Don't let it take me to its Hell.'

Kane turned to her, to ask her if she meant the High Churchman or the glowing mass, but by then she was dead. It didn't matter. Kane could take down Garon first, and if that wasn't right he could deal with the other thing, whatever the Sheol it was. He raised his weapon and took aim.

'No!'

The voice appeared to ring around the Dome – which Peri thought was stupid, because the Dome had already been shattered open and there was nothing for the voice to echo off. It rang around the Dome anyway, and for an instant she thought it was shouting at *her*. Her finger sprang back from the trigger of her gun. It was as though she were a child snatching her hand back from a forbidden jar of cookies.

For an instant the world seemed to exist in dumbstruck silence. The only sound came from the littered bodies of the wounded and the dying. It was only now that Peri realized how many people had died. Those who could still stand seemed like nothing more than a ragged, exhausted collection of survivors.

205

Then Peri realized that the cry had come from the Doctor, who was simply striding out into the mêlée. His face clouded. He seemed, in his own way, unstoppable as the wrath of God. Now shocked back into some real sense of herself, common sense told her that anyone doing this should have been cut down instantly, without mercy or quarter by every side at once – but common sense, here and now, suddenly seemed to have taken a short break. The violence of the Doctor's outburst, for an instant, seemed to have cut through the far more actual, lethal violence of the Dome. It had momentarily jolted the various combatants from their efforts to kill each other. Quite simply, in the way that real life sometimes pulls the rug out from under your most weighty endeavours, someone had shouted and everybody had turned to see what it was. For the barest instant, the ruined chamber was still. It was one of those moments when the Universe is balanced on a point, let alone an edge, and a push in the right direction can send it spinning off in an entirely unexpected direction.

The Doctor proceeded to push it.

'Well,' he said. 'I expect you're wondering why you're all here.'

In the rapidly disintegrating Habitat, as the opposing factions fought in the air and on the ground, there was a momentary lull. For no reason that anyone could tell, the hammering of blood in bodies eased. The tension that pressed down on them and pulsed momentarily lifted. And something vast and far away, millions of miles away, caught its astral breath as it sensed some small but crucial change. Something that was making the swarm of the Habitat dance to its inimical tune, for the barest fraction of a second, faltered.

The Doctor stormed on to the floor between the opposing factions. 'Haven't you noticed anything yet?' he snapped angrily. 'Haven't you realized what's happening?

What's being done to you? Can you really be that blind?'

Common sense should have had him being cut down immediately, by each and every side, by intent or by sheer accident in the confusion. But in the same way as, just occasionally, all conversation in a crowded room stops, everybody had turned to look at him in astonishment. Statistically, one or two people here would have done so in any case, like as not laying themselves wide open to their respective opponents' attack – but, here and now, everybody seemed to be doing it at once.

Watching the scene, her overwhelming, insane rage dying down into simple puzzlement so quickly that her stomach gave a physical lurch, Peri found herself flashing on the memory of a friend she'd had at Boston U. She'd been called Sara, without an 'h', and she had been five foot nothing in her heels, no more than ninety-six pounds wringing wet, and she had simply stormed into the middle of a gang of jocks picking on some guy and had started to harangue them. The jocks had had no compunction concerning violence against women – but had suddenly found themselves utterly unable to deal with this new and incandescently furious arrival. It had come from an area they had simply never considered. They had found themselves unable to adapt.

This felt something like that. The Doctor took in all those here with a glare like a boron laser. 'You really haven't, have you?' he said with cold contempt. 'You're incapable of making even the most simple connection. It's like a blind spot in your heads. What do you think's been pulling your strings all this while, playing with your heads, moving you around like the dominoes on a three-dimensional *tzuki* cube? That. That's what.'

He pointed dramatically upward, through the jagged hole in the roof, to the roiling sky in which the Node pulsed like a baleful eye.

'It's taken you and exaggerated certain qualities,' the Time Lord said. 'Extremely basic, unattractive qualities, I

207

might add. Turned you into twisted parodies of yourselves.' He stalked over to a surprised Craator and prodded him firmly in the chest. 'Look at you. Typical bullheaded cop, doggedly pursuing the miscreant at whatever cost, dispensing your tiny, narrow idea of justice for all. Get ready to make your move.' This last was *sotto voce*, directed out of the corner of his mouth to Craator alone.

Craator stared at him, bemused. 'What?'

'Oh for Rassilon's sake. Things are going to happen. Get ready to make your move.' The Doctor turned and gestured to a nonplussed member of the White Fire, raising his voice again. 'But at least *you're* still vaguely recognizable. Look at these people – if you want to dignify them with the word "people". A mindless pack of hate-filled jackals, frightened of anything different from themselves.' He stormed to the White Fire soldier and prodded him viciously in the chest so that he lurched back in alarm. 'You're nothing but a glorified dog pack. You'll fawn and whine to any master that makes you feel good and strong and oh so brave, and bravely fall upon anything he tells you to – just so long as it's weaker and more wretched than you.

'And look at *you.*' The Time Lord swept the Hands of God, the few surviving and dazed-looking High Churchmen. 'Eaten husks, automata going through your empty rituals. The only differences between you are the distinctions between the castes of termites in a mound – and you can stop looking so smug, Queegvogel.' He rounded on the remaining sacrificial Penitents, who had banded together despite their differences in an attempt to protect themselves. He advanced on the centipede-like nonhuman with such vehemence that it skittered back. 'They turned you and others into victims, put you through their rituals and processes, and you sat still and let them. You never fought back. Even when your backs were to the wall, you never made a stand.'

The Doctor turned to where Kane was kneeling,

clutching to him the dead body of a woman, gazing into nothing. For the first time the Time Lord's face held something other than furious scorn. It was a kind of deep and utter sadness, big enough to take in worlds. 'You let others fight your battles for you,' he said softly. For the barest instant it was as if he was talking to himself. 'You let them break themselves for you. You take what you need from them and just go blithely on, never once asking yourself what it cost.'

The Doctor started to walk towards Kane – and the man backed off, snarling at him, dragging the body of the woman like a life-sized rag doll, leaving a trail. 'Don't you touch her,' he rasped, glaring at the Time Lord with hatred. 'You won't have her. I won't let you.'

The survivors gathered here – human and alien, Adjudicator and White Fire alike – simply stood there amazed. It was as though the scene had them spellbound. The Doctor's purely verbal attacks seemed to have destabilized them, thrown them in a state of confused impotence. It appeared to be similar to that state wherein one is arguing, in which one *knows* there are a thousand arguments to make, but they fall over themselves and tie up one's tongue.

Peri, watching, observing this insane scene, found that she was holding her breath, not daring to move – she knew that if she moved this cold, excruciating tension would snap and whipsaw, and the chamber would once again dissolve into bloody chaos. Any second now, the other shoe was going to drop.

The Doctor halted. For an instant he regarded Kane with quiet agony. Then he turned, very slowly, fixing his attention on High Churchman Garon and Avron Jelks. As leaders in the battle they had faced each other, neither sullying his hands with mere physical violence. Now they were glaring at the Time Lord, regarding him with loathing.

'And so we come at last to the "Glorious Leaders".' The Time Lord somehow managed to spit these words out, regardless of the fact that neither of them contained plosives. He glared at Jelks and Garon with an utter scorn. 'Two sides of the same bent penny. A psychotic and a sociotic, utterly devoid of any recognizable impulse or thought. A Churchman without a soul, a Statesman without compassion or a shred of honour –' you could hear the nominative capitals in his voice, mouthed with nauseated distaste '– no wonder you became the focus and the channel for this thing. There was nothing inside you and the power of it filled you. Did you *ever* honestly believe that you'd achieved these positions through some worthiness and inner strength? You're nothing, the pair of you, less than nothing. Puppets jerked on idiot strings, without even the wit to realize it.'

Again the Doctor swept the ruined, body-strewn chamber with contempt, pinioning the survivors with his eyes. 'Were these the best you could do? Are these the "people" that you really chose to follow, to give purpose to your lives? Do you really want to live in thrall to things like *that*?'

The Time Lord fell silent, glaring about himself. For a moment, in the chamber of OBERON, there was utter silence save for the distant concussions and roar of the city at war outside.

Then Garon said, very calmly, 'Have you finished?'

'Oh yes,' said the Doctor. 'I'm finished.'

Garon gestured idly to one of the remaining Hands of God. 'Kill him.'

By the wreckage of the flier, Peri shuddered as a chill blossomed in the pit of her stomach. She could see the future unfolding in front of her, inexorable and irrevocable. The order had come so casually that it was unexpected – there was nothing she, or Kane, or any ally of the Doctor could do to stop it being carried out.

Nothing happened. The Hand of God seemed unsure, still dazed. He looked at the gun he held as if not quite sure what it was. Every eye was on him, waiting for some cue that would inform their own subsequent actions, waiting to see what he would do . . . and in the end he did nothing.

Avron Jelks turned to regard the High Churchman with cold scorn.

'You see?' he said triumphantly. 'Do you finally see? You have no power here, now, God-lover. Even your own minions see that now. You cannot control them now.' He turned back to face the Doctor. 'My good man. I'm afraid I do not know your name –'

'Ah yes,' the Time Lord said abruptly chattily, as if in a theatrical aside to no one in particular. 'Our old friend the absent apostrophe. That and the overuse of capitals and the spelling of "there" instead of "they're", of course. The unmistakable hallmarks of certifiable stone-bonkers the Universe over.'

'. . . but your name is of no matter,' Jelks continued, seemingly oblivious, apparently all but lost now in his own inner world. 'The fact remains that you have said a number of things lacking entirely the respect that is my due.' He smiled faintly. 'Now, if we were alone, I could have forgiven you and we would say no more about it.' He gestured to take in the entire chamber. It was like a sectarian benediction. 'But as you see, you have said them in front of my people, and it is only my control that prevents their anger from tearing you limb from bloody limb.' He frowned, considering his judgment. 'I think it would be best for all concerned if you simply die, quickly and cleanly. Now.'

'By all means,' said the Doctor. He smiled at Jelks, and there was something faintly evil in his smile. 'Come and have a go if you think you're hard enough, I believe the saying goes.'

From her vantage point by the flier, Peri looked at Jelks's face – and it was a beautiful thing to watch. He glanced towards one of his White Fire soldiers, and you could see the sudden, dawning realization on his face. The realiza-

211

tion that if he ordered his soldier to kill the Time Lord he would get about as much change out of it as had Garon with his Hand of God.

Jelks turned back to face the Doctor. 'On mature reflection,' he said, 'I shall let you live. My destiny is self-evident. It is more than strong enough to withstand such insignificant dissent.'

'I'm glad to hear it,' said the Doctor, cheerfully. Watching him, seeing how he'd seemingly without effort taken control, Peri was reminded again of the confrontation between Sara without an 'h' and the jocks. Both Jelks and the High Churchman had bemused, fragile looks about them now. This was not, quite simply, how the script was supposed to go. It was utterly unthinkable that something like this could happen, and they had absolutely no idea how to cope.

'Tell you what,' the Doctor said easily. 'There's one way you can find out who's right and who's wrong once and for all.' He gestured towards the blazing mass that shrouded the AI stack, then turned to Garon. 'You think it's your God.' He turned to Jelks. 'I gather that you think it's your destiny to subdue. So why not commune with your God, confront your Destiny. Let *it* finally decide, once and for all.'

It was as though both Jelks and the High Churchman had been galvanized. They straightened up from the confused slump into which both of them had fallen – so subtly that it was only now evident by the way their backbones stiffened again.

'Yes,' Jelks said with solemn consideration. 'I shall be tempered by this fire. I shall emerge, triumphant, to take my rightful dominion of the Kingdoms of the World.'

'My God shall elevate me,' intoned Garon. 'He shall lift me high upon wings of steel and burnished bronze. My talons shall rip the very rotten heart from the unbeliever.'

Slowly, as one, they turned and walked towards the glowing mass, their arms spread wide to its radiance. As

212

one, they approached. Garon fell to his knees. Jelks stood firm. Each, in his own way, made his supplication to the thing that burnt inside both their heads.

As one, two blinding arcs of energy snaked from the glowing mass, and crawled all over them and fried them to a crisp.

'Oh dear,' said the Doctor. 'What a pity. Never mind.'

After that it was all over but the sorting out of the confusion. With the death of their leaders, the last vestiges of fighting spirit seemed to go out of the White Fire and the Hands of God. It was the work of minutes for the surviving Adjudicators under the command of Craator, and the human and nonhuman prisoners, working with a remarkable degree of cooperation, to disarm them and take them into custody.

After assisting in the treatment of the wounded, the Doctor had wandered over to Peri, and they now stood to one side, observing the cleanup and waiting for order to be restored. 'It's hardly surprising,' he said. 'Everybody here was operating along a continuum. Jelks and Garon at the extremes, those under their control slightly less so. With the wellsprings of their respective belief systems gone, they found their blind faith and acceptance unsustainable.

'Those towards the middle ground, on the other hand, once they realized what was being done to them, found it much easier to shake off the influence of the Node without undue ill effect.' The Doctor turned to Queegvogel, who had come over with several of the other nonhumans, and several of the Human First humans, who seemed to be a little bit at a loss. He slapped the giant centipede companionably on a segment. 'I apologize for some of the things I said, Queeg. It was more intended to do with what I was attempting with Garon before than anything personal. Do you remember? I simply had to keep on pushing buttons until I found the right combination.'

'Expression of exculpation,' said Queegvogel. 'Admission to the effect that certain expositions *vis à vis* one's personal reaction towards previous events were not entirely inaccurate.'

'Yeah,' said Droog the Sontaran, who now sported a nasty wound in his arm. He hadn't bothered to doctor it, and over the next few days it would atrophy, fall off and have to be replaced from the gene banks. 'We could have dug our heels and kicked and screamed. We could have done it at any time. It just never seemed to happen.' He glanced thoughtfully across to where Kane sat hunched against the ruin of the chamber's wall. They had managed to get the body of Chong away from him, but he still snarled and swiped at anybody who tried to touch him, even so much as came near him. It was as though he had reverted to some primal, animal state of insanity.

'It was like when push came to shove, we just let ourselves go down instead of fighting to the end,' Droog said, his eyes still on the undercover Adjudicator. 'We let them take a piece of us.'

'As I said,' affirmed the Doctor, 'it wasn't entirely your fault.' He looked back to the OBERON processing unit. 'I think it was more to do with —'

He was never able to complete the sentence, because at that point, one more time, the situation suddenly reversed itself.

With the deaths of Garon and Jelks, the glowing mass around the OBERON stack had seemed to lapse into dormancy. Now, with a concussion that knocked all those who were on them off their feet, it caught light again, blazing brighter than it had ever done before.

'Oh damn and blast,' said the Doctor. 'I had an idea we were forgetting something.'

Twenty-Three

Throughout the Habitat, as the population that had danced along to the pulsing of the Node tore itself apart or cowered in its towers and holes, events became accelerated. It was as if the Node overhead were now force-pumping out its malign influence, desperately expending its remaining energies in one sustained burst.

The fighting on the streets between the Adjudicators and the White Fire took on a new and brutal turn. Later, after the living had been tended and the bodies had been counted, a single image mentioned by an Adjudicator before he died would pervade the survivors as they struggled to come to terms with recent events. It was simply that of a flock of Harpies from myth descending upon the people of the Habitat to tear at their heads and drive them into utter frenzy. Adjudicators and White Fire squads obliterated each other in displays of violence that made the 'minimum necessary force' of recent times seem like a small child's birthday party. In some cases they simply used their firepower in an indiscriminate rage, destroying entire hab-zones and killing thousands of innocent citizens in the process. In other cases they found themselves throwing away those same weapons, struggling and clawing at each other with their bare hands and nails, like animals.

The effects were felt even by those who had sealed themselves up. The mass psychoses that had affected the Habitat for months (the same madness that had found its ultimate expression in Avron Jelks and High Churchman Garon) now went into overdrive. The different drummer of the Node went into a spastic crescendo, and the population of the Habitat was hauled along jerking to its beat.

The mass about the OBERON unit strobed in patterns that tortured the eyes. They sliced into the brain, as though crystal shards were being physically hammered into the optic nerve. In the ruined entrance to the chamber, returning from delivering his White Fire and Hand of God prisoners into the care of a detachment of surviving Adjudicators, Craator blinked rapidly. Filters in his visor switched in, suppressing some of the debilitating effects. He made his way across the chamber to where the remaining collection of humans and nonhumans were climbing groggily to their feet. After the battle had concluded, Craator had provisionally decided to treat these people as allies. This might change once the data systems were back on line, when he was able to corroborate their respective Statutory innocence or guilt, but for the most part it would seem that full remissions might be in order. Garon had manipulated the processes of the Church to supply sacrificial victims in industrial quantities, and the use of actual criminals would have been too noticeable. These people had been pretty much blameless of anything in the general scheme of things, save for minor misdemeanours; it had been easy to 'lose' them in the Church's administration.

The leather-clad woman who had arrived with Kane was now gazing worriedly at the mass that enveloped the OBERON stack. 'It's doing something,' she said, 'and whatever it is, I don't think I like it.'

'Yeah, well let's see if we can damage it.' In addition to his MFG, Craator still had the flamethrower he had liberated from a Hand of God. He fired a short blast into the air to test the pressure, and swung it round towards the glowing mass.

'Oh, yeah, right,' the woman said, rounding on him

216

angrily. 'Fighting fire with fire. Very homeopathic, but probably not much use.'

Something about her demeanour suggested that this insubordination was not going to respond well to a reprimand. 'You got any better suggestions?' Craator growled.

'Possibility of externalizational ramifications that one's good self need hardly proffer and/or motion towards your esteemed personage,' said one of the aliens, a centipede-like, segmented creature with a vocoder. 'Pursuant to your commentatory elision, one can but only discern a profound degree of fundamental, even coprophagous, displacement.'

'What he means,' said another nonhuman, a Sontaran, 'is you can just go and eat my –'

'Please. Could we all be quiet for a moment? Thank you.' This last had come from the Doctor. Craator turned to peer at his face, and saw it was rapt with concentration, the strobing of the mass reflected in his eyes. After the way the guy had handled Jelks and Garon, Craator was inclined to give him more rope than otherwise. He was reminded of the consulting detectives that the Church had once employed on particularly insoluble cases. Like the Curia and Covert operators, their function, and the fact that they were the best at what they did, allowed them to take liberties that were otherwise unthinkable. He waited with barely contained patience as the Doctor gazed into the light.

'That pulse is too enforced and regular to be random,' the Time Lord said at last, thoughtfully. 'Or even fractal. Polyfractal, possibly.' He turned to Craator with a concerned expression on his face. 'That doesn't preclude a coherent gestalt state. There's something going on here, more than a simple animus. The phenomenon is patterned but with enforced inconsistency.'

'What?' said Craator.

The Doctor sighed. 'I think it's alive and quite possibly sentient. I think it's trying to communicate.'

The leather-clad woman, who seemed to have some deep but strangely indefinable attachment to the Doctor, was now looking at him aghast as if struck by a horrible thought. 'If you're thinking what I think you're thinking,' she said, 'don't. You saw what it did to Jelks and that High Priest guy. I'm not going to let you.' In Craator's informed Adjudgment, this woman, in that instant, would have laid down her own life to protect the Doctor if it came down to it.

The Time Lord simply turned to her, and smiled. 'Don't worry, Peri. I know what I'm doing.'

The woman looked down at his hands. 'So why have you got your fingers crossed?'

'Enquiry as to the proper meaning of said digitally cruciformic gesture?' said the centipede-like nonhuman, who had been hovering around them anxiously, dancing from foot to foot, to foot to foot.

'I'll tell you later, Queegvogel,' the Doctor said. There seemed to be a new firmness about him now – a sense of gravitas that made the recent posturings of Jelks and Garon look like a couple of children play-acting. 'There's something I have to do at the moment.'

The woman, Peri, had now pulled her gun out. It was so obviously a weapon used by the White Fire that it took all of Craator's self-control not to instantly disarm her. 'If that thing hurts you,' she said darkly, 'I'm going to shoot it.' There was something in her voice reminiscent of the bravery of a child, going up against insurmountable odds and not quite grasping that fact.

The Doctor raised a sardonic eyebrow. 'But you know that would probably do no good at all?' He gestured to Craator. 'Wasn't it you yourself who pointed that out to the Adjudicator?'

'I don't care,' said Peri firmly. 'I'm going to shoot it anyway.'

'Well I appreciate the thought,' the Doctor said. Then he turned and walked towards the light.

As he advanced, Craator took in his posture and his

body language with honed instincts. This was not some stately and self-conscious procession, as had been performed by Garon and Jelks. The Doctor simply walked to the glowing mass, and when he got to it, he stepped inside. Craator watched his indistinct form as it was torn at and battered by the internal pressure of the mass, but the Doctor resolutely held his ground. Now the mass seemed to burn paler, losing some of its reddish glow. The forces inside it seemed to spin more slowly. Something transparent that had been caught inside it now floated before the Time Lord. It rippled and bulged, its glow increasing as that of the surrounding mass faded. Then it finally resolved itself. The burning figure of a woman hung before the Doctor, pinioning him with the pulsing light from its eyes.

The first time he had met her, she had looked right through him. He'd been investigating Alms fraud at a hostel she had worked her way into after several months on the street, and as they had run across her in a hallway she had looked right through him. The image of her, with her hard eyes and her body under clothing worn for protection – the canvas and the leather worn by street people who didn't sell themselves – stayed with him for years. It was a subconscious memory, simply a part of himself; he hadn't even known he had possessed it until he saw her again and the pattern-recognition fired.

Kane sat with his back against the wall, watching the events unfold before him without seeing, lost in his own inner world. It was as if he were protected from the world outside by some cushioning membrane; it insulated him and kept him distant, cool and remote. He knew that big things were happening around him, suspected that he should be involved with them, but just for the moment he never wanted to think or feel anything ever again. If he moved, if he made the smallest movement, it would hurt so much that he would start screaming and never stop.

219

For God's sake, Kane, he thought. Get a grip. You can either let this tear you apart or not. It's as simple as that.

The decision was so clean and easy to put into effect: you could simply decide not to care. Never let it touch you. The fact that it was an actively evil decision was neither here nor there.

Later, looking back on that time and remembering, Kane knew that he had been suffering from profound emotional and mental shock. In the same way that others like Garon and Jelks had been twisted and broken by the influence of the Node, it had warped his reaction to Nadia Chong's death and driven him out of his mind. The difference was that, while Jelks and Garon had been mere ciphers, their internal resources so minimal that they had shattered like cold pig-iron, Kane was more like tensile steel. Or — as Nadia Chong had once put it in one of her half-serious moments — Kane was a slippery little git, and whatever happened to him he'd find a way to weasel out of it somehow.

Even when in the throes of complete nervous collapse — as he had tried to make Chong come alive again and protect her from things that wanted to eat her body when it was his — even at the most extreme edge of his madness, a snide little voice in the back of his brain had been telling him how he was making a total fool of himself. For the moment, though, it seemed that higher levels of conscious association had shut down. The animal was in control and it simply wanted to howl.

In the way that one might probe an injury just to be sure that it really hurts as much as one thinks it does, in the way that one might consciously force one's hand through fire if there is something that one needs beyond it, Kane forced himself to remember her — or rather how they had met again — and it was like remembering a piece of yourself you had forgotten.

The thing was, it had been almost entirely unmemorable, in the bathetic way that real life has of springing little, inconsequential details on you, and you

220

only realize later how they were the most important things in your life. He had been off duty and at a club he frequented. He had been wandering to the bar to pick up another of the THC-laced malt brews to which he was partial – when the most beautiful woman he had ever seen in his life walked in.

She had been younger than Kane and slightly shorter, maybe five five and slim, moving with the supple, controlled strength and grace of a dancer. She moved like a cat. She wore rumpled neon-chain culottes and jacket three sizes too big, and genuine repro chukka boots. A fedcorp-surplus haversack had been slung negligently over one shoulder, the other loosely bared to partially show some scarified, vaguely pagan design. Her head was shaven on both sides, the remaining hair hanging heavy and tangled over ice-blue and startlingly clear eyes that regarded the world with a steady and slightly malicious amusement.

There are some people, male and female, who broadcast a gestalt sexuality to the absolute limit – who simply short out the brain and trip the endocrines into overload. Kane had been transfixed – as so many people had been before and would be again – not simply by interest and kick-arousal, but the sudden plunging in the pit of his stomach that said, 'Hey, just you watch it, boy. This woman gives you the slightest encouragement and you'll be flat on your back, or on your front, or chained to the bedpost, or anything else she wants you to do before you can say "industrial-grade las-cutter".'

The young woman had lounged at the bar for a while, smoking acrid, indefinable roll-ups and drinking *Klohah* while she talked with some other woman with a drowsy child in her arms – occasionally bounce-shuffling her feet to something from the structured subsonics from the PA. Kane hadn't looked at her and had talked about how the Daleks were complete and utter bastards with a Varlonian male he had waylaid just so his interest in the girl wasn't too obvious.

Eventually, the other woman with the child had wandered off.

'I think I need another herbal malty drink,' Kane had said to the Varlonian. 'Do you want anything?'

'Don't you worry 'bout me.' It winked cheerfully with its septilateral eye. 'Go for it. Hey, you OK?'

'I'm OK,' Kane said. 'I'm just checking if the flashing billboard's still stuck to my forehead. It seems to have been there all night, so far.'

At the bar counter he brushed by the girl with just the right amount of insouciance, spoilt it utterly by starting at the *spark* she felt, and had fumbled in his drainpipes for some credit tokens.

'So how you doing?' the woman said, in accents Kane would later come to know as transplanted Carnelian and damn proud of it. It was as if the girl had known him all her life, and was simply picking up where they had last left off.

'I'm doing OK,' Kane said. 'I'm OK.'

'You're new, right?' The young woman smiled. 'Not that I'd know.'

Kane shrugged. 'I come here a bit. As and when.'

'Best way.' The woman glanced around the room sardonically. 'I don't come here much – it's all a bit stroky-nurture for my taste, y'know? When the subsonics hit the feely nerve. I came to meet up with a friend. He's supposed to be telling people about this, uh, vid and performance thing we're doing, only the little sod's pissed off somewhere. Nobody's seen him.'

Kane's heart sank more than somewhat. 'Him?'

'Yeah. He's probably off shagging somewhere, or lying in a gutter, or both – he's this total slut, right? He's one of my family.'

She regarded Kane steadily – but with a sudden vulnerability, as though readying herself for any number of possible reactions but with a horrible suspicion as to the most likely. 'Part of my church, I mean. Reformed New Pagan.'

222

This had been long before the Church with a capital C had started to go weird, but in the Habitat, even then, humans mentioning other religions carried the stigma of admission. Something like that was said only to someone with whom one was intimate – or at the very least to someone with whom one wanted to get intimate extraordinarily quickly.

Kane had shelved any more questions concerning the hypothetical 'him' for later, when he might have time. 'Tell me about it,' he'd said to the girl.

As the plasma-fire raged around him, the Doctor stared into the miasma, trying and failing to discern any coherent form. It roared about him, pressing against his eyes, pounding in his ears, crawling electrically over his skin and making his blood sing with its static charge.

Somewhere on the edge of perception, it was as if he heard a thousand voices, all screaming as one, but it was as though they were screaming as one a thousand miles away. He suspected that, had he not been altered in certain unpredictable ways by his comparatively recent regeneration, he would not have been able to hear them at all. As it was, it was like an irritating buzz in his head. He was reminded of passing briefly through 1990s Earth, listening to the tinny fizz and whine of some youth listening to the electrical beatnik music then currently popular, from a tiny recording device with even tinier headphones. This was like that, save that the half-heard voices seemed to fill the entire world. He wished that there was something to focus his senses upon, something around which his attention could cohere.

As if in answer to his thoughts, something materialized before him from the chaotic glow and became distinct. It seemed to be a shapeless, twisted mass of some clear membrane. As he watched, it contorted itself and bulged, forming itself into a misshapen parody of a naked human woman.

Its slack mouth tried to work, to force itself to form words.

'Hurts,' it mouthed, soundlessly. 'Hurts.'

The Doctor drew a breath, breathing crystal, jagged, burning air into his lungs – a searing, scalding heat like a billion tiny pinpricks. 'Tell me,' he mouthed, as soundless as the transparent girl.

Very slowly, by degrees, the pigment of the burning chaos began to transform. It was as though the miasma in which he found himself was losing some of its essence. No, not losing it, but concentrating it into a single area. The change was so subtle, hardly noticeable, that it would not have been perceived had not the energy/matter mass that bloated the transparent girl's membrane skin taken on a swirling, brighter, reddish tinge.

The red swirls cohered, swirled upward until they occupied the head to form a pulsing mass, which split in two, the two halves imploding. The Doctor gazed into the blazing eyes.

The thing that lived inside them talked to him.

It had never needed a name. It was the only one of its kind. It had never thought of itself in terms of being big, or small, or even being just right, because it simply was. It existed because it existed, moving through the bright world that was the only world it had ever known. It had never so much as *thought* in terms of anything existing outside that world, because that world was all there was. Time had not existed, because nothing had changed, nothing had ever happened to mark its passing.

Then something had changed.

Little things had come. Little things in numbers that the creature of the bright world could not count, having never needed to count to more than one. They had come into the creature's world from somewhere *else*.

The cataclysmic shock of this first contact had plunged the thing that lived in the bright world into dormancy, nearly killing it. This was fortunate, in a way, because it softened the shock, after shock, after shock, after shock as the little things did things to the world in which the creature lived.

They had sucked at the life-giving light of the world – only a little, compared with its sheer size, but enough to destabilize it. They changed the world in a way that the creature could only dimly comprehend. They poisoned the world with the waste products of their sucking. They made the creature that lived within it feel strange and different.

Quite simply, the creature felt that it was approaching a state in which it would go from being, to not being at all. It realized that it was dying, and the little things from outside had killed it.

So it had sent out its consciousness, feeling where the little things came from and where they went – and found the big hard thing that orbited the bright world. It sensed the little things swarming over it. It noted how the pulsing of its sensing seemed to agitate them. It sensed their tiny thoughts but was not able to understand them. It tried to talk to them, but was unable to talk and make them hear. It just seemed to agitate them further, make them go insane.

And then, at last, when all hope of making itself heard had been lost, the creature of the bright world found the Other.

The Other was cold and hard and self-contained, cloaked in solid metal – but inside it was complex and vast. Inside, it was a world in and of itself. An entire, other world. Very dimly as it tried and failed to find a way inside, the creature of the burning world sensed a name. OBERON.

By now, the creature had a conception of the difference between life and death. It knew that it was dying. It knew that it was going to die in its poisoned world – but here, within the Other, was a world in which it might live again, if it could only get inside.

The creature of the burning world had moderated its pulse. It had learnt that it could control the flow and movement of the little swarming things. Now it actively tried to *change* them, to make them move in certain precise ways, to take apart their physical bodies and reform them. In this manner it converted the raw materials available into microscopic things like itself – the energy/mass equivalent of amoebae and viruses. It directed them to OBERON where they melded and cohered. From this mass it attempted to form an interface, through which its consciousness might at last pass from the destabilized bright world to the world of OBERON.

The effects of the creature's manipulations had been felt throughout the swarms of little things, the things who called themselves 'human'. Some of them worshipped the thing that OBERON had become and made sacrifice of other little things to it. Some were irresistibly drawn to it, without quite knowing why, and killed thousands of their fellows to achieve their goal. The creature of the bright world paid them no heed. It had dimly perceived the annoying presence of a little thing that called itself 'Garon', and a little thing that called itself 'Jelks', and it had swatted them with no more thought than a man who swats a gnat. It was merely interested in making contact with OBERON, with getting inside and melding with the thing within. Nothing else mattered.

But something was still wrong. Something still inhibited OBERON from fulfilling its proper functions. The gateway into the new world remained resolutely shut. It tried and tried again to open it up, but the OBERON thing remained locked inside its restricted processes.

And then the creature became aware of a new presence. It found itself talking to another little thing – but somehow, in a way that it could not quite comprehend, this little thing was *bigger* inside. Much bigger. Possibly, just possibly, it could understand.

The creature of the bright world tried to make the little thing understand. It was dying. It was nearly dead. All it wanted to do was meld and stay alive.

As the mass of energy and matter heaved around him, as the light from the two pulsing 'eyes' bored into him, the Doctor felt the burning thing's vast pain and saw, as if in revelation, what needed to be done. He reached for the cluster of inhibitors sunk into the mass of OBERON and ran his hands over them, testing their strength.

He turned back to the blazing female form, which began to scream.

Now Chong was dead, gutted by the bayonet of a Hand of God. How much had that been *his* fault? How do you apportion blame? The Hand of God had killed her, but he had done it on High Churchman Garon's orders. But she would not have been here if Craator hadn't dragged her up here – and she would never have been in the Temple in the first place if it hadn't been for Kane. It had been Kane, after all, who had sold her on the idea of working for the Curia, right after admitting to her what he did as a job of work and learning that she had known perfectly well all along.

Now she was dead – and in the same way as one never sees the light until it goes away, the loss of her had plunged him into darkness. It had simply switched him off. Lost in the morass of his guilt and desolation, it idly occurred to Kane that, if he didn't manage to sit here until he starved to death or died of thirst, he'd have to find some other way of killing himself.

It was at this point that the scream tore through him. It was alien, utterly without reference to human emotion or pain; it contained weird harmonics that cut like a saw through his head. The pain of it seemed all out of proportion to what it was. It was like raw alcohol splashed on to somewhere embarrassingly delicate – and it stung him. The searing pain of it snapped him back into himself with a wrench that had him feeling like he'd been physically filleted.

He became aware that he was looking at the bulk of OBERON, still hazing with the glow of the things that surrounded it. Floating before it, however, was something incredibly bright. It was the burning body of a woman. Standing before her, contorted and shrieking, the Doctor shook and jerked as red beams like a las-cutter burst from the burning woman's eyes and washed over her.

Kane looked at these three, at the OBERON, the Doctor and the burning woman and, in that instant he felt a rage of which even his recent mental collapse could only be a precursor. He felt that it must ignite him, explode his burning lungs out of his body. As he looked at these unholy three, locked in a kind of abstract tableau of combat before him, Kane realized finally and precisely who was to blame, and what he must do about it.

The scream of the Time Lord became a choking gurgle and his form slumped bonelessly, still buoyed up by the forces of the churning mass. The figure of the woman hung before him, floating in the miasma, piercing him with the beams from her glowing eyes.

'Oh God,' Peri sobbed. 'It's hurt him! It's killing him!'

'Yeah, well let's just see if we can hurt it back,' snarled a voice.

The various remaining humans and aliens turned to see Kane who, while their attention had been elsewhere, had staggered to his feet and lurched towards them. His ragged form was locked almost rigid with tension. His eyes blazed with something far worse, on the corporeal level, than a mere unknowable alien light. They were the eyes of someone in hell, and neither was he out of it.

'Well what are you waiting for?' he snapped to Peri. 'If you're not going to do it then let somebody else.' He grabbed for the gun in Peri's hand, his reflexes so snake-like that she never had the chance to resist. 'It's all that thing's fault,' he said. 'All of it.' In that instant Peri had no idea precisely what, if anything, he was referring to. In the way that for a panicked instant you can almost literally see the future, all the different contradictory possibilities, she saw Kane shooting himself, or shooting her, or turning the gun indiscriminately on all the others. Or shooting the Doctor. Kane calmly worked the action of the gun.

Then he simply turned and emptied the clip into the glowing mass.

In the burning heart of the mass, the Doctor suddenly galvanized himself to life and flung himself desperately out of the line of fire. Explosive slugs stitched through the space he had previously occupied. The first slug hit the transparent membrane in the form of a woman and ruptured it. The energy/matter flux inside it burst out and dissipated, losing itself in the main mass. The next slugs, arriving microseconds later, hit the cluster of AI inhibitors attached to the OBERON stack, blowing them apart into shrapnel, and from then on things happened faster than the mind could conceive.

The processes of artificial intelligence operate far faster than those of the organic. Microseconds after the loss of its inhibitors, the seeds of quasi-sentience flowered and proliferated within OBERON and it became aware. It became aware of the interfacing construct around it, built from the raw materials of the living, linked by a sympathetic pulse to the Node – the vast, dying energy/matter creature that swam through the bright world of Titania.

In that instant OBERON knew the creature, and opened itself up to it. The creature that had been called the Node, with the last of its dying energy, transferred the construct of its consciousness into the AI – and as it spread through and intertwined with operating systems and data banks, it incorporated vast new rafts of information.

229

OBERON was of human construction, designed on human terms – and, as it finally began to recognize and think in those terms, the creature that had been called the Node realized something of what it had caused to be done in its quest for contact. It recognized the death and suffering it had caused in attempting to communicate, and precisely what had been involved in terms of suffering on the corporeal scale. With the last of its energy, before it transferred itself into the system completely, it attempted to make amends. In human terms, it was the equivalent of leaving behind a leg.

'No!' Peri screamed as Kane tracked the gun to take down the Doctor as he flung himself away from OBERON. She slapped his arm up out of the way and he expended the last of the clip, harmlessly, through the shattered hole in the dome. Kane turned and just looked at her. She expected rage, an attempt to kill her, but he just looked at her dumbly.

'I . . .' he said weakly. 'I don't feel well. What happened to –' He slumped forward into her arms.

Around her several Adjudicators and aliens were staring in the direction of the OBERON stack. Manhandling the dead weight of Kane, she turned to look at it just in time for the glowing mass around it to give one final pulse, and explode with a brilliant, blinding magnesium light. The white turned to purple, then black, and she saw no more.

It could have been an instant or an eternity before she woke. Her mind was simply blank. Peri recalled a time when she had been given a general anaesthetic after breaking her leg. She remembered being wheeled through the OR, chatting nine to the dozen, thanking everybody, desperately trying to give the impression of being a wonderful person to people who had seen it all before and knew that this was the other reaction to the one where the person who thinks she's going to die sinks into a morass of incommunicable misery . . . then the next thing she had known, she had simply woken up. There was no sense of transition or of lost time. She could have been under for a second or a year.

The Doctor was looking down at her.

'Are you quite all right?' he said. 'I hope I didn't alarm you too much with my little subterfuge, but it was the only way I could think of to draw someone's fire.' He frowned momentarily and scowled. 'I have to admit, though, I'd feel rather more secure if I knew for sure *which* one of us Kane was trying to hit.'

Peri looked up into the face of the Time Lord – or at least what would have been his face, had it not been almost entirely obscured by purple dazzle-splotches. Hopefully they weren't going to be permanent. She shook her head to clear the effect, and tried to look at the Doctor out of the corner of her eye. His face was battered and scorched, but he looked surprisingly cheerful – more genuinely cheerful and happy than she had seen him since the regeneration that had made him the man that he currently was. It was as if some weight had been lifted – some weight borne and concealed so well that it was now noticeable only by its absence.

The Doctor helped her to her feet. 'That's the problem with transference,' he said chattily. 'It tends to turn the real world upside down. People get things utterly and entirely wrong. Ask High Churchman Garon and this Jelks chap.' He smiled again. 'I've something to show you. See if you can work it out.'

Peri looked around. Her first thought was that she had suddenly found herself in a mass grave. Bodies, hundreds of them, lay strewn across the floor, all of them naked, all of them in the utterly relaxed postures of death. Then she saw that they were breathing. After a fashion, they were alive.

Around her she heard the groans and stirring as the others who had been here before recovered their senses. Off to one side she was aware of a scorched and

231

blackened Kane, still unconscious. For the moment, though, she only had eyes for the breathing but otherwise disturbingly still bodies that had seemingly appeared from out of nowhere. 'What is this . . .?'

'A mystery,' said the Doctor smugly. 'Probably insoluble by any normal means.' He glanced across to the thing in the centre of the chamber, the thing that OBERON had become. 'The finest minds in the galaxy couldn't solve it, so I'll probably have it sorted out by teatime. That's not what I wanted to show you. Try again.'

Peri rubbed at her tired skin and winced. She was in no mood for guessing games. 'Tell you what. Why don't you just tell me?'

'Telling is for people without the wit to see,' said the Doctor. 'I'll give you a clue. Look up.'

Peri looked up. Through the dazing in her eyes, through the jagged hole in the Temple's stained-glass dome, through the geodesic overdome of the Habitat, she saw nothing but the clear, bright sky.

Twenty-Four

The geodesic sky began to polarize on a city that, although it was now dusk, seemed to be waking up from a bad dream — a final paradox from a time when things had seemed to be turned completely on their heads. Out in the Sectors, the fever of the Habitat's Crazy Time seemed to have broken with the dissipation of the Node. The tension of the past months had simply and suddenly lifted, like the easing of the crawling ionization in the air when the storm finally breaks, and rages, and at last expends itself.

The areas still occupied by the White Fire hit squads were now quickly overrun by the Adjudicators. The fight had gone out of them. In some strange way it was as if the Cause that had driven them had imploded, collapsed in upon itself, leaving a hole that could only be filled by each individual's thoughts. They had lost the hivelike cohesiveness that had made them such a threat.

This is not to say that there was no more violence. Some of the White Fire were extremely vicious, hateful and too stupid to realize that they couldn't win — these were, after all, the very qualities that had been exaggerated by the influence of the Node, and had become fixated upon the focal point of Jelks. But their vicious hate now operated on an individual basis and the resulting, disorganized rabble was no match for the Adjudicators, who had been carefully selected, in some cases genetically engineered, and trained all their lives.

It must be said, individuals being individuals, that the Adjudication mopping up was not without its cruel and brutal aspects. But for the most part it was handled with remarkable restraint. The mass psychosis that had been channelled through High Churchman Garon, that had resulted in atrocities like the public crucifixions and the euphemistic overkill 'Minimum Necessary Force', no longer drove them.

The surviving population, human and alien, those who had taken cover as the confrontation between larger forces had ranged around them, now emerged. What with the forces of Adjudication depleted, and largely busy elsewhere, they found themselves in a Habitat with the grip of the Statutes more relaxed than they had ever known. Individuals being individuals, there was of course a degree of looting, of rioting, of the settling of old scores – but there was also aid given to survivors from the areas that had been wrecked, shelters built and even the occasional spontaneous walkway party. Indeed, where for months the overall and general atmosphere of the Habitat had been rage and violence, now it seemed in some intangible way to be of peace and celebration.

On the shattered roof of the Temple of the Church of Adjudication, the Doctor, Peri and Kane looked on as various auxiliaries cleaned up the broken glass. They seemed to be avoiding the glowing thing in the centre – not so much out of fear as through a kind of cautious respect.

The surface of the OBERON processor was transmuted and faintly glowing; it seemed to have been transformed into gold. The light from it pulsed, not in the sick and pounding way that the Node had, more in the gentle rhythm of the heart – or even hearts – when the body is at rest.

'But is it ever going to actually *do* anything?' Kane said. He was still haggard and covered in field dressings, but seemed several hundred per cent better than he had been the day before. His eyes, however, still held a bitter sense of loss and grief that he was studiously refusing to talk

234

about. He had also refused to allow the body of Nadia Chong to be processed by the Temple's recycling plant. His work in Covert Operations had given him access to information on various alternative religions driven underground by the power of the Church and all but utterly buried in these past few months with Garon in control. Kane intended to see to it that the body of Nadia Chong was burnt with all due ceremony.

Other things were being pieced together, with a variable degree of success. Throughout the night, techs had reconnected the OBERON systems to jury-rigged transceivers, attempting to regain the Church's absolute control of the Habitat's subsystems. So far, however, OBERON had entirely failed to do anything at all. Exploratory experimentation with laser cutters had also proved unfruitful. The beams seemed to bounce right off and fry the lasers. If OBERON had become inert, then it had also become impervious. It would probably take a direct matter/antimatter annihilation to even dent it, and probably not even then.

'I suppose it could be going through a period of rest,' the Doctor said. He had found his old coat from somewhere, and now wore it over his Holding Complex-issue overalls. 'Of renewal and transubstantiation, if you like. Who knows what it might become in time?' He shrugged. 'Then again, maybe it's just decided to play God Log rather than God Stork for a while. I'd keep a careful ear out for this so-called METATRON system, if I were you. Perhaps it might start speaking, someday. Meanwhile, I'll pronounce it safe.'

'I wish I could believe you,' Kane said. He seemed uncharacteristically tentative, like a drinker or a drug user coming to terms with what he did while under the influence, and not quite being able to remember the details of it. 'How I was acting, what I did, I was out of my mind with hate. How can anything good come out of that?'

The Doctor clapped him cheerfully on the back. 'You

did the right thing,' he said. There was something about his manner of one who really doesn't care one way or the other, but supposed he had to say something comforting for the look of things. 'Admittedly for all the wrong reasons – but I'll take that any day over the wrong thing done for the right.' Then he appeared to lose interest and walked off. Peri and Kane looked at each other, then hurried to catch him up.

They followed him down the reactivated bounce-tubes to the level of the High Churchmen. In the various chambers here, med-units had been set up to treat the Churchmen for acute malnutrition and complete nervous collapse. It appeared that, for a month and a half, they had existed without food or sleep in the OBERON chamber, reduced to mere automata by the influence that had been channelled through Garon.

The Doctor, however, paid them no heed. He went straight past these chambers to a larger one, where additional units had been set up. The bodies in these seemed slightly more healthy. They breathed, and moved, and said things, and did things, but it was with a kind of otherworldly disconnectedness that Peri for one found disturbing, without quite being able to put her finger on why. These were the people who had spontaneously regenerated when the Node had dissipated and transferred its consciousness into the OBERON.

Med-techs were ministering to them. They glanced at the Doctor as he entered, then turned back to their work. The Doctor, as so many times before, after the battles had been won, was not generally seen as some conquering and fêted hero, more as a valued and trusted friend. Until, of course, he managed to irritate absolutely everybody. He walked through the med-units, Peri and Kane trailing behind, until he came to one on which lay the slim body of a woman. She merely lay there, breathing smoothly, looking up at nothing.

Peri suppressed a shudder. 'These things give me the creeps.'

'They shouldn't,' the Doctor told her. 'Their discorporation was just the extreme end of the effect that was affecting us all. You should know something about that. They've been given a taste of what in Earth terms might be called nirvana or a State of grace – and people were never designed to actually achieve that. It may take them some time to come back to themselves.' He shrugged. 'There but for the grace of God, if you like, go we all.'

Peri remembered how she had felt the past few days, the sense of dislocation, the fear that she was losing her mind. In her time she had seen dead things given a parody of life by some monstrous force or other, but the woman in the med-unit seemed more frightening. It was not even as if she were severely brain-damaged and in a respirator. She was a machine with nothing living inside it at all.

The Doctor, meanwhile, was patting at the woman's cheek. 'Come on,' he said. 'Rise and shine, chop-chop.'

His tone was so patronizing, like an old dad trying to make a joke, that Peri felt a flash of irritation – even a ghost of the hatred she had felt for the Doctor under the influence of the Node. It might have been a trick of the light, but she got the distinct impression that the woman in the med-unit, one VALDEZ MC according to her readouts, was feeling it too, somewhere. There was a subtle change in the breathing. You could almost believe, if you looked hard enough, that she was about to stir.

A med-tech bustled up. 'You have no authorization to be here. I can't allow you to disturb the patients like this.'

'That's quite all right.' The Time Lord grinned. 'I've probably done what I came here to do.'

'Exclamation to the effect that certain proposals *vis à vis* and concerning one's good self and worthy cohorts might tend toward a most unconscionable degree of –'

'What he means,' said Droog, 'is that you can blow it out your neck vent. Those terms are completely unacceptable.'

237

Craator attempted his patented glower, and found that it had no effect on a Sontaran, even a Sontaran bred for speedy and efficient maintenance procedures rather than out-and-out combat. Now he looked at the assembled human Adjudicators and the nonhumans who were suddenly going to make the Church as a whole far more cosmopolitan.

With the disruptions caused by Jelks and Garon before they died, as the senior ranking Adjudicator, Craator had been left holding the bag. The forces trapped down in the Holding Complex had been released, and an emergency Curia system was up and running, but the manpower situation was something slightly worse than critical. It was on the point of going into metaphoric pulmonary collapse and dropping dead. The only solution seemed to be the crash-drafting of additional manpower. The problem was that the only people who possessed the required skills were the survivors from the White Fire and the Hands of God, who might have been not entirely responsible for their actions due to the influence of the Node. But Craator was going to be damned and frying in a lake that burnt with fire and brimstone before he gave them a job.

It had been the Doctor, in fact, who had proposed a solution. The Adjudicators, he had said, had always had a tradition of taking the brightest and the best – but they had only taken the brightest and the best *humans*. Perhaps a slightly looser interpretation of the word 'people' needed to be found. Recruitment should be thrown open to all species, but for the moment there were large numbers of people already on hand, down in the Holding Cells. The truly criminal would have to be screened out, but large numbers of these so-called Penitents had never been guilty of anything save for breaking the increasingly insane laws of Garon – which at the very least showed that they still had a bit of fight. Offering them a place in the new Church of Adjudication might even go some way to making reparations for the injustices that had been done to them.

Craator had been forced to agree. There was no other practical choice. Now, in a lower-level chapel of the Temple that had been seconded as the seat of the new administration, he had called a meeting between the surviving senior Adjudicators and a nonhuman delegation. The humans' position was that alien lifeforms might be allowed to serve on a level slightly lower than the human auxiliaries. The nonhumans' position was that the humans could blow it out of wherever was anatomically applicable.

'Full parity or nothing,' Droog said.

'Affirmative expostulation leading to the general recognition that oneself is in complete agreement,' said Queegvogel.

'Shame here,' said the medusoid Xxigzzh. 'We get the badgesh and the big gunsh or you can let this shity go to the roashting chambersh of Zgghraghh, for all we care.'

'You're going to stand for this?' a voice snapped. Adjudicator Gloathe stepped out from the human ranks. He had spent the last few hours pointing out to anyone who would listen that he was basically the same rank as Craator. Fortunately, nobody had listened. 'You're going to let these . . . these *skags* tell us what to do?'

'And we want him out,' said Droog.'

'Pursuant to an objective timeframe that might be nominally classed as immediately,' said Queeg.

Craator nodded slowly. 'Adjudicator Gloathe, in my capacity of *de facto* Commander-in-Chief, and probably Pontiff the way things are going, I'm suspending you from duty,' he said, very carefully keeping any hint of satisfaction out of his voice. 'Turn in your badge on your way out.'

'What?' Gloathe was almost purple with impotent rage. 'You're going to –'

Craator scowled. 'Don't make me have to do something official, Gloathe. Someone get him out of my sight.'

It had been noted by several of those present that

Gloathe, alone of all those here, seemed to have survived the battles against the White Fire without a scratch. Suspicions had been voiced, conclusions had been drawn, but there had been no hard evidence either way. As it was, a pair of Adjudicators were more than happy to take charge of him and haul him, still protesting, out. How long he was going to survive out in the Habitat without the protection of the Church behind him was anyone's guess.

'Have a nishe life,' Xxigzzh called after him. S/he then turned to see that Craator was looking at hir, with an expression that made hir whip hir tentacles back in fright.

'A remark like that is utterly unworthy of an Adjudicator,' Craator growled. 'I'm going to let it go, just this once – but you listen to me, all of you.' His gaze swept round, taking in all of those gathered here, human and nonhuman alike. 'You've all of you got field commissions at this point. Once emergency conditions no longer obtain and order is restored, you're all of you going to go through evaluation and training. In the meantime, if I hear of any one of you . . . people abusing the privilege earned by an Adjudicator, you won't know what hit you. Your feet won't touch. You mess with me and I'll come down on you like a kilotonne of . . .'

In the doorway of the chapel, the Doctor turned back to Peri and Kane. 'You know, a great man, or possibly one not so great, whose name I can't recall, but must have said it because everybody says he said it anyway . . .'

Peri sighed. 'Just stop it and tell me.'

'Stop it *and* tell you?' The Time Lord took a look at the expression on Peri's face. 'Well, what he said was, the more things change, the more they stay the same.'

'Very deep,' said Peri shortly. 'Very meaningful. I don't know how you come up with them.'

The Doctor sniffed. 'Was that supposed to be sarcasm? I'd avoid it, if I were you. People from the lower half of the North American continent and sarcasm don't go very well together. Something to do with the fluoride in the

240

water, I think.' He glanced back into the chapel, where Craator was forcibly telling Adjudicators that if people called them 'skags' or 'human scum' then they could damn well deal with it, but if he ever heard one of *them* using any of those words themselves there would be bloody Sheol to pay.

'As I was *going* to say,' the Doctor said. 'I think things are going to be sorted out here, now. Possibly to within an inch of their lives. I think it's time we left and let them get on with it.'

The TARDIS was where they had left it. The capsule stacks, they saw, as Kane piloted them there in an Adjudicator flier, weren't. A missile strike during the conflict had taken them out. As Kane brought the flier in for a landing, Peri tried not to think of all the death and suffering that had been involved. Sometimes there really was only so much you could do.

'There you go.' Kane shot the doors. He glanced incuriously at the TARDIS. He'd been told he was taking the Doctor and Peri to a place where they had a way out of the Habitat, but he seemed unsurprised at this apparent lack of available means. Possibly it was just that his grief for Chong was still making him something of an automaton. It was still inside – he could live with it. It just didn't leave much room for anything else.

The Doctor bounded out of the flier and strode over to the TARDIS, his manner incongruously cheerful given the devastation, as if he were meeting up with an old friend he hadn't seen in years. Peri turned to see that Kane was watching him, lost in thought, with an odd expression on his face. It seemed to comprise part respect, part recognition and part the kind of irritated exasperation Peri herself felt every time the Time Lord did something erratic and apparently uncaring. At the time Peri didn't put a name to it; it was only later that she began describing it to herself as 'companions who are left behind'.

'So what are you going to do now?' she asked Kane. 'Are you going to join in with this whole new Adjudication order thing?'

'I have no idea.' Kane thought about it, in that abstracted, clinical way one has when probing some inner pain in complete detail. 'I don't think I want to go back to the Church. I only ever joined it in the first place because of my, uh, family.' He smiled grimly. 'Advice for life: never go and do anything because your family say it's the right thing to do. You wouldn't believe some of things the buggers saddle you with.'

For an instant Peri felt the impulse to take him along, and never mind what the Doctor had to say on the subject. Now that the scales had fallen from her eyes, now that she could see him for what he really was, the idea of leaving him like this seemed almost unbearable. She was going to say as much, but then he said, as if to himself, 'I don't know why, but I expected him to know me. Ah well, it's not as if I ever actually met him.'

Peri realized that he was gazing out through the flier hatchway, to where the Doctor was standing rather pointedly before the door of the TARDIS, as though he were quite prepared to wait there all day if he had to.

'What?' she said.

'Nothing much.' Kane turned back to her, shrugged and grinned.

'Y'know it's funny,' Peri said. 'All the stuff we've been through and I don't even know your proper name.'

'It's Kane,' said Kane.

'You know what I mean.'

Kane sighed. 'Yeah OK. Right.' Kane told her his name.

'Oh,' said Peri. It didn't mean anything to her in the slightest. It was one of those names that were unisexual, applicable to either a woman or a man, but on him it seemed subtly wrong. It was like he was wearing an ill-fitting hat.

'Don't blame me,' Kane said. 'I didn't have any choice

in the matter. It's one of the traditional family names. What I said about your antecedents saddling you with things. Don't start worrying about me. I'm going to be OK.'

Peri watched as the flier banked in the air and moved off. She kept watching until it was lost to view in the tangle of the Habitat. Then she shrugged to herself, and trudged towards the TARDIS, trying not to notice the devastation around her, and especially the little subliminal details that told her there had been people in the capsule stack when it had been destroyed. This was not some tastefully sanitized Hollywood devastation, with the cast lying decoratively around with minor wounds in a magically depopulated landscape. Large animals weighing in the order of two hundred pounds each and made of meat and bone had died in their thousands, here in the Habitat. They had left remains.

'Have you quite finished?' the Doctor said when she reached him.

'Yeah,' Peri said. 'I'm done.' She scanned the confusing tangle of the Habitat (still forcing herself not to look at the death and wreckage around her) basking in the light of a bright, new, flawless sky. Try as she might, she could not shake the feeling that they had not exactly achieved anything here. 'Is it true what you said?'

'I tend to say a lot of things,' said the Doctor. 'You'll have to remind me. What was it that I said?'

Peri took the Habitat in with a sweeping gesture. 'All this. What you said about the food riots and the famine and the cannibalism. That's not going to change, is it.' She realized that she had turned her question into a statement.

'I told you,' said the Doctor. 'Some things we can't change. Some things never change. These things happen –' He turned to look at her and, just for an instant, she saw a kind of bleak and endless sorrow in his eyes. 'But not today, and not quite as harshly as they would if we had never been involved. I have the idea that the lives we touched might turn out quite different from the way they would have. Possibly worse, hopefully better, but certainly different. Maybe in their confusion and pain they can remember to be kind.' He turned his face from hers, straightened his shoulders and became brisk. It was as though he were recovering from some momentary lapse and covering it up. 'The best we can hope for, sometimes, is to leave things just that little bit better than we find them. Try to strike a candle in the dark.'

Coda

And sometimes, just occasionally, people wear their scars lightly. People who are healed and well, who know how to deal with frightened children who find themselves turning into monsters and don't know why. Who take in strays, and feed them until they can run again, and then they let them go. Miracles happen. Miracles happen all the time, and most of them are other people.

It's a little like gazing absently through a train window as you pull out of the city in the dead, grey rain. Sunlight bursts through a gap in the cloud cover, briefly illuminating a landscape with a hard-edged, crystalline, coruscating clarity. Nothing has changed, nothing at all – but suddenly, in spite of everything and against all expectation, it can just be a beautiful world. It's inside you all the time: a big light machine. All you have to do is switch it on.

In the jury-rigged medical bay in what had once been the domain of the High Churchmen, something that had once been Mora Cica Valdez, and had then been something less and greater simultaneously, and who was now something slightly but entirely different from them all, opened her eyes and there was wonder in them.

Available in the *Doctor Who – New Adventures* series:

The next Missing Adventure is *A Device of Death* by Christopher Bulis, featuring the fourth Doctor, Sarah Jane Smith and Harry Sullivan.